## Praise for PATTY FRIEDMANN and
## the The *Too Jewish* Trilogy:

"A trio of eccentric women and the city of New Orleans come vividly alive in this diverting debut, an entertaining coming-of-age novel ... Quirky, irreverent and irresistible."

—*Publishers Weekly*

"Patty Friedmann may be the greatest New Orleans author of the past quarter century. If you like New Orleans, if you're interested in its Jewish community or Southern life or simply the rhythms of America's most unique city, you'll love *Too Jewish*. And even if you don't give a hoot about NOLA and its Jews, buy *Too Jewish* for another reason: it's a great read."

—*Failed Messiah*

"The story is by turns humorous and heartbreaking, and the author is adept at capturing that quirky combination of love and resentment that characterizes so many families."

—*School Library Journal*

# Do Not Open for Fifty Years

*Too Jewish Trilogy*

Part III

BY

## PATTY FRIEDMANN

booksBnimble Publishing
New Orleans, La.

*Do Not Open for 50 Years: Too Jewish Trilogy Part III*
Copyright © 2014 by Patty Friedmann

Cover by Kristen Ruth Smith

*Do Not Open for 50 Years: Too Jewish Trilogy Part III* is also available in mobi format.

booksBnimble Publishing

Print ISBN: 978-0-9904543-6-6
eBook ISBN: 978-0-9904543-5-9

www.booksbnimble.com

First booksBnimble electronic publication: January, 2015

Print layout by eBooks By Barb for Booknook.biz

# PROLOGUE

I wonder whether I ever will ask any of them if they remember what the man said. We were on the school trip that everyone takes, learning to kiss, to run away, to backbite in new places. "The National Cathedral will not be finished until around the year two thousand," the man said, and I heard an inrush of breath. Who could be indifferent to that? I pictured space travel and air cars, dead grandparents definitely, dead parents probably, dead me possibly, gray-haired me surely. And he was telling us about these people, up in Washington D.C., chipping at stone.

I remembered little else of the civic lessons, such as they were, from that trip, but that man's talk came back when I was writing my book about my father, born Bernard Kuper, renamed Bernard Cooper at Ellis Island. *Werner Weiss/Werner Vice* was a bestseller. I found an interview my father had done in 1958 buried away in an archive in Mississippi. I also saw interviews done by my mother Letty and me, but we're alive, so I couldn't look. I don't know why someone at Tulane had been doing oral histories back then when individuals weren't terribly important in history, but she had. I shivered when I read the first page of my father's transcript. He had decided to tell three things about himself. First, he said, his favorite TV show was *The $64,000 Question*. Had he known what that would do to me now? Such a knowing man, with no schooling, all because of history. Next, he said he and my mother just had brushed past each other, escaping Europe at LeHavre the last day before war broke out, but he wouldn't tell that story, because telling how he had left his mother behind was enough of 1939 for him. And finally he had said he didn't want his story read for fifty years because right then he had a twelve-year-old girl he wanted to protect. I was that girl, of course.

Fifty years. It's finally that far into his future. I want to know what he was thinking. Was this just a number he picked because it's the one everyone picks? Kennedy's secret assassination files were sealed for fifty years, but Kennedy was a senator in 1958. What did my father imagine about fifty years? I was easy to predict, within very wide parameters: an older woman with something of a familiar genetic profile. But the world? When I see electronics, I think of him, but more often when I see public nudity or the banning of cigarettes on television I imagine his reaction. I never bother with international borders that shift. Like his mother who believed nothing could go wrong in Germany in 1939, my father became blind to the wider world to protect himself, believing that everything turns. He did not live to see Vietnam.

He wasn't good enough for the Jews in New Orleans. He was Jewish all right, but not the kind they wanted. They wanted Jews who could ride in Rex and look dumbfounded in a synagogue. My father knew how to pray, though he had learned the hard way that there certainly was no God. His was not a good life.

\*\*\*

Of the Jews in New Orleans who chose to drive my father to sadness, no one was less subtle than my grandmother. My New Orleans grandmother. The only grandmother I ever met. The one who, despite my father's objections, sneaked me to Bergen-Belsen to try to find out how my other grandmother died. My father didn't want to know.

Grammy may have gotten what she deserved, but then I think a lot about myself in the future, because I've had so many chances to get into minds projecting into the future, and all in all I would like to die the way she died—at least up until she actually died. She slipped away a fingerful of brain cells at a time. She never knew what was hitting her. The nastiness dwindled in a way that probably was pleasant to her, but not to anyone else. First she lost specificity, so she couldn't be picky. Then she lost face recognition, so grudges were impossible to hold. When meanness still lingered but censors did not, she began using the N word, which tickled her staff: "Now we know what the old bitch been thinking all along." Finally she was reduced to mumbling about hunger. When she died, Grammy surely didn't know anything was going on.

It was the letter she wrote me before she began losing sense that made me wonder about her prescience. It wasn't a prescience couched in decency, because the letter was dated October 29, 1961, and that alone gives it a triumphant quality. If I want to, I can read the letter to say, *All right, I'm finally rid of Bernie, so now I'll be just wonderful, simply wonderful!*

I have a copy in my files. She was explaining why her will would give me a choice of which of her two houses I would like to have when she died. I was the only child of an only child, so the only alternative would have been to sell both and leave the money to Tulane or the Museum, but the houses weren't enough to get her name on another school building or another Degas, so why bother?

I have the city house and the beach house, and you may choose. I can't tell right now which will be of more value ten, twenty, or thirty years down the road. Right now the city house is assessed higher, but that could change. There is only so much beachfront property in the world. (On the other hand, a hurricane may come in the next decade or so, and then you'll have only a pile of sand, and the decision will be easy.) Anyhow, value doesn't really matter, does it? If you have grown up to be the sort of lady who wants to hold her head up in polite society, then the city house is about the best you can have; the boulevard will never go down in value. Or you may already have a fine home, and then the Pass Christian house will be a nice little extra. But something tells me that you are high-spirited, that you may want something besides sitting in New Orleans and hanging on your mother's skirts the way Letty has her entire life.

She went on for a little more, musing about the future, and I admit she missed the target by hundreds of thousands of miles, imagining me being too high-spirited to have children, or living on the moon. But one line was on the mark, hidden in parentheses, even, and I showed it recently to my daughter Honor. "First of all," Honor said, "she was off by a really long time, like probably, what, thirty years at least? And second of all, it doesn't take a genius to think it could have happened. After all, it *did*."

# Chapter One

I was probably the only person to evacuate *to* New Orleans for Hurricane Katrina.

It wasn't easy, given that I had to work around contraflow, the system of routing all major highways out of New Orleans, turning westward roadways into eastward and making westward travel impossible for most coming from the east. But no one cared about the backways, the ones I'd used before the interstates, the ones on which I'd been a child in the backseat when my grandfather drove criminally drunk. I drove this highway west, remembering. The storm was going to make a direct hit on the Mississippi beaches, and I had chosen the beach house when Grammy died decades ago, saying in her letter that my imitation Beauvoir somehow preposterously was going away and leaving a pile of sand. I would go to Honor in New Orleans. Even if Honor wasn't there.

Honor was in graduate school at Tulane, but not to learn anything. She was getting a PhD in English, which had an I-dare-you quality to it. I could not tell her it was a chimerical pursuit, because of course it was. Though I actually had found money in writing. Her degree would prepare her for finding some money in teaching, but money didn't drive Honor. Honor said she wasn't in school for any reason other than the joy. I thought school meant a lot more work than real life. Finding joy in work was a promise Karl Marx made, and surely he didn't make it with a straight face. Karl Marx did not have a repetitive tool to love.

Honor lived in Grammy's house on the boulevard. Alone right then as far as I knew, though it was her right as owner to rent out the extra bedrooms and make enough money to be the wealthiest graduate student in the entire university. The boulevard ran straight into the campus. Honor owned the house because of a legal history that was foolish and boring and involved my mother and her late second husband. Right then I was grateful for a place of refuge, no matter how ridiculous it was for a single woman to be living among couples who thought they were on their second, final, well-deserved homes. She was living in a home, but she thought it was a house. Far too often she brought home lithe men with good haircuts who paid rent for a few months, became boring, and were sent away.

If I didn't feel the power steering or notice the CD player and airplane panel on my dashboard, I could pretend I was driving back into the New Orleans where I first was a driver. The houses had not changed, the streets were as damaged as ever, and most of all, few people were on the streets. I never knew how safe and quiet the city felt in my young days until that moment. I drove onto the boulevard, and I could have been a newly licensed driver. Right until I saw Honor's little Mercedes Kompressor parked in the driveway and realized I couldn't pull in and block my grown daughter.

I rang the doorbell and waited ten seconds before I used my own key. She knew I was coming. We hadn't seen each other in about six months, and for that I deserved a lot of credit. On purpose I had never given her a father, so I had the right to be a cloying mother, a mother who could say she was all I had. She would say that she never had let that happen; I would say that I had used remarkable restraint. She would say that depriving her of a father made me owe her something, but it wasn't more of me. I would say that she should be grateful for my sparing her great sadness. She would never grieve over a father the way I did. "Oh, there are all kinds of grief," she would say back.

I also could say that I was a person in my own right, that people far and wide knew who I was, but I never did that. It was a very big issue for me, never to identify myself as anything but Darby. Not Honor's mother, not the author, just Darby. I had to be figured out new each time. I knew where that came from. I didn't know why though, except probably that I was decent. I tried to explain it to Honor once. "I think you'll be honest with yourself one day," she said.

What did that mean?

"You're dying to tout your identity, that's all." I looked at her funny. "Aw, come on," she said. "There's a compliment in there somewhere."

Honor came down the steps double-time, the same steps where her great-grandmother had died. "God, Darby, we thought you'd never get here," she said. *We?* With Honor it was always a "we."

Behind her came her friend Amanda. Honor first had known Amanda in Newcomb Nursery School. Amanda had been one of the main reasons I had chosen the beach house. Honor had played with Amanda in that sandbox that had accommodated so much future Carnival royalty. And Amanda at age three had put forth so much innocent racism that I knew Honor would be better off even in Mississippi. Public school in Mississippi evidently had done no good with Honor. The truism of child development is that everything gets set in stone in the first three years, so Honor already was destined to be a

New Orleans sort of rich girl before I took her away. New Orleans rich girls had a peculiar view of their comfortable place in the world, even if often their families had gone broke two generations ago. Honor had the peculiar view if not the genteel poverty. My choice of single motherhood had gone from Letty's ignominy to my film-star prescience in less than a generation. It took Honor about three weeks in her freshman year at Tulane to find Amanda in what I imagined to have been an "oh, God, are we cute or what?" moment.

"You have got to take us to the airport," Honor said. "If you'd gotten here sooner, well, we could've just taken the car and left it there. We would've had time to hang out."

Clearly they didn't plan to ride out the storm with me. Good news for the mother in me.

"It might drown here, you know," Amanda said.

Honor tried to give her a hush-up look.

"What."

"Think," Honor said.

"She's trying to tell you that if her car gets killed, I'm going to get killed, and she doesn't want to think that's possible because she's leaving me behind," I said.

"Stop it," Honor said.

I asked her why she'd waited for me.

"Because maybe you *will* die, and I don't want to grieve. You know, *grieve*," she said.

Amanda was trying to stifle a giggle, though I didn't know why she bothered. It wasn't as if she hadn't heard such talk before. Amanda was one of those girls who had worked five days a week in college to make cum laude, but had stayed almost fatally drunk on weekends to make sure she never became intelligent. Now she worked five days a week in her father's law office doing absolutely nothing but dressing nicely in front of clients so she one day might stop being a burden to

12

her parents. "Thank goodness your father's a real estate attorney," Honor once said to her. "But all his clients are old," Amanda said back. "Hey, you want him to be a criminal lawyer?" Honor said. "Now those guys are really hot," Amanda said.

"This is not Nazi Germany," I said. Honor had heard the story of my German grandmother and my father's guilt over leaving her many times. It was one topic about which she dared not be funny.

"As long as you don't think so," Honor said.

"I think New Orleans is going to be messed up, but New Orleans is always messed up," I said.

"You guys are so different from my family," Amanda said. She looked as if someone just had given her a big bowl of ice cream.

"She knows how much I love her," I said. "It eases her conscience a lot."

"You never make any sense," Honor said to me, and probably I alone heard affection in her voice.

Honor drove her car to the airport. It was a winning choice. She wouldn't have to remember seeing her mother for the last time ever as having struggled through traffic to deliver her into a three-deep pile-up at Southwest drop-off. She could park in the long-term high-rise that looked strong even if it was built by Louisiana contractors. She would have a ride waiting when she came back in three days. "Oh, and Darby, you won't use up twenty miles' worth of gas in case you need to get out of here." Honor's relationship with her conscience was now on great terms, and she flew out of the house probably ten minutes after I arrived. She and I weren't the kisses type, though I never knew why. Never having had kisses, I'd been sure I would have them with my child. But Honor saw some things she liked in my mother, and my mother kissed only the air.

\*\*\*

Now I had the house.

I'd never *had* the house, and I'd always *known* it. Grammy had had it built to her specifications, wanting French provincial design, so its bones were unchanged. So were most of its contents. Letty had bought it from the estate, from sentiment or power I didn't know which, but I thought an element of anger figured in one or the other. Now it had touches of a young woman in it, but mostly in a bedroom or two, and of course in the kitchen. What mattered to me, though, was outside. A child will explore the small spaces inside that never change—the closets and storage spaces—but the child knows the gardens and trees best. Take a New Orleans child back to her first house, and the first thing she will notice is the oak tree.

The boulevard had oak trees in front of most of the houses, and only a child who roller-skated would have noticed this. Oaks have weak branches that fall for the smallest reason, but oaks have tenacious thick roots that push up sidewalks with first maturity. On that boulevard, no child could go a smooth hundred yards without coming upon broken cement. Paving was the job of the city, and no one wanted to be the one to hack at those important roots for the sake of a flat sidewalk. My tour around the house started at the street, at the roots of the oak tree, trying for perspective. They seemed unchanged, but I had grown and lost balance, so I stumbled on them just as I had when I was seven. I was glad no one was around. I saw no cars in the driveways in either direction. The boulevard was deserted. I knew some of my high-school classmates lived there, having become wealthy as dumb dermatologists or their wives or personal injury attorneys or their wives, and I didn't want to be in a lifeboat with them. If I didn't look as far as Claiborne or Fontainebleau, where a car might pass every minute or so, I could imagine being completely alone. I closed my eyes, tried to pretend away most of my life, tried to frighten myself. Even in the tree shade, it was brutally hot. The heat staved off the fear. I couldn't be afraid in the heat. I'd always believed that bad people stayed indoors at the height of summer days. No one had told me that. Bad people were all that scared me.

I had no need to stay out in the heat. I could have gone to explore the back yard, but I was going to have the house for three days, so I could wait. I stayed off the grass, went up the stone walkway. When I was a child, the walkway had been bordered by boxwood, but Letty had had it ripped out as soon as the act of sale had passed. It was too "Metairie," she had said. Letty had grown up in that house, and I didn't understand why she never had noticed that boxwood didn't need its uniformity, that underneath the boring tiny leaves were astonishing bonsai branches, individual two-foot trees she could have allowed to live. I'd seen them at eye-level, hated that they'd been made into boxes.

I put the car in the slightly elevated driveway and unloaded it. I'd taken no chances. All of my history was going to be in one place. I hung my paintings in my beach house, but I didn't wear my jewelry. I'd packed it all. Grammy's prediction that only sand would remain made me consider that anything inside would go into the Gulf, worth money or worth remembering. My only rule had been whether an item could be replaced. Refrigerator, yes. Books, some. Computer, not the hard drive. Snapshots, no. Clothing, of course. My car was full of decisions. They had been decisions I'd thought Honor was going to make after my funeral. Possibly the week after, knowing Honor's taste, lack of sentimentality, and general disinterest in hanging anything but photographs on the walls.

I made a little shrine to myself in the dining room. It all fit on or up against the dining room table. As tempted as she surely had been to take the table to her own house, Letty had left it there, using it as her measure of tenants. "If I can trust them not to spill on the table and to keep it polished, I'll lease them the house," she'd said. She went through Sotheby's and got film people mostly, who never stayed home much and had a house staff that outnumbered them. When she eventually gave the house to Honor, Letty cried for hours until Honor said, "Hire me a housekeeper who'll boss me around. It'll be our family tradition." Letty had not been angry; Letty had brimmed over with her own special kind of love.

The phone rang in the back hallway, too muted to startle me, but sudden enough in the silence to annoy me. As I moved toward the phone, I realized why the sound bothered me. It was not the same ring that was there for all the years I knew this house. Even when pushbutton phones came in. Even when portables came, and then Caller ID. I knew it was nothing more than disinterest, but I appreciated Letty's having left the heavy black dial phone. It was the one I'd memorized so well, the one I'd figured out 911 on, seeing how fingernails had worn away the paint on the lower numbers, realizing that it was impossible to dial that 9 by accident, but it was easy to dial those 1s.

Honor had replaced it with a portable phone. Not even a landline. I was sure it was she on the phone, and I was going to do a little worry-easing fussing at her. A house in a storm needed a landline. When electricity went out, so did portable phones. Landlines had their own wires to lose.

Caller ID showed Letty's home phone. I answered because this was not a time to play games. I even used my own voice. "Why are you still home?" I said. Letty had an aversion to saying hello. She said it made people uninteresting.

"Who's this?" she said, as if she hadn't known me for quite a while.

"What number are you trying to reach, Letty?"

16

"Well, it sounded like you, but what in God's name are you doing in New Orleans?" she said. "In case you haven't heard, there's a hurricane coming here."

I told her I supposed I could say the same thing to her.

"I'm more than eighty years old and a widow. What am I supposed to do?" she said.

"I don't know. Stay home, I guess. You've got a generator. Though most people are leaving, generator or not."

Letty was as fit and steady-handed as anyone half her age. She was as sharp as she ever had been, though I didn't know how to gauge that because dumbness had a tendency to overshadow intellect. That especially had been true inside of marriages, the first with a man who ached to be seen as the smart person because he had so little else, the second with a man who spoiled her so rotten she had to act like a fool. Letty was as capable of driving to Texas or holing up in New Orleans as anyone with as much money as she had.

She asked me what Honor and I were doing. I told her that Honor and Amanda were gone on vacation to Florida. I thought that was enough information. She was quiet, processing. When Letty processed, it never was good.

"Do you need me over there?" she said finally.

I didn't bother to stifle a laugh. "Oh, God, no."

I'd just made Letty very happy.

"I don't need any reminders of how useless I've become since Eddie died," she said. "Much less how vulnerable I am. I've always had a man to take care of things. You'll never understand what it feels like to rely on someone stronger than you in a crisis. I was trying to give you an easy way to offer to help me out. You're no man, but you're all I've got."

I wanted to be alone with the house. I wasn't selfish. I wanted to stay away from selfish people. That had been my one choice in life, to go to a very lonely place, the most silent edge

17

of Mississippi, where I could keep my child's selfishness to her minimum, then send her away and be alone with no one around to take and take. I wasn't a taker. I just didn't want to *give* to crazed, solipsistic people. I needed to write in silence. I'd learned long ago that when I sat at the computer, I was inviting bored people to interrupt me. I needed to have no one around. Not even a cat.

"I can't have another person here," I said.

"*I* gave that house to your kid."

"But that's between you and Honor," I said.

She said she was going to call Honor, and I looked at my watch. It was far too early for Honor to be airborne. "Please don't do that," I said. "You already have a house, though what you need to do is get out of town. You're really healthy, but at your age you can't tell if you'll be all right in an emergency."

"That's why I need you," she said, and she hung up on me.

I noticed she didn't invite me to her house. Thank goodness. A generator was low-hanging fruit.

I kept my hand on the phone. I considered calling her back. But I imagined the alternatives. On the one hand, I had the sure knowledge that I had food and water and unself-consciousness, so I would have peace at a difficult time. On the other hand, I could give it all away to Letty, just as I always had done, if she came to be with me. In ordinary days with air conditioning and running water, she could make all of my muscles tighten; she could make me want to cry after ten minutes of a nonstop monologue. Letty always survived. I let my decision stand. Better to fail as Letty's daughter than to have an emotional breakdown. If I thought about it, this probably had been a choice I'd been making for a long time.

# Chapter Two

I didn't spend Saturday and Sunday in regret. The house was a dream, the way New York was a dream, full of places that came to mind in regular life because they were so important. When I wrote *Werner Weiss/Werner Vice*, I imagined scenes in the house even though they had taken place before I was born. The furniture had not changed since Grammy built the house and moved in, and as a fiction writer I had been lazy, placing my characters in her solarium, at her dinner table, that permanent table that had made permanent small troughs in the Persian rug where each foot was placed the day it arrived. I wasn't one to describe furniture, but I did need to seat the parents, Letty's parents, renamed, of course, in big generic bergere chairs so that Werner would seem like a sad mendicant, squeezed next to their daughter on an undescribed loveseat. The loveseat still was there, a diminutive directoire piece, but in my writer's mind a seat of shame. The book had been strange to write, done when Grammy had been stripped of most of her faculties, almost to the point of being pitiable, but I had written in memory of my daddy, and in interviews I had not been afraid to say so.

Now I was wandering through the house, not listening much to the televisions. I was largely indifferent to Katrina. I had filled the bathtubs, I had brought my battery recharger station, I had checked to make sure windows were not painted shut, I had brought all of the food from my house, I had checked Honor's pantry. So much non-perishable food. I even had learned that she had kept the dial phone in the bedroom that once had been my grandfather's but also had put a landline in her bedroom. Living where she did was no protection from losing electricity, and even though Honor was a cell-phone kind of girl, she was not giving up having a listing.

With no contact, I slept for pure pleasure. I didn't allow myself more than three hours at a time. That way, when I fell asleep, it was almost instant, the way a baby would go from wakeful to gone. I ate that way, too. A small, meaningless meal at three a.m., an apple and cool buttered bread. I was keenly aware that the refrigerator might not last forever, and I cooked up meats and fish too plentiful for one person in three days. I didn't care. If it appealed to me at the moment, I ate it. I did that with half a pound of salmon Sunday morning at ten. I sent all the skin down the disposal. Anything I didn't want to live with went down the disposal. Except banana peels.

This was a perfect time to write more on my new novel, my sequel, *Lily Stern/Lily Vice*. People would know it followed the book about my father, but I was writing it about the woman who lived on after him, and I was succeeding in ignoring the fact that she was still alive. Sitting in that house, indulging myself as much as Letty and Honor indulged themselves, the first thing I did was to go into the software and put the title on every page. The title to me was the most important part of writing. I had worked hard at naming Honor, I only allowed us to have a dog when we had the best name possible for any pet ever owned among all the people we knew, though that had limited us to Ansel Adams and FedEx. Naming my mother Lily Stern still made me feel slightly drugged. *A flower in the sky*, the flower lily, the German for star, irony, the grandest dame in New Orleans, Edith Stern, and of course the English word itself, stern.

I spent Sunday afternoon writing about Letty having a nude photo taken of herself for the man who became her husband after my daddy died. That was a true story, but I put flourishes on it. I made myself present at the photo shoot so I could suffer the images of my own mother trying to look sexual when she was past fifty. Now I was far past fifty, and I could go into my grandfather's old bathroom and do research. The same mirror was there that always had been there, small spots of black silver here and there where it had aged. I took off my clothes. It was cold in the house. I was keeping the thermostat at 70, saving the cold, even though I knew it would dissipate within an hour of losing electricity.

I first stood face forward. The price of nursing Honor, the drooping breasts, was what I noticed first, though it seemed to me that far too many women complained of this same trait. We couldn't all have nursed our babies for a year. I didn't know anyone who had, but then I hadn't been among too many other mothers. Otherwise, I looked all right. As long as my arms hung at my sides, and I stayed three feet from the mirror. It was a good mirror for my purposes, old and smoky.

I remembered Letty's final pose, the one Eddie had been forced to hang on his wall to scare away other women. Left hand on hip, left knee bent slightly in front of right, head tossed back as if she had long hair. I struck the pose. Oh, skin, skin. I had been good to my skin, never stretching it except to carry a baby, but it gave up anyway. A little on my arm, a little on my thigh, too much on my neck, at least for my purposes. And my belly, too round for the rest of me. No one was going to see me, no one was going to know these would be the details in the book, but I would know. That was the trouble with writing stories, having the true images in my head.

The storm came in that night, and of course nothing happened other than the shedding of a lot of oak branches. And the loss of electricity. I went out in the morning and walked around the property. It would fall to Honor's yard service to clean up. I was not going to haul debris when I had no air conditioning and little possibility of gratitude.

The garden wall had held fast, just as it always had, but all above it and below it had suffered in the wind. Grammy's ancient azaleas filled the upper bed, but now were so terribly broken and uprooted. The St. Augustine grass at the foot of the wall might have been all right, but it was covered with old oak leaves and mulch that must have blown in from a neighbor's yard. My memory of this space was gone.

I would not go out again. The house already was hot, and I opened all the windows in the corner back bedroom. It was on the second floor, and no one was in the city, and it seemed to me that if anyone was going to brave the heat for crime he would do it by going to empty houses. I set up my computer and recharger in the coolest corner of the room, soaked a t-shirt in tub water and put it on. I caught only puffs of breeze, but I wasn't hot.

I plugged my cell phone into the recharger and tried to decide whether I wanted to turn it on. I had checked, and the landline was dead. Only two people mattered, if anyone did. Honor and Letty. Honor would be coming back, possibly tomorrow, and I didn't know if Letty even had left at all. I decided I could turn it on and leave it in another room so I wouldn't have to answer it, but I could check it at night for messages. I didn't want to call anyone. Since the storm had given the city a pass, my time alone in the house was not going to be very long, and I didn't want it broken. I wasn't worried about my mother and my daughter because I wasn't worried about myself. I was at ground zero, safe and sound, so how could there be danger anywhere else? This was the way New Orleans always felt after escaping the brunt of a storm.

\*\*\*

As history tells, what I expected turned out not to be true. Katrina gave New Orleans a pass all right, but by Tuesday morning even the boulevard was flooded with lake waters that had breached the levees. If I stood in the front doorway, I could look in either direction and see nothing but an unmoving river that stretched from the Tulane campus to Fontainebleau Drive. I had no way of knowing what lay beyond either boundary. I could gauge the depth of the water by how well I knew the oak tree, the oleanders on the neutral ground, the house across the street. I could measure my own troubles, such as they were, by the wheels on my car and the steps to the house. I didn't own the house, but I treasured the house. The first floor had wide pine floors. By midday, the water level seemed to have peaked at three feet. Grammy had built the house with a partially submerged basement; my car had a high wheel base. The losses would be a washer and dryer. I knew Honor had stored all her treasures in the attic. When she was very small, I'd taught her to enjoy the smell of new lumber in the attic. As old as the house was, the hot attic always smelled of new lumber.

Everything above the basement was safe. I was safe.

Not just safe from the flood, not just safe from criminals, but safe from anyone I knew. I could be more alone than I ever had been in my life. Of course, as a writer I had the company of my imagination, and as the writer of a book that thinly disguised my mother I had the company of the figures in my history, but I would control all intrusions. If I was going to monitor the city at all, it would be to find out how long my privacy would last. I had enough water to last a month, at least for drinking. I had enough food, too, good food. I even had found a stash of handi-wipes so I could sit around in my underwear and feel fresh. With all the power I needed for my computer, I couldn't imagine what more I needed. If the computer died, I'd remembered pencil and paper.

I honestly didn't feel selfish. Never in my life had I been selfish, and here I was, with the grandest, most unassailable excuse to take care of only myself. I knew very well that Letty was somewhere safe, surely with an audience, ranting about the thoughtless daughter who had no interest whatsoever in saving her life in this catastrophe. I knew Letty. When Letty learned I was not going to drive over to her house and pick her up with her terrible bubble-wrap Chanel luggage and bring her to the house so she could have me use up all of the food and water on her, she had called a taxi and headed to the airport, boarding the next flight to a fun place. Possibly she had tracked down Honor and found out where Honor was going. And, knowing Honor, she'd been lied to.

As for Honor, she was on an unscathed beach. The storm had crossed Florida gently the week before. I assumed Tulane was closed—the only information she needed. The boulevard was a stretch of high ground, its value invisible except during floods, when it ran into below-sea-level Fontainebleau, reminding everyone of New Orleans's secret lines of demarcation. Tulane was at its other end, and surely Tulane was not on high ground. Honor was in for a nice little vacation.

I bunched up my t-shirt, poured a cup of bathtub water on it so it was soaked, put it on, set myself up in my breezy writing corner, and slipped away. I told myself I might reward myself later by going online to find out what was happening, but then I remembered I had no Wi-Fi. I decided instead the reward would be to find a radio in Honor's house. I didn't know if I wanted to.

*** 

I never found a radio; in fact I gave it an hour and decided I didn't care for much news that could come from reporters. I owned a house on the Gulf Coast, and it was my refuge. The news would give me an idea of whether it was damaged. I didn't want to know. Radio wouldn't announce that one Letty Cooper was currently lounging on a beach on the west coast of Florida. With no signals in the New Orleans air or on its wires, the only way I could learn anything was the same as it had been in centuries long past. It would have to be in person. No one was coming to me, so if I wanted to know anything I would have to venture out. And the only person I felt some obligation to know about was Letty. I figured her house could tell me a lot.

Getting into my car and going to her house told me a lot, but not about Letty. I learned about the topography of the city —or at least of some part of the city that lay between Honor's house and Letty's. I could not get from one to the other. I would take a street running lake-river, and I'd come to water too deep to drive through. So I'd try to cut over on an uptown-downtown street and find it blocked by a fallen oak limb. No one was out except a few military; certainly no one from the Department of Streets was clearing debris. When I was growing up I learned every year during Carnival season to find alternate routes around Uptown, and sometimes I would find it impossible to go from one place to another; I would go home, missing a party and wondering if anyone showed up. I would have to turn back this time, too. But now I didn't blame the

25

city. I was going to stay at Honor's and feel sorry for New Orleans. Even her pretty streets looked war-torn.

I had no interruptions until the National Guard came two weeks later. I know now that I was a spoiled rotten rich white woman, everything that was wrong with New Orleans. While I was eating Honor's Pepperidge Farm cookies and washing them down with sealed cartons of vanilla soy milk, people were drowning and starving and being shot by police in distant parts of the city. I had seen smoke over the trees from my back window and heard no sirens, and the smoke kept going for hours. I had a sense that it came from a thickly populated part of Carrollton, so I got my news the way I would have two hundred years past. Big fire, no firemen, or too much water for fire trucks. But I saw no way to try to help.

I'd become accustomed to the kind of silence only possible with fingers in ears, and even fingers in ears make an exaggerated noise if they move. So any sound could be heard from quite a distance. I heard the banging from about ten houses down. When it came closer, I opened the front door a crack and saw a half dozen men in military uniform moving from house to house. I bet they were terribly hot in those uniforms, which included hip-waders. That seemed a little much, since the water had gone down almost to dry in the past few days.

They would pound on a front door, walk around, confer as if they were serious, then one of them would spray paint on the sidewalk. As they left the house next door, I stepped out just as one was saying, "Hey, there's a car here." He was terribly excited, and I almost felt bad for him, the way I was ruining his detective work. "You don't have to paint the sidewalk," I said. It felt funny talking. I hadn't spoken in over two weeks.

"Every other neighborhood, we paint on the front doors," the blond one said. He looked terribly proud of his power. I could hear in his tone that he was authorized to paint my door if I got out of hand. He was possibly twenty years old.

He approached me as if I were dangerous or fragile. "You know there's an emergency here?" he said.

I laughed. He took a step forward. He'd added crazy and subtracted fragile. "You can't stay here, you know," he said.

"I've done a good job so far," I said.

A black kid, possibly even younger than the blond guy, stepped forward. "Ma'am, you know the whole city closed?"

"That sounds like good news to me," I said.

"You got to get out of here," the blond guy said. He was close enough now for me to read his nametag. Roberson. I looked at the other one's tag. Nash.

"So, Mr. Nash," I said to the other one, "if the city is closed, I think I'm pretty safe here."

"You not the only one didn't evacuate," Nash said. "But you just about the only one setting up in her house. The rest, they running in the streets. They especially like dry streets."

I could see clear, unblocked blacktop in both directions. I also could see my car, high and dry. I had turned over the motor and let it run the day before. I always did that in Mississippi when I went several days without leaving the house. I didn't know if that was necessary with cars made after 1970, but as soon as the water had started to go down I'd been doing it anyway.

I could have tried driving again and exploring as far as dry streets went. But my city was ruined, and to me that meant my writing was destroyed. I had told my first of these two parent stories in small measure in Germany and in smaller measure in New York, but everything else took place in New Orleans. New Orleans as I knew it was gone. My landscape was more than the St. Augustine grass and oaks and crape myrtles that tourists sometimes noticed. It was a social fabric that could not survive a diaspora. No one was going to share our local private jokes and shared history again. I had to stay inside my memory and write about the past.

I asked if Nash and Roberson had a way to find my mother. That was when I learned I could have her name broadcast on the only radio station in the region by telling these two guys. She would call my number if she heard. I didn't have a number, I told them. "That's a problem, yeah," Nash said. "But what you do, you put in your cell and your landline. They got to come back eventually." My mother, too, I told him.

I offered to let them come in from the sun and have a cup of water. Each looked at his comrades as if I had suggested putting on formal wool jackets and sitting down in the parlor to have steaming tea. "You could come sit in the truck and have a' ice-cold bottle of spring water," Roberson said. "We got AC."

It was tempting, but I knew it would lead to my choosing to let them give me a half-dozen bottles of water so I could load up my car and leave town to some colorless place where I could live this same life in a hotel room with no memories. I knew my memories for the book were always with me, but the memories that came from objects and smells and filled me up so I was complicated could not be found in a hotel room in Texas.

I told Roberson and Nash that I was doing fine, that I could wait for the city to come back, that they could tell I was in no hurry, that I had to wait for my mother and daughter. They gave me a case of bottled water.

"If you can get to River Road, you can get anything you want," Roberson said. "Jefferson Parish is all good—long as you kept your roof. Remember the Wizard of Oz? It's all in color over there."

They painted the smallest possible red tattoo at the foot of Honor's driveway. A cross with a zero in two of the quadrants.

Then they left me behind, forgetting how easily sound traveled.

"That's one tough old bitch."

"Well, I'd fuck her."

Old?

# Chapter Three

Honor came back to the house at the same time as electricity, gas, water, and cell-tower signals.

It pays to live on a street with important people. Services were not restored democratically in New Orleans. The boulevard came to normal faster than most of the city.

I should have known better than to think she had extrasensory powers or great good luck. I would learn that, in spite of feeling young and single, Honor had made a point of getting on speaking terms with a few of her neighbors, though in Honor's world speaking terms meant having e-mail addresses. She would not have known these people if she had seen them in any public places other than directly in front of their own houses. This included the headmaster of the school that Letty and I had graduated from. He lived free in what I'd always called the worst kind of house possible, a two-story brick house. To me the two-story brick house had been the hallmark of the truly unimaginative rich. The headmaster got a pass because he didn't choose the house; at least he got a pass on the rich part.

So Honor had had no problem texting the headmaster for

news about the street. Even though he probably was being bombarded by spoiled mothers who wanted to know if the school was too flooded for them to come back from Atlanta and Houston to get their money's worth. The headmaster had gotten fake press credentials a week after the storm and had come in and out to know everything. I'd seen him from the front window once or twice and had felt violated. I loathed that school. After what happened to me in high school, anything associated with that place filled me with rage and a need to find a way to unleash that rage.

Honor had waited until the boulevard was close to normal, just when I was air-conditioned and showering and going the back way to get handfuls of fresh fruit from Rouse's out near Kenner and trying to steel myself to try to get to Letty's. I'd become irrational about Letty. Getting around, I'd heard the water was down in her part of the city, but a lot was not navigable in between. When she didn't come find me, I was afraid to go find her. I'd seen a number of tattoos on houses that said a dead body had been found inside.

Honor's house was just as she'd left it, aside from the yard. But the yard matched the city. The city was gray. That's the word for it. All the grass was dead. All the shrubs and trees that had sat in salt water were dead.

Honor did not come back alone, and her companion was not Amanda.

She honked when she pulled into the driveway, though she had no reason except to announce herself. I'd started parking on the street days ago, expecting her to show when I didn't expect her. New Orleans had become such a polite city, people letting one another cut in line, no one using car horns, everyone sharing. In this changed city, Honor was like a New Yorker, loud and barking.

I didn't move from my computer. I was in the middle of a

paragraph that would be a fine piece of language if I spilled out all the words I had ready for it. I typed fast, hearing the rustling in the driveway, voices, one male, the key in the door, more rustling, clomping on the steps; I typed faster. "Darby!"

"Who the fuck is Darby?"

"Like, my *mother*." I finished the paragraph.

"What." That was the reaction cool Honor would want. I hoped her companion would think it was hilarious.

I could hear her coming closer. I was happy to have her back safe. A little unnerved to have to share space with her, but terribly happy to have her back safe. I met her at the top of the stairs. "Where've you been?" I said, letting out gratitude.

"You could've called me," Honor said.

I gave her a hug. We weren't the hugging type, but we also weren't the type to be separated for such long stretches of time. Four weeks without power are a lot longer than four ordinary weeks, but Honor didn't know that. I could feel her arms coming up like little robot arms, but I let her go before she had to commit to the hug.

"Darby, this's Sciutto Gotti. Sciutto, this is my mother, but everybody calls her Darby, like, everyone."

Shooto, as his name sounded to me, put his hand out to shake mine and said, "Hey." Out of the side of his mouth, he whispered to Honor, "Don't go telling people my last name."

Honor ignored him. "You should go to Ybor City," she said to me. "It's like the Quarter, only way cooler. You just take a taxi to Seventh Avenue. Beach in the daytime, party all night. Amanda knew exactly where to go. We didn't see one person from New Orleans the whole time, probably."

"And you found me," Shooto said.

Honor put her arm around his waist. I'd never seen such a boy. Or man. Or whatever he was. Certainly not with Honor. He was possibly six-five and I would have guessed over three hundred pounds of solid muscle, though gauging people over normal size wasn't something I did well. What struck me was the way his hair was so full, actually balanced for someone his size. He was streaky blond, and his waves were long and unkempt and almost scary. He was too tall for me to see directly the color of his eyes, which to me was the most important feature on a man. The green that had made me choose Honor's father probably would have shone down in this boy, so I guessed his eyes were dark. He had a few days' of untrimmed beard; that was the look, and I could see why girls liked it. But Honor always had brought home chiseled boys who looked as if they had large allowances. I had taken one look at their clothes that surely came from the Perlis shop and had hoped she would get over them so she would not become boring. This Sciutto was not going to make her boring. But I was sure that was the only difference. She would move him in, possibly charge him rent, get annoyed, and send him away. As long as I kept my mouth shut. Honor clung to the boys I didn't like. "If I'd had a father, you could have some rights about my judgment," she'd say.

Honor gave him a little squeeze. I saw triumph in her eyes, a good kind of triumph.

"You didn't choose to visit New Orleans at its best," I said.

"Maybe he's not visiting," Honor said.

I asked him if he was from here. He looked at Honor, she looked at him, and I knew I had to leave soon.

"I want to stay here," Shooto said.

"Are you fucking nuts?" I said.

"I told you she was pretty cool," Honor said. I relaxed for the first time in weeks, which surprised me.

Before they unloaded the car in a safe city with no crime, they stood right in the upstairs hallway and told me everything. Honor and Amanda were out drinking, like, the third night they were there. They were not paying attention to the television because, well, nobody in Tampa that they knew of had even heard of New Orleans practically. So anyway, Amanda has met this guy, and Honor hasn't picked up anybody, so she's probably a little too drunk, and they come out of this bar, and Honor trips on, she swears, nothing, and this giant of a gentleman catches her, and she feels like she's found the man to take care of her for the first time in her total life. And Shooto, whose name you just have to picture in your head as Sciutto because it's short for prosciutto, see, which is a long story, anyway, he says Honor is like this delicate little angel who's fallen into his arms. They spend all their time together, and they know everything together. It's amazing, what with his father being in the business, and her family owning Cooper Transportation, and how maybe one day something will come of it, but for now they're just falling in love. And eventually Sciutto turns on the radio and hears about New Orleans, so Honor figures she better pay attention. After all, she owns a house, and she can't stay in Florida in a hotel forever. That's how they got their information. "I tried your cell, which doesn't work," she said to me, "so I texted you, but you never answered."

"Do I look like someone who knows how to text?" I said.

"You could've read what I wrote."

"Do I look like someone who knows how to access texts?"

"Well, it's all over now," Honor said.

Except for the small matters of my home and my mother, I thought, but I didn't want to mention them and act vulnerable in front of this boy, so I said nothing.

\*\*\*

I lay awake that night on the sofa in the solarium. I thought if I slept in there I could avoid hearing bedroom noises that Honor would make, now that she had Sciutto in her home. Having a man between one's own sheets is romantic, I think because a woman thinks he has been imagining this for a long time. She can think of herself as his dream, and she can move, dreamlike, in the low lights and the soft spaces. I never had minded seeing Honor naked, and I probably would not have been bothered by hearing her make love, but this man unnerved me. His sexuality and his possible noises could not come even to my thoughts. I kept my eyes open, made plans for the next day. I would have to move out, of course, and that meant dealing with my house and Letty. I could not find a way to think logically about either. All news was extreme news in those days. I had all means to find it; now I needed means to face it.

I dozed fitfully, did not get up when my watch said it was nine o'clock, slept until almost eleven. Only a narrow hallway separated the solarium from the kitchen, and I had heard no one in the kitchen. This was a creaky old house, with fine thin rugs on wide pine floors. I would hear Honor, just as she would hear me. I decided I would leave behind anything that was in the dining room and untouched since I had arrived. That meant I would take clothing and toiletries and papers and my computer, all of which were upstairs. I went up noisily. If they wanted to get out of bed, they needed to do so with covered bodies.

Neither showed as I loaded my car. I pulled off not knowing where I was headed. I had two choices, Letty's house or Mississippi. I wanted the wheel of the car to pull like the planchette of a Ouija board.

I got halfway to Fontainebleau Drive and decided to let go of the steering wheel to see what it would do. The car immediately began veering to the left. That would take me to the interstate, which would take me to Mississippi. Either this was a divine moment, or I needed a front-end alignment. I felt a small wave of nausea because neither outcome was good. I turned onto Fontainebleau, straightened out, let go of the wheel, found myself veering right. I pulled over. I got out and looked at my wheels. Dan Usner Shell station was closed, and that was the only place I knew to get my car fixed in New Orleans. I didn't know what to look for in a wobbly tire anyway. But I did know what a bad street looked like. And that stretch of street had pushed itself up in the middle the way I'd seen mountains form in slow motion in school films. It wouldn't be visible to a driver, at least not yet, but it was there all right. I doubled back to the boulevard, and it, too, was buckling. The flood water had melted the streets.

Now I was back to having no outside influence on my choice of where to go, so I chose logic. Logic wasn't my favorite course of action. Logic wasn't the friend of a fiction writer. I needed natural ambiguity, so I tried to live inside it. Ambiguity would have left me where? Driving around town until I passed a landmark that made me say, *All right*. But logic was the friend of pragmatism, and pragmatism said, *You just might run out of gasoline in the wrong place*. Of course pragmatism would dictate through fact, and I had the fact that gasoline was not an available commodity on the Mississippi Gulf Coast. I actually also had the fact that the beach had been decimated, but I was sure my house was the exception. It was old, with a stone foundation and a brick chimney. Wind could not move stone. Fact. Logic.

But the logic I was using weighed only Letty against my house, and it was a matter of which to do first. If I went to Letty first, I would learn how she was doing, but I would go without the safety of having a house of my own. If I went to

the house first, I could go check on Letty, knowing she couldn't
have power over me.

I got onto the interstate. And I fiddled with the radio all the
way to the highway so I wouldn't see what had happened to all
of my landmarks. The closer I came to the Gulf, the less I saw
that was recognizable out of the corner of my eye. When I got
onto the beach road, I began to sob. I had only my odometer to
guide me. Not a house, not a tree, not a fence. Maybe a slab,
but I didn't know slabs. I'd played games of distance often
enough to know exactly how far my house was from the exit.
As I came within one-tenth of a mile, I expected to see at least
the frame of the house, standing alone, wind-damaged, but
standing.

I saw nothing.

This was where I had brought Honor when she was three
to escape the closed minds in New Orleans. She had played
alone in the gazebo, and I had washed tiny shorts with wet
sandy circles on the backsides. She had gone to public school
here, and I had written a novel about my father, surrounded
only by Cooper souvenirs, no Adler souvenirs. Jewish people all
over the world cherished the book I wrote, and now all they
could come to see would be an empty lot.

I got out of the car, started to walk the property, looking for
anything tenacious enough to have stayed, tears streaming,
grieving. I was alone, with an unobstructed view, to Florida, to
Texas, or so it seemed. Probably other people were nearby, also
grieving very specifically for memories of swimming in the Gulf
and sitting on a deck at sunset. I was grieving for what I, like
everyone else, would call a total loss. It seemed to me that there
were degrees of total, even if that wasn't logical.

A box truck came up the beach road and stopped when the
driver saw me. Never had I had less wish for company. But it
was the Red Cross, and I couldn't be rude to the Red Cross.

Even if I thought they needed to be helping people with no money to start with.

A woman no older than Honor came toward me, and as she came closer I could see she had a hot dog in her hand. A hot dog. These were nauseating times, and the Red Cross had chosen hot dogs. She also had a can of Coke that had beads of sweat on it. I started to cry harder. As she came closer, I could see that it was a good hot dog, probably all-beef, not the scrawny, red-dyed kind. This was a little kid's comfort snack, and I wanted it. She held it out, and I took it.

"Guess this was your house," she said. I nodded. "You have insurance?" I nodded. "You contacted FEMA yet?"

"This is the first time I've been here since the storm," I said.

"I'm sorry," she said.

I told her thanks for the hot dog. I wasn't trying to get rid of her. I meant it. Though I hoped she'd leave soon.

She said she had some stuff to give me before she went away, and she held up her index finger, freezing me in place, as if a woman with half a hot dog and a cold Coke would have any desire to move.

All she gave me was a sheet of paper with a list of things to do and how to do them. Calling FEMA was on the list. I'd never before seen a list that I didn't throw directly into recycling. This was a list I was going to use for a while. Besides, I couldn't imagine recycling ever would matter here again. Who could take the earth seriously?

# Chapter Four

This time I went all the way through to Letty's neighborhood, which was high, but which had been surrounded by low lakes of water. Letty's car was in her driveway, giving me instant relief, so I rang her doorbell. Letty and Honor were so much alike that maybe she had gone to a beach and found an astonishing man and brought him home to her bed. I waited, rang again. It was late afternoon. Driving to Mississippi and back had taken its toll, mostly because I'd discovered while driving that I was homeless.

Listening to the radio left me with nothing but thinking time, and the daydreams of writers can go just so far on a highway. In city traffic, I could daydream because I knew ideas could be jotted down at stoplights. But on the highway I would take bad risks to scribble while driving, especially on a highway that had taken a beating and hadn't had all the broken signage fixed and jetsam removed. So the practical thoughts came on me long before the Louisiana line. And they all had to do with my having no home.

I'd left Honor. I'd long ago learned I couldn't live with Letty. I could use Letty's house today to get my bearings, but

I'd have to figure out something quickly, or I'd be destroyed. Letty had had so much practice. In an empty room, Letty could take back her old powers within hours. In a filled house that she owned, I would go back to being my father's sad child in minutes.

I gave a woman of Letty's age ample time to come to the door. Letty didn't need that much time because Letty still worked out on the treadmill. Besides, Letty still had an intercom in the upstairs hallway, and she had startled her share of young people with a blasting "who's there?" I let myself in with my key.

No trace of Letty. The AC wasn't on, but Letty long ago had run out of estrogen, and she turned it off in mid-September every year. It was light out, so there was no reason for lights to be on. If she didn't have electricity, she surely had gas, and gas would run her generator. I saw no mail, of course, because mail service hadn't been reinstated anywhere in the city, even in the neighborhoods like Letty's that had been unscathed. Letty lived in that sliver by the river that had had no water. I tiptoed around, afraid of leaving traces of myself. If she walked in on me, I didn't want to be caught being a snoop.

I gave her an hour. Without her car, she surely would be dropped off soon. No one could put up with Letty for more than an hour. When she didn't show, I went into active snoop mode. I wasn't sure what I might find.

I went upstairs first. Everything was in what Letty called dying order. The bed was made, which for Letty was pretty much what constituted dying order. Letty did not do her own housekeeping. Letty also did not generate much dirt. At least not by my standards. Dust was not a factor in my life. Someone had left the upstairs neat, but I couldn't tell when. I had a feeling it wasn't that morning. I opened the guest room door, a brave act. The guest room existed only as a shrine, as far as I could tell. Its last occupant had been her stepdaughter Linda, who last had visited when her third child was a few months older than infant Honor. Letty had done something of an exorcism on the room, putting in high Early American beds that announced that any small child who slept on one would fall off and suffer brain-damage. This is where Letty stored her luggage in the large closet. The two large Chanel pieces were gone.

I felt all my muscles loosen. I could roam free in the house. Letty was out of town. She had come back after the storm from wherever she'd gone, taken a look at the inconvenient city, and booked the next flight out. As long as I didn't mind the fear of her walking in on me, I could stay there and get my bearings.

Then I made the mistake of opening the refrigerator.

Refrigerators were the emblem of Hurricane Katrina. On every block, all over the city, perfectly good refrigerators sat curbside, waiting for special trucks to come haul away ruined white goods. That was what Honor would lose, white goods, washer and dryer. That could be her Sciutto test, to see whether he was clever enough to do her only recovery act, to drag those two appliances to the street. Knowing Honor, she would not think to ask.

Letty's refrigerator was not going to have to be jettisoned for one reason. Letty did not eat food that rotted like a graveyard. Letty never ate meat or fish, and Letty ate vegetables that were hermetically sealed tight in individually wrapped servings. Her milk never had been opened. The vegetables were dark soup in their bags, and her milk had separated in its container, but to restore her refrigerator, all a person needed to do was remove its contents. It was all cooled with restored electricity or a gas-powered generator. I didn't even have to do it immediately, though I would do it the next day.

If Letty had been home, she would have done it. Clearly Letty never had been home.

Letty wasn't the person who ever had filled me with homesickness—until that very moment. It seemed to me that Letty was missing. New Orleans was full of the spirit of missing people. Even now, when the borders were open, and some phone service was coming back, tens of thousands of people could not be found.

I checked every room. If Letty were dead, even with air conditioning, I would smell something. There was no reason for her to be dead. Unless she had had a heart attack or stroke. New Orleans had had no emergency services for a long time. Calling 911 was not an option. The trap door to her attic was closed, but in a dry part of the city, Letty had had no need to go up into the attic. She had two dormer windows up there and laughed before most storms that she didn't need an ax; she could kick out a window to get on the roof.

She was nowhere dead. She also had been nowhere alive. There was no water in the bathtubs. If she had stayed, there would be water in the bathtubs, wouldn't there? Though no bathtub was watertight, not even in Letty's house. They could have emptied out. I couldn't know. She could have stayed. She could have left. She could have gone, come back, gone again. If I'd been able to get through the uptown streets earlier, I might have known. But probably not.

I was surprising myself. I was frightened about the woman whose disappearance from my life always had seemed like a milestone to be reached so I could breathe more easily. Though I remembered when I first was pregnant with Honor, and she had been in London, and I had told her long distance, and she had screamed long distance that she was coming home right away, and then there had been a bombing at Heathrow, and I had panicked, sure she was dead. Overnight she had forgotten about coming home, but I had seen myself panic.

I lay down on the sofa in her television room, feet up, small pillow over my face. It was a fearless act, but I wasn't sure what it meant. If Letty could have tiptoed in on me at that very second, all she would have seen were shoes on a good-as-new sofa. I kicked off my shoes, sensed my feet weren't fresh-from-shower clean, let them hang down. I had to think. I knew already that Letty was alive. I'd just told myself that.

I'd been alone too long. I'd forgotten how to sort out matters by talking to anyone but myself. I knew I was a good kind of crazy, and seeing a psychiatrist would destroy my good kind of craziness. Eventually that belief had drawn me away from any kind of conversation that had anything to do with me. I was a splendid listener, never resentful at all, sucking lives from other people to use for my own purposes. I never allowed myself to have dilemmas, because I had only myself to talk to, and I frankly bored myself. Now I knew I had dilemmas, and I couldn't stand being alone with them. Only what some people were calling a natural disaster could force me out of complacency. It wasn't a natural disaster; it was a man-made disaster, said the pundits I liked. I don't care, I said silently; what counts is that it wasn't my damn fault.

The last time I had had someone listen to me as a whiny child in the guise of an adult had been when Honor was born. I had been rotten to Charlotte, but Charlotte probably had been the person who had taught me how to hide my own stories and listen to everyone else's. She was Honor's godmother, a cruel choice when I knew she had lost her only baby to crib death. But I had been nothing more than a whiny child, and I had thought I was doing her a favor. Over the years, as Charlotte had watched Honor's hand-on-hip ferocity evolve, no matter where I took her, Charlotte slowly lost her ache for motherhood and settled into a distant affection for both of us. I included Charlotte in the world of people to whom I didn't confide, and we talked often, amazed that we found stories that made us both laugh. She was between me and Letty in age, a nowhere in particular generation, but her cynicism ran deep.

I checked Letty's phone, and I heard a dial tone. That was not a given, and it was a delight, as if I'd found an open safe filled with cash. I dialed Charlotte's number. She answered with genuine fear in her voice. "Hello?"

"Hey, you're okay!"

"You scared the holy crap out of me," she said. I didn't know why. "I saw your mother's number on Caller ID, I figured she was calling to tell me you drowned in Mississippi."

"Think," I said. "If I were dead, would Letty bother to call anybody?"

\*\*\*

Charlotte's house never changed, and a brutal storm wasn't enough to make much difference. Even her yard had the colors of Jefferson Parish, patches of green, foliage that was fighting its way back from nothing more than wind. The first thing I ever had noticed about Charlotte's house had been the beveled glass panel in the front door. I would have protected it with plywood or tape, but when I came up on the porch I saw no nail holes, no sticky residue, no cracks in the glass. Charlotte came to the door and saw me inspecting. "The house doesn't face directly south," she said. "I didn't worry for one second."

Charlotte had a bottle of Cold Duck. Charlotte always had Cold Duck, even when I was pregnant and couldn't drink it, just could watch her put away enough for both of us, needing to put away enough for both of us. "You can buy this stuff anywhere," she said. "Except here right now."

I asked her where she went. That was the question all over the city. Stand in line at the grocery, and a stranger was an old friend. "So where'd you go?" That could start a story lasting all the way through checkout, and that was a long time.

"The one place where Arthur can always get a room," she said.

Their parents were dead. Though in my personal experience, parents were the last people offering an open invitation. I shrugged.

"Las Fucking Vegas," she said.

I couldn't picture Charlotte in Las Vegas. I thought of big feathers and neon, and Charlotte was not the big feathers and neon type. She probably wasn't even the type to tolerate a sleek sky suite, and I was sure whatever muckety-muck room awaited Arthur was not a ground-level mildew pit. From what I knew, Las Vegas hotels comped rooms for high rollers. Arthur was past retirement age, with all of his shopping centers securely constructed and sucking money from the right demographics, so maybe he was a gambler.

"Why?" I said.

Charlotte flopped back on the sofa. Charlotte was plumper than ever, and I loved seeing her fall into the pillows. "He brings half a dozen guys there to the convention every year. They love him. I just never had to go before."

Charlotte never talked about herself, and in truth she made a point of never doing anything worth weighing. It happened, it was over, there was nothing to discuss. Up until now, I had tried to do the same. I stayed at Honor's, I lost my house, I was back in town, I was staying in Letty's empty house, it was over. Except, I wouldn't add, the actual finding-Letty part.

"You're in deep shit," Charlotte said. I was glad she put it that way. It kept me from bursting into tears. "You call

FEMA?" I shook my head, no. "You know where that mother of yours is?" No. "What's with Honor?"

I could answer that one. "You don't want to know."

Charlotte smiled. Her smile always was benevolent, and I never minded. "Try to surprise me."

"If I tried to make you guess, you'd never get it," I said. "She came back with this humongous boy named Sciutto Gotti. They act like they're serious. Get this: she told him her family owns Cooper Transportation, and he said maybe the two families could do business together."

Charlotte let out the loud, wild cackle that I earned only if I was truly, deeply funny. It was a big payoff usually. "You're not making this up. You write fiction, but even you aren't this good."

"Nope."

"You're in deep shit all by yourself," she said.

I took a long, nonstop draught of Cold Duck. It didn't seem to affect me, but it tasted good. "I need to think," I said.

Charlotte gently took my glass from me, looked at her watch, and told me I needed to call FEMA. "They can't expect much from you," she said. "And give them my address."

The Cold Duck had affected me after all. I couldn't follow. "All I mean is that you can use this for mail," she said. "Think about it."

\*\*\*

I didn't stay at Charlotte's. I probably could have asked, and she probably would have said yes, but over the many years we had known each other, I had had to prove to her that I was an adult. She had been my supervisor at the St. Francis College library, and I had been a big baby, and begging for refuge would have eradicated all the years of functioning without mewling. So I went back to Letty's before dark. I'd left no lights on, and the place made me feel surrounded by shadows even in daylight.

\*\*\*

I had two chores for that day, to call the insurance company and to find Letty. I called the insurance company first, of course, because it was concrete, tangible, manageable, or at least not Letty. I had all of the right papers with me, so I had the right string of numbers and capital letters, and I thought I was refreshing to the representative on the line, who surely was talking all day to angry, empty-handed victims. I was too numb for anger, and my hands were full of papers. When I said that all that was left was an empty lot, the man on the phone said I would not have to meet the claims representative in Mississippi. "Oh, I need full disclosure," I said, rifling through the papers. "I evacuated with a lot of valuables, all of which are listed in my policy."

"Are you serious?" he said.

"Uh, huh."

"Most people are just claiming a total loss."

"Oh." I was glad I didn't have a total loss. Besides, how was I going to insure my paintings the next time? Wait, was there going to be a next time? A rebuilding? Was I going to have another home? Anywhere?

"We'll be in touch," the man said. I gave him Charlotte's phone number. I didn't want my messages coming to Letty's house. They were far worse than fingerprints.

Hiding my own traces was easier than finding Letty's. Probably because I'd been hiding my traces most of my life. At least the part after my father died, and that was the longest part, because I lost him when I was in tenth grade, a young girl, which made him tragically young, too, though I hadn't known it then. Once she no longer had to pretend to fight so hard against her parents' meanness, Letty became spoiled herself, and that meant everything she owned suddenly was valuable. Grammy giving her costly gifts made that especially true. And marrying Daddy's boss a respectable year later had sealed Letty into pure cleanliness. I could not come into her house with wet umbrellas or dry shoes or bags of fresh corn chips.

I got clean, leaving porcelain clean behind myself. I wore cotton. And I poked around, memorizing where everything was before I moved it. Her cosmetics and toiletries left in the house seemed to be enough for many months for an ordinary person, but Letty didn't think of herself as an ordinary person. Finding traces of Letty in the house was going to do no good. Letty would have liked to be like her mother, actually would have liked to surpass her mother, who had two separate houses. Letty loved reading about film stars who had houses, no, homes, on both coasts and on the Mediterranean and maybe in Paris. Letty could leave behind several wardrobes, and it would give me no clue about how she had left. She might have taken a year's worth and still have left three years' worth behind. She definitely took *something*—she would not have walked out with empty bags. Not even if she planned to fill them at her destination.

I found a lot of her papers in her desk. That meant nothing, because Letty saw no reason to keep most papers. For all I knew, she was smart, saving only annual statements for her CPA, throwing away anything else that came in the mail. Letty didn't recycle. "Oh, it's the right thing to do," she said, "but I'm going to die long before the earth will, so why bother?"

Her 1040 from 2004 was in a cabinet where she saved only 1040s for the past three years. That's what she'd once told me to do, but I'd been too superstitious. I wanted to see her 1040 very badly, and I didn't want to see it at all. Maybe the top of the second page? No, that was the information that would tell me everything I wanted. I sat still, the neat folder from the CPA on my lap. My own 1040 reflected earnings from my work, and that was good. I needed to remember to have some pride. Maybe not dignity, but pride. Letty never had worked. That was not a source of shame, not in any way, except she had become one of those women who acted better than others because she had money. I couldn't wait to tell her that her granddaughter had in effect given her Cooper Transportation simply by saying it was so.

I decided I would look at the form for clues.

Letty took in a lot of money from investments, but she also took in over half a million in straight revenues from part ownership of Marino's Market. Marino's! I hadn't thought about Marino's as a family place since before I got a phone back, when I'd made a small mental list of people Letty knew. Linda had crossed my mind when I peeked in the guest room, but it was the Linda of almost thirty years ago. Marino's was a connection outside of the house. Not only did Letty have to maintain cordial relations with the store, she also probably exchanged greeting cards with Linda. I had liked Linda because, from the outset, she was too lackadaisical for her blondness, and she had little use for Letty's ways. Maybe Letty had gone to stay with Linda in Atlanta; I would go to the store personally to have Linda checked out. Oh, God, what was her name? They would know at Marino's. Linda got money, too.

Phoning Marino's didn't feel quite right. Having a missing mother, particularly one whose name was Marino, probably had a certain gravitas at that store. So I went there.

It was astonishing that Marino's was open. The woman next door had been there a few days ago, and she said the aisles had been packed with people whose arms were full; no one dared use a cart. Few other stores had opened. According to the neighbor, everyone from the back was working checkout or stocking the shelves. Even the general manager was doing customer service. I was afraid they'd have no time to answer my questions. Well, question. Yes or no. Letty or no Letty.

I couldn't find a space in the parking lot, so I left my car a block away and started to walk toward the store. I'd been fearless since the storm, sensing danger had only slowly slipped back into the city, and I wasn't looking in all directions. When the voice came at me from the street, I was startled. "So you're not gonna talk to me, huh, Cooper?"

I turned to my left, where by then the woman was walking alongside me. She almost was too close for me to be able to look at her. Louise Silverman Whatever-Her-Name-Was-Now. "I wasn't paying attention," I said.

"Like hell you weren't," she said.

I shrugged. I usually was vigilant. For me in New Orleans the danger was not the blood sport of street hoods, the danger was the destruction wrought by the women with whom I'd gone to school. It was this Louise and her friends who had read my grandmother's letters from Germany and written a note on them where my father could see it: "The Nazis didn't kill your mother. You killed your mother." It all came back.

It always came back.

The hurt still was fresh.

Last year Louise's father had been on the society page of the *Times-Picayune* for some LSU Alumni event. He was still alive, and while I had looked a little sentimentally at the photo of a harmless old man, I resented his continuing existence. Louise not only never had grieved, but when his time came, it would be a natural time.

"Excuse me," I said.

"You think you're better than everybody," she said. "You think you're so smart."

I told her she needed to stay away from me. I'd always intended to find a way to come to terms with what those girls had done, but this wasn't the time to do it.

I was within ten feet of the security guard. I almost never went to the store, but Ulysses knew me. "Hey, Ulysses," I said. "I need to come into the store by myself, all right?"

Ulysses stepped forward with as much menace as a bald, round man could. "I'm a come in, Ms. Darby."

"I don't want to shop in this crappy store anyway," Louise said.

That was good enough for me. Marino's was the best store in Uptown for pre-cooked meals, long before the storm. I knew if she came back, Ulysses would recognize her and ask her if she hadn't said she didn't want to shop in this crappy store.

\*\*\*

The general manager had been with the store since before Eddie died, and I was glad he hadn't been replaced by a typical executive, thirtyish with comb lines in his hair and a gold wedding band that always shone. That sort liked to be called chief of operations. Harry Stone even was Jewish. The difference between Harry and my father, who'd been Marino's manager, was that he had grown up in New Orleans speaking its form of English. But Harry had gone to Fortier instead of my private school, and being the manager at Marino's was pretty excellent for Harry. In New Orleans, where a person went to school meant high school, and Fortier was the great unwashed public school that my classmates looked down upon. Of course, when I was in high school, Ben Franklin opened for the truly brilliant kids from all over the city, and my classmates, who never were truly brilliant, still scoffed, because all that mattered was how much school cost.

Harry liked himself just the right amount, and I liked him for that. When I found him in the store, he was doing a good job in calming down a woman who could not understand why she couldn't get lump crabmeat.

"I had the same people over for dinner in Houston, and they *expect* me to serve crabmeat salad tonight," she was saying. "Houston is landlocked, you know."

"New Orleans was kind of waterlocked for a while, remember?" Harry said, giving her a funny little grin. Harry had something of a Don Rickles face. Harry could say almost anything, and I would want to giggle.

"Joking about a tragedy does not show much respect to your customers," the woman said. "You have no way of knowing about my struggles. I have no help with this party. *No* help. It ordinarily takes three people in the kitchen, and I have to do this all by myself."

"Hey, you can use mock crabmeat," I said uninvited. "It tastes exactly the same."

The woman opened her mouth to say something contemptuous, but Harry said to her, "Oh, my, this is Darby Cooper. You know, the famous author," and the woman suddenly looked as if she thought mock crabmeat was a good idea. She could tell her guests she learned about it from me, whoever me was, though in a small town like New Orleans anyone with pretensions of importance should have heard of me. That wasn't bragging; that was just a wish for a basic level of literacy.

Harry had jacked me up considerably to save himself, and I could not possibly complain. Though I couldn't think of anyone else I'd have let pull that off.

"So," I said, my arm wrapped tight around his neck, leading him away, "I think I get your undivided attention for five minutes, right?" He nodded slowly, as if I might choke him. I kept my arm around his neck, playfully dragging him through the crowd of shoppers, back to his office.

"You're actually the easiest customer I've had today," Harry said. His face was an adorable shade of pink. I concentrated on his face, didn't want to look past him. Time had passed, enough time that this office seemed to have taken on a new configuration, walls moved though they could not have, desks moved and removed, walls recovered several times. Yet the store muzak still was piped in, classical, and I could swear it still smelled of stale cigarettes, and I had so many senses besides visual, and the visits to my father came at me. It was here where I'd told him that girls in school thought Oreos and Coke were acceptable, and the Hydrox and Pepsi Letty insisted on buying were wrong, and he told me he completely understood. "Oh, this office," I said.

"Never changes, huh."

I shook my head, no. Oreos and Coke.

He waited for me to speak.

Finally I said, "Letty's missing."

He clearly tried to suppress a smile. "People like your mother don't go missing," he said. In New Orleans that meant that she had not been evacuated from a neighborhood that was under twelve feet of water and transported out west—or drowned in that same neighborhood. Those were the two ways to go missing in New Orleans right then. Letty's house was in the dry sliver by the river. Letty never even had heard of the Ninth Ward, much less had had any reason to take herself into a part of the city where she could disappear.

"Well, she's nowhere to be found," I said. "Her house is empty, her car is there, and her luggage is gone."

"I'd say Letty's taken herself a cruise."

I told him I didn't think that even Letty would be that callous, to go without even a note.

55

"Forgive me for talking bad about your mama, but Letty is exactly that callous."

"Look," I said, "I didn't come here because I thought she'd decided to volunteer to man the cash registers when you're overloaded. I just thought that since you guys send her money, you'd have some paper trail, you know?"

He had to think, but I could see he was moving his mind from crabmeat to half-million-dollar checks. "Baby, I'll tell you the truth. For that kind of information you got to have power of attorney. Which you probably lost in the Gulf of Mexico—you had that house over there in Mississippi, right?—or you got to get from your lawyer. But it don't matter, because I don't have anything for you. We send out checks quarterly, but I'm sure with somebody like Letty, we got direct deposit. Which is good, on account of there's no mail, you know?"

That made me remember Linda. I asked him if he was in touch with her, if he thought maybe Letty had gone to Linda's house.

"You promise you won't get your feelings hurt?" he said.

I sensed what might be coming. "I'm sure I won't."

"I'm pretty sure if Letty was drowning, Linda wouldn't throw her a piece of string," he said.

I gave him a *got-it* smile. I hadn't been at the reading of Eddie's will but I'd heard a one-sided account of it. I'd tried to listen sympathetically, but only on the outside.

"Anyway," he said, "you need to talk to whoever handles her money for her. But whoever that is won't tell you anything unless you got power of attorney to show him. And at that you might not see what she's spending. What about her bank?"

All I was hearing was power of attorney. I didn't have power of attorney. If Harry hadn't been half undone by spoiled, undamaged women, he'd have been logical enough to know that Letty never would have given me the satisfaction of that level of trust. Power of attorney meant a trust of judgment. Even if Letty ever trusted my judgment, she could not possibly have acknowledged it, either to me or to binding law. She probably had given it to her cousin William who surely would predecease her any day now. William's legal skills had been so scattershot that he'd had to have his own little one-person firm, and I'd been sure all of my adult life that my grandparents and mother had been his only clients.

I told Harry I didn't have power of attorney. He asked where she banked. Where do you think? I asked. The Whitney, he said, grinning. I nodded. The Whitney always was a decade behind the state of the art, but the downtown office had an all-marble lobby, so women like Letty never switched. "You might get sympathy there," Harry said.

I doubted it.

# Chapter Five

William had me make an appointment. He was in a make-shift office. His building had flooded in the basement, ruining the elevator mechanisms, effectively shutting down the full seventeen stories. He was using one room in a suite of law offices in the warehouse district, and it was bare bones. A desk and his laptop. Like a motel room by the hour. I hoped he didn't think he was fooling me that he had survived the storm. There was no need for anyone to pretend.

"Not much anybody can do for anybody," he said. "But I'm here for you, baby girl."

William was as old as Letty, but attorneys never quit practicing in New Orleans. And old men in New Orleans never quit seeing women younger than themselves as baby girls. For some reason William no longer annoyed me. Even though he'd been the one to tell my grandfather that the will he wrote, cutting my father out of any real peace and acceptance, wasn't legal, but abiding by illegal wills was done every day as long as nobody protested. I translated that to mean, if you protest a will where you've been cut out, then everyone will say you're greedy and never loved anyone.

"Letty's missing," I said.

William let out a phlegmy chuckle, which was to be expected of his type, except that he never had smoked. "Oh, honey, Letty is never missing. You know as well as I do that wherever Letty is, that's the center of the universe."

I told him I was serious. William probably hadn't noticed the storm. He might have noticed that the streets he drove on were terribly messy, and that annoyed him, but otherwise he was unaware that lives had been affected. Since most lives had been of black people getting out with only the shirts on their backs, Katrina had been a world event in another part of the planet. It had nothing to do with his life. And it couldn't possibly affect Letty. As for Letty simply disappearing for no reason, I supposed he figured no one had any use for a spoiled woman in her eighties. Letty was O'Henry's Red Chief. An abductor would have returned her by then. Or killed her in a public place.

"She'll be back," he said. "I guess you're not living in Mississippi, or you wouldn't've noticed."

I told him he was right, that my Mississippi life was gone, at least for now, and he brightened a little, thinking I might need some help having lost a "wonderful, wonderful" house where he had made a lot of memories in his Tulane days. Cecile never knew he went there mid-week, he said. Cecile was Grammy. "I bet Grammy knew everything," I said. *Have your fun, William, so you won't decide to bill me by the hour.*

Even though I bored myself, I gave William all the reasons why Letty's disappearance alarmed me. By alarmed I meant that I suspected something wrong, not that I felt fear about her for only the second time in my life. I gave him a verbal tour of her house; I told him of her uncustomary silence. I didn't tell him that my last conversation with her had left Letty annoyed. "Not a damn thing I can do, honey," he said, and for the first time in my life I fully understood what a keen legal mind was—and was not.

"A spendthrift leaves a paper trail," I said.

"Then you need a private investigator." That wasn't a bad idea, but it was overkill.

"Who's got power of attorney?" I was going to go all Socratic on him, or I was going to go all frustrated.

William shrugged. His face said he genuinely had no idea.

"Letty has maybe three possibilities. Me, Honor, and you," I said. "Now no one in her right mind would trust Honor with five dollars to go to the grocery, and I know I don't have power of attorney, so you want to guess who's left?"

He stared at me for a few seconds, just long enough for me to consider the possibility of senile dementia, then said, "Not Honor, not you, must be me. I can look in my files." He swiveled in his chair, saw a blank wall, swiveled back. "Oops, force of habit," he said.

It wasn't in his computer. Well, not in his laptop. He used the laptop for e-mail, but all of his files were on his desktop and in a cabinet on the tenth story of a shut-down high-rise.

"Oh, hell, you remember my grandfather's will?" I said. "You said you don't have to go by the letter of the law as long as you *expect* everybody to go along with you."

"Damn, girl, you forget anything?"

"Well, it kind of drove my daddy—" I stopped. "Never mind," I said. "Look, all you need to do is walk into the Whitney Bank and tell them you're Letty Marino's attorney and she gave you power of attorney and you need to see her latest bank statement, and I guarantee you'll have a printout while you wait." William didn't have any sense, but when a man who looked like him walked into the Whitney Bank, he looked as if he belonged. William's hair was white, and he was still in seersucker after Labor Day because New Orleans had missed

61

Labor Day, and he could have been king of Carnival for all any bank vice-president knew.

\*\*\*

I had waited on one of the benches next to the corral of vice presidents' desks. Those men—and women—could strut around town with their titles, but they were Dilberts. It didn't matter. A young woman in a suit with pressed-straight, even-cut hair made a pretense of asking William questions, then went off for what seemed to me like a short lunch break and came back with a few sheets of paper. I quit pretending not to watch them now that we had what we wanted, and as soon as William got up from his chair, I walked into the corral and said, "So?"

So Letty had had no bank activity since August 25, the Thursday before the hurricane, and that transaction had been to get her hair cut. I could tell from the price. It was thirty-eight dollars. If she charged more at the salon, it meant color and brows and nails. She'd tried to take me there once when I'd been in town. I'd told her that I wasn't going to fool anyone at my age, and she certainly wasn't going to fool anyone at hers. Of course, my hair had gone from a honey color to streaky with white to more streaky with white, and in truth it looked at all times as if I'd paid for it. I matched myself. Letty would have been striking if she had let her hair go silver, as it surely would have by now. But Letty kept up the darkest brown, her curls covering the roots, and Letty loved herself. So the thirty-eight dollars was her three-week trim. By this time, she needed color. But not according to her Whitney account.

\*\*\*

I had what I called my stomach cancer pain. In the part of my abdomen where I knew my stomach lay, I had a burning that shot and stopped. I wasn't the type to have ulcers because ulcers were a 1950s problem of men who worked eighty-hour weeks for tyrannical bosses or were tyrannical bosses themselves. Never mind that now ulcers probably were caused by bacteria. And never mind that cancer didn't cause pain until it was too late. I was distracted by a quick, sharp pain that might very well have meant fear.

I left William at the bank. He said he'd bill Letty for his time, a generous plan when his cousin probably was dead. I told him I didn't care. I said I would phone him with the contact information for Letty's stockbroker. It was surely someone he knew. No matter how un-Jewish a man was in New Orleans, he knew every other un-Jewish man in New Orleans. Un-Jewish was not non-Jewish. Only the former started out Jewish. Being un-Jewish meant acting philanthropic. Not altruistic, but definitely philanthropic. Philanthropy came with black-tie dinners in air-conditioned ballrooms. Altruism came with handing out hot dogs on killed streets.

By close of day, I learned how Letty's money flowed, great, crazed sums of it, and I learned that it had found its way in quite smoothly and then had sat, waiting. Letty had a checking account and could write checks from Morgan Stanley. She had an American Express black card and could have bought herself a new house in one of those few states untouched by natural disaster. But she hadn't.

She was dead.

Or someone's prisoner.

Or the prisoner of the state.

In New Orleans after Katrina, everyone could have been a good fiction writer, because everything impossible was possible. Imagination was part of all thought, and much thought slipped into conversation, even and especially with strangers. We all needed to laugh, usually in a macabre way, and no one thought it strange to walk away from the counter at Walgreens pharmacy, bag in hand, and say right out loud, "What do you think I can get for this in Hollygrove?" expecting a chorus of, "Shot."

It was perfectly reasonable to think of a half dozen ways in which Letty could have allowed herself to get arrested right before or after the storm. The few police who stayed, and the many military who came in, were not in the mood for foolishness. They would see Letty as a bantam hen who squawked too long and needed to be caged. And once caged, no one was getting out. That was the way law was enforced, unless it was possible to shoot noisy people on bridges or burn them on levees. Usually they weren't Letty's color, but usually they were less annoying.

Dead. Jailed. Kidnapped. Really, I saw no other options. I had a secret life of watching reality television, even using my cable bill as a tax deduction because it seemed to me that A&E and TNT and even TLC and Oxygen were legitimate sources of enrichment for my work. I knew how people disappeared. Even with a hurricane, "dead" covered a lot of possibilities.

I rang the bell at Letty's house before I entered, in case she'd come back, even though now I was sure she was dead or locked up. She didn't answer after a full minute, so I let myself in. I was going to have to leave on lights and air conditioning to keep out smells and shadows. I didn't want to come in guessing about whether she had been there; I didn't want to come in and think about her former presence, either. It was a free place to live while I was homeless, but I didn't think I could last more than a few days.

This was one of the very few times when I was a little sorry to be single. My never having married once had been a huge issue, because women "of our station" did not go out and have babies by themselves. I had tricked a beautiful man into having unprotected sex with me to make a beautiful baby, and Honor was a beautiful baby, and as far as I knew her only disagreeable characteristic was her unpredictability, which lately seemed to come from my matrilineal line. Now, of course, most terribly chic women thought having a husband—in the house or outside of it—was purely optional, but no one who had scoffed at me three decades ago had apologized. Though most of them were dead. Letty hadn't apologized, but I didn't know whether she was dead.

Her last take on the subject had been, "You'd never have pulled this stunt if your daddy was alive." I thought that was true, but not for her reasons.

I was sorry to be alone because I needed someone to work with me. Not be with me, but carry some of the confusion. Having made it clear to the world that I would ask nothing of Honor's father, I was reluctant to ask anything of anyone else. This was a point of pride with me, but it had made Honor alternately furious and sullen. Telling her we had the sweetest life of all did no good. I hadn't been the sort to have a wild circle of girlfriends, and of course alone with a child I would have had no time for a lot of them, either. Maybe in New Orleans I would have made friends with Honor's friends' mothers, because I'd seen the way that worked with private-school children. They didn't live in walking distance of one another, so their mothers shuttled them back and forth, and of course the mothers talked, and then they confided, and then they counted on one another, and then they talked one another into divorces, and then they had only one another to depend on.

In Mississippi I had one friend, Chelsea, Honor's pediatrician. She was a perfect friend because she was too busy to be frivolous, but she was black, and I knew it was just a matter of time before she'd get the hell out of state. Her daughter was Honor's age but went to private school because it was necessary for survival. Generally Honor stayed in the neighborhood, and the neighbors were married couples, and I stayed holed up, writing, and my steadiest emotional tethers were to my agent and editor. But those were tricky connections because I saw them as the ones with power. My success gave me power, I read, but I knew better. I was only as good as what was coming next.

I could have called my agent. Shoshana Miller. She had been sincerely frantic with worry when I couldn't be reached during the storm. Whether her worry had to do with my living to finish my Letty book or not, I couldn't know, but I liked to think she had a certain affection for me. I definitely had something close to love for her. But then she was a woman ten years older who took care of me, giving me what a person needs most, validation, which made her something of a mother, or at least what I would have imagined a mother to feel like. Naturally I would love her. Maybe she chose agenting to be a sweet mama duck, sitting on her eggs, waiting for them to hatch little ducklings who'd follow her anywhere. I'd seen that clip on the news of that mama duck whose ducklings had fallen down a city sewer drain and noticed how flapped she'd been until a human had rescued her babies.

I could justify calling Shoshana in the name of narrative drive. After all, I was writing the Letty novel, and what could be a better twist than the disappearance and death of the protagonist? It was late afternoon. Shoshana had a tendency to get cranky as the day wore on. It was an hour later in New York. I would e-mail her. I preferred e-mail anyway. I could make sense. This was probably why I was a writer. I could make enough sense on the page if I had time. Though I had permission—in fact I gave myself a mandate—to be ambiguous. No one reading what I wrote would blame me for being difficult to understand. I was supposed to be that way, and if my reader couldn't figure me out, it was his fault for not being nuanced enough.

I wrote out all the details, of coming into her house, of finding it in dying order, of checking the closets, the bathroom cabinet. I gave her general facts about the bank, the credit cards. I knew how not to be boring, because I wanted Shoshana to see sure murder and mayhem in every bit of information. She would agree with me that I was moving toward an ugly ending to my book, then she would work me toward needing to feel something. All along, she had said the *Werner Weiss* book had made the public cry because I loved my father. If I didn't work on loving Letty better, she was never going to get an editor for this book, no matter how funny, no matter how complex. Doesn't anger sell? I would ask her. Readers will hold your hand for just so long, and then they'll slam the book and tell you to grow the fuck up, Shoshana had said.

I hit send when it was after office hours in New York. I'd been to her office on West 20th Street a number of times and admired it for its pure lack of pretension. Other agents and all publishers had polished wood and clear glass dividers and displays of all current books. Shoshana's office was one large room filled with large messy desks. If paper was a thing of the past, no one there knew it. She explained to me on my first visit that she had tried for six months to work from home, giving over space to herself and her staff, and she had grown to loathe everyone except herself. She'd decided to pay office rent before she landed on her own list of unacceptable people. Her apartment was about five blocks away, but I'd never been there, and I didn't know how early or late she went home. She had the same phone number in both places.

Ten minutes after I sent the e-mail, Letty's phone rang. Any sound scared me, especially the phone. It was Shoshana.

"Your mother's not dead," she said. No hello.

It was like getting an acceptance letter to Brown after resigning myself to going to Tulane.

"She's with you?" I said.

"Oh, God, no," Shoshana said. "How would your mother know me?"

Too little time had passed since I sent the e-mail. Shoshana had had no opportunity to have done anything clever. Even in New York, where New Orleans could be seen under a microscope. I waited for her to explain.

Shoshana had read my book about my father. From there she knew about Letty secondhand, so she'd had no surprises when I'd sent her the first sections of the new novel. My disguising of actual persons was very thin, and in that time's world of publishing, it didn't matter as long as there was a disclaimer at the front and a pretty good sense that the bad people who recognized themselves weren't going to come out in public and proclaim for all the world that they were in the book, especially when my retort could be, *Well, you're certainly true to life, so where's the libel?* Shoshana knew Letty in print well enough to say, "No kidnapper walks in and says, 'I'm going to grab you and take you off to be my sex slave, and, oh, by the way, please pack up your lovely Louis Vuitton or Chanel or whatever luggage before we go; I wouldn't want you to feel anything but chic while I have you.'"

I had to think that one over.

Shoshana and I on rare occasions talked about feasibility of plot lines, but only on rare occasions. Being a storyteller wasn't what being a literary writer was about, and we both knew that. But Shoshana had a few mystery writers in her stable, and she was willing to play fantasy in real life.

"I didn't say she was taken from her house," I said. "Maybe she was taken somewhere else."

"Is her car there?" Yes. "Did she buy a plane ticket?" No.

I was getting confused. "I hate logic," I said. "You know that. I don't want to be the one to think this through. I definitely don't want to be the detective who tracks her down. Fucking selfish Letty."

"Hey, chill," Shoshana said, and we both laughed because people our age were not entitled to say chill. "You are working yourself into a state that will poison every word you write in this book. Besides, you don't look so good, y'know?"

"I'm worried sick about her when I'm honest," I said. "But I'm never honest except when I'm by myself."

"Thank God you don't work with the public."

"You love me anyway?" I said, knowing love meant nothing in this kind of conversation.

"Yeah, I love you anyway. I've got to love somebody who writes a bestseller and then keeps trying to ruin herself."

"I guess we can both thank Letty."

# Chapter Six

When the phone rang the following afternoon, I wasn't alarmed. I had Shoshana, and I needed Shoshana. She was in my mind as I wrote. Actually as I rewrote. I went back to the first page of the manuscript and propped a slip of paper on my keyboard. On it I'd written a note. *Have sympathy for Letty.* It had to be a tiny note so it wouldn't interfere with my ability to see the screen, and I felt those words did the trick. I remembered the Letty in the Werner book. Before my father died, and Grammy reclaimed her soul, she had been the daughter of snooty rich parents who was trying so hard not to be snooty and rich. Well, she wasn't trying not to be rich; she and Daddy struggled to survive and wouldn't have minded comfortable money. But my grandparents were determined to keep my parents in poverty as long as their Letty was married to that too-Jewish immigrant. When he was gone, Grammy threw enough money at Letty to half blind her. Letty had been so uncomfortable all her years as a Cooper that she forgot whose fault it had been. She let Grammy buy her all the way towards greed. She'd even remarried for greed. Eddie was a good man, but he spoiled her. I needed to remember the mother who had been married to my father. I had sympathy for that mother.

I was going fairly quickly through the second chapter, finding it possible to transform badly behaved Letty into two-sided Letty, and two-sided was fair. When I answered the phone and said hello, I didn't look at Caller ID. The familiar voice on the line said, "Letty, is that you?"

I peeked at Caller ID.

"This is your mother," I said.

"Are you serious?"

I told Honor I didn't know much these days, but I was pretty sure I could vouch for who I was. She told me that she was only calling Letty to try to find me. "I don't know why you don't have a cell phone," she said. I told her I did have a cell phone that I used to carry during emergencies, but the cell towers fell in the storm, so what was the point? "You could've texted," Honor said.

"You could've e-mailed me," I said. Why did we always go to this level?

"God, Darby, if you can't text, why'd I think you could get Wi-Fi?"

I told her I even could get Wi-Fi in Letty's house. Letty didn't have it, but at least three of her neighbors did. But wasn't this all beside the point? Was she looking for me for a reason? I was hoping for housing, but that was foolish. I missed Honor whenever I wasn't with her, but I never let Honor know that. Mothers weren't supposed to depend on their children. I'd seen too many adult women—and men—come on Dr. Phil and complain bitterly that their mothers' lives were so empty that they had nothing better to do but live vicariously through them. My life wasn't empty, but Honor never saw that. If I slipped anywhere close to what Honor saw as clinginess, she would imply that I was pitiful. I would do a lot of fighting with myself to avoid getting my feelings hurt.

"Me and Sciutto went to Gretna this morning and got married," she said. "You have no idea how hard it is to get a license in this city. I mean, half of the government buildings are shut down, so you, like, have to park in one place, go around and find a sign on the door, we're closed, blah, blah, blah, go back and get your car, go all the way to Jefferson Parish. And then do you have any idea where Gretna is? I mean, you really have to *want* to get married."

"Holy shit," I whispered.

"What."

"Have I taught you nothing?" I said. It was the first thing out of my mouth, and I didn't like myself the instant I said it. A marriage was a marriage.

"Yeah, you taught me that if you have a kid by yourself, you're messing up the kid bad. And look at you now. You're all by yourself."

"That's not very nice." I'd have told her it was extremely cruel, but she'd have enjoyed hearing it. She always wanted me punished for giving her no daddy. "Listen, congratulations."

"I'm sorry." She said it sweetly, like a newlywed whose handsome fresh groom was standing right by her. I wondered if Sciutto had worn something better than a t-shirt to the courthouse. My only consolation was that Honor was young, and this could not last. I just had to hope that it ended before I had grandchildren who looked like Macy's Thanksgiving floats.

"Are you trying to tell me you're pregnant?" I said.

"I just got married this morning," she said. If she'd been in my presence, she'd have been batting her eyelashes at me. "Now how could a good girl like me be pregnant?"

I told her the message was received. Not the answer, but

PATTY FRIEDMANN

the message. This must have been what shock felt like. It felt
like nothing, absolutely nothing.

"Have you told his parents he's married a girl who's half
Jewish?" I said finally.

"He says they love Jews, that lots of Jews are in the Mob.
He can't wait to tell his dad about Cooper Transportation."

I said nothing about her having gotten the name Cooper
from a penniless man named Kuper who met a confused clerk
at Ellis Island and then came no closer to the trucking industry
than the produce delivered to the loading area behind Marino's.
I might have been on speaker phone.

I asked her if she was calling because there was something
she needed me to do. I couldn't imagine any sort of celebration.
If only because I had no place to hold one. All hotels were full
of FEMA evacuees, whose ranks I had considered joining until
I thought about the noise. I certainly wouldn't have a party in
Letty's house, which I supposed meant I thought Letty was still
alive. And would I need to call his father? I had no use for his
father.

"I thought you'd want to know, that's all," she said.

"You don't want some kind of celebration?"

"Do we look like that kind of couple? Besides, there's
nobody to invite."

I didn't bother to mention sending out announcements.
Announcements were for innocent little couples who needed
kitchenware, and Honor had a house. Her appliances might
have been decades-old, but then Honor wasn't the type to use
them. I asked instead whether I would meet his family. Sure,
she said, his dad traveled all the time. She was positive he'd be
in New Orleans soon. "And he won't stay *here*." I wondered
how John Gotti, Junior, would enjoy sharing hotel hallways
with FEMA evacuees.

\*\*\*

I learned what it felt like to be a mother-in-law within the week. The phone woke me at three a.m. I answered, and in a lot of dead air I heard a recording say, "You have a collect call from —" silence then "Sciutto—" then "at the correctional facility at Orleans Parish Prison. Will you accept the charges?" It took me a moment to figure out I was awake, then I said yes. "Hey, Darby," he said, taking to my name as if he'd been saying it for years, "I need your help."

"Where's Honor?" I wanted to go back to sleep. I'd never known anyone to go to jail before, but I was sure this was a regular occurrence in this boy's life.

"The cops split us up," he said.

"Oh, great, just great," I said. "Is she in girl jail?" I said it with lightness, but I wasn't feeling lightness.

"Oh, fuck, no, that's why they split us up. See, I'm the one talked back to the cop, and I'm the one getting ready to take a swing at the sonofabitch, so they just haul me in. Look, you don't treat my wife like crap and get away with it. They tried to tell her her ID was fake."

"So where's my daughter?"

"Don't get all worried. She's with her friends. Look, I married your girl to take good care of her."

I asked him why he wasn't calling her and her girlfriends, though I knew where the lockup was, and I didn't want her down there. Honor might have considered herself to be a married woman, but she was all married and no woman.

"You can't make a collect call to a cell phone," he said. Clearly everyone except me knew that.

All right. What next. Next was a three-way call to a bail bondsman. All the bail bondsmen had cards posted next to the pay phone. "You like this one?" Sciutto said. "They call themselves Abracadabra Bail Bonds."

Right away I wondered if there were a way I could work it into my fiction. Probably not, and besides, it was an actual place of business. Whoever owned it had a wicked sense of humor. I told Sciutto to give me the number, and I clicked over and dialed.

The woman who answered clearly had been working the night shift for a long time. She was as clear-voiced as daylight. Can I help you? "Yes," I said. "I'm calling on behalf of a young man named Sciutto Gotti who was arrested a few hours ago—"

"Hold on, please," Sciutto said. "Darby, you can't go around using my real last name. It'll get the wrong kind of attention. And Sciutto's only my nickname. Ma'am?" The woman said yes. In her job she'd heard everything. "I'm listed under the name of Devin Morrow." I wondered if Honor knew this. Devin Morrow sounded more like a TV anchorman than a mob boss in training.

According to her computer, it would cost five hundred dollars to get Sciutto bonded out of lockup. That was five hundred dollars I'd probably never see again. And according to the system, I had to go all by myself to Tulane Avenue, pay the bond, then go over to the jail, retrieve Sciutto, take him back to Tulane Avenue, and let him sign himself off on his bond. "What if I find his wife and give her five hundred dollars and let her do it?" I said. I assumed Honor would have a protective posse.

"That works," the woman said.

"I don't like the idea of Honor walking around here all by herself," Sciutto said.

"The man got a point," the woman said.

I figured finding Honor to ride along and protect me would be counterproductive, so I just told them, "Well, all right, if it doesn't bother you to let a woman of my age walk around over there, I'm on my way. I'll probably be killed at the Whitney ATM anyway."

"Oh, we take credit cards," the woman said.

***

It was still dark when I delivered Sciutto to Honor's house. Her car was there. When I pulled up to the curb, Sciutto hopped out as if I'd just given him a ride from the bus stop, though he didn't bother to stick his head in to say thank you for the ride. Before he could get halfway up the walk, I stepped out of the car and hollered after him, "Hold on, there." He turned around, as if I'd found something of his in the car.

"Get Honor out here."

"She's probably sleeping."

"Are you serious?" I said. It wasn't what I wanted to say. I was sleep-starved, and rage when I was sleep-starved took away my censors if I wasn't terribly careful.

"I'm sure she got in real late."

I walked toward him, clicking my door lock as I went. I told him I'd be happy to wake her up if he was worried about upsetting her.

"Hold on, hold on," he said. "In my family we don't like upsetting people. What you need?"

"Well, generally I get eight hours of sleep, you know?"

"You can't just sleep during the day?"

I told him I worked during the day. I supposed that was a foreign concept to him.

"Honor says you just write books."

Just?

"Look," I said. "Your father owes me five hundred dollars.

The two of you stay away from me until I get my five hundred dollars."

***

It took me until almost noon to calm down enough to fall asleep, and that is when Honor chose to call up and scream at me.

"How can you say that kind of thing to somebody like him?" No hello. She hadn't learned that from her grandmother. She had inherited it. The screaming was more recently acquired. I'd say since the storm. Sciutto was making her even more sure of herself than I had.

I'd been in that deepest well of sleep that comes from deserving it. But I came up remembering the last thing I'd said to Sciutto. I whispered because I was trying not to wake myself up completely. "I told Sciutto or Kevin or whatever his name is that I didn't want to hear from you two until his father sent me my five hundred dollars." My eyes were closed. I put my pillow over my head.

"Do you know who his father is? Can you imagine what the man thinks when you say something like that?"

"Probably that he wants me working for him."

"He thinks you're a bitch."

I thought that sounded pretty good, too. I told her I needed to go back to sleep, and I gently hung up the phone. I put a pillow over it so I couldn't hear it, and I didn't wake up until after three. I tested my mind by going straight to the computer and making myself write. I was softening up Letty, and I found it easy to do. I knew the difference between her and Honor. At least between Letty of the book and Honor of Honor Gotti.

By the time I realized that I hadn't eaten or drunk anything since the night before, it was getting close to nightfall. I had many calorie-loaded options to make up for the day, but all I could think to do was brush my teeth. Toothpaste always killed my appetite, but at least I was doing right by my mouth in a way that a trip to Haagen-Dazs would not. I totaled up the day and found nothing but pure virtue, and I was a little ashamed of myself. Being called a bitch was about the only moment when I could say I misbehaved, even if I didn't. I was known publicly and privately for breaking rules—social, grammatical, thought —and now, here I was, a woman pushing retirement age for those who were quitters, and I took care of business and tolerated no nonsense and even softened my prose.

I rinsed my mouth over and over, went to Haagen-Dazs and bought a quart and a pint, the first for tonight, the second for breakfast.

# Chapter Seven

When I chose the Mississippi house over the boulevard house so long ago, Honor had been my reason. My spoken reason, and so the reason I carried with me as I moved over there from New Orleans and set up a life for her. But I also set up a life for myself, and slowly I began to find meaning and comfort in escape. Not just from Letty, but from everyone I had known. New Orleans had been a small town then. With the ravages of the hurricane, it was becoming a strange kind of smaller.

So many who could not afford to leave had been taken away in buses and then could not afford to come back. They were the ones who still were walking around in Idaho or even California trying to find their food and humor. Those with resources and insurance or criminal wiles were back, recreating just the right kind of familiarity and appeal for us who chose to ignore the phony gloom and instead to restore the darkness of our old ironic selves. I could sense from television that before long carpetbaggers were going to come and stay and feel they had discovered something special, but for the time being New Orleans was my own personal scary place. It was the New

Orleans of my childhood where everyone was personally mean to me.

Seeing Louise Silverman Whatever in front of Marino's had been a cautionary tale. I long ago had learned that if I visited New Orleans, there were certain places I could not go. As a graduate of my school, I had that Oreos and Coke mentality. People from my school went to gourmet groceries like Marino's; they did not go to Sav-A-Center. They did not go to Walgreens; they went to Castellon's. Galatoire's on Friday was a school reunion, and Galatoire's on any day of the week was just asking for trouble. For some reason Stein Mart drew more shoppers from my high school than any Magazine Street retro shops, but Walmart was safe. If I wanted to go anywhere tainted by too-discerning shoppers, I would wear sunglasses indoors and home right in on what I was there for. I did not feel like a celebrity, but it came back to me through Alyce that word on the street was I'd been acting like I was some kind of movie star. Alyce was a girl in my class who'd floated above the nonsense; we'd found each other in a book shop when we were in our mid-twenties, and eventually she'd become my financial advisor, even after she moved to Chicago. I'd figured, rightly, that she'd had good practice in sorting out. Now that it couldn't affect her in any way, Alyce got a huge kick out of reading the *IN News* and following all the e-mails that came from the school and her classmates. I had given the school no address, and the school had not made the effort to find me. Alyce forwarded school communiques and said they were a value-added part of her financial services.

I was becoming accustomed to living at Letty's without fear of her walking in, instead hoping to hear her key in the door. But I also was rebuilding my old habit of skulking around the city, looking both ways, fearing I'd be ambushed by one of those women Louise probably talked to on the phone every day. I had to make some kind of decision about my beach property, and I was having small daily reminders that if I rebuilt on the sand I could escape once more. In New Orleans most people feared the night, but I feared the day. In Mississippi, I could walk freely at any hour, with no crime, no cruel people from my past. I had a past by now in Mississippi, and while I could say that there was nothing more vicious than a swipe delivered in a drawl, no one over there lived for pure meanness. The women from my childhood were nourished by it and fed it to their children.

An e-mail I'd sent the day before asked Alyce the practical questions. I had almost nine hundred thousand dollars in insurance on the beach house. That was replacement value. I had no conflicts the way some people in New Orleans did, differentiating between water and wind damage. This was water damage, through and through. Somewhere in the Gulf of Mexico, as I imagined it, was my intact house. I could have enough money to build a compound of small houses on the property. Or a brand new replica of Jefferson Davis's house. Or leave the lot as it was intended, a piece of beach, and walk away with the cash. And buy in the city. I hoped this was a practical matter.

But Alyce was nothing if not a rising-above kind of woman. She wrote me back. "You're obviously not ready to make a decision," she said. "Use your FEMA money to rent. Wherever you want. That'll tell you something."

And then she forwarded me a couple of the value-added e-mails that distracted me so well, making me angry instead of practical and frightened. News from our school sounded as if Katrina was all for the best. Most New Orleans people who reported in said something to the effect of, *Just want to say we're all right. Thank goodness for our summer house in North Carolina!* Alyce knew how much I liked to get disgusted.

The big newsletters were from out-of-towners, and they had nothing to do with the storm. They, too, disgusted me. The first came every Thursday, no matter what. Alyce never read it. But because everyone thought Alyce was his or her best friend, everyone sent stuff to Alyce. For all I knew, all these rich women used her as a financial advisor, but I didn't want to know that about Alyce because then I'd have to judge her badly. What came every Thursday was the Internet newsletter from the woman who was called Joni in school but now was Joan. Joan was a psychic, though her powers hadn't manifested themselves in any way whatsoever in her younger years. Now she did what seemed to me to be parlor tricks to small audiences, if I could judge from the credits she listed under her photo on the newsletter. Each week she made sweeping predictions about world affairs. She had about a fifty-percent accuracy record, but most of those predictions could have been based on even the most casual reading of a newspaper—and a local one at that. She had predicted the invasion of Iraq, but only when Colin Powell testified at the U.N General Assembly the month before. She had published three books, but when I looked for them on Amazon, I didn't recognize the publisher until I realized it was her husband's name, and that he had published nothing else. I knew my wish to debunk her work made me as mean as everyone else I knew from school, but I was enraged. Her newsletter was so full of misspellings and grammatical errors that she gave both the title "writer" and our high school English department a bad name. I supposed I should have found some delight in that, but I didn't. I searched my angry little soul. Maybe I envied her puffed-out little chest. She thought she was entitled to forty lines under her name. I had my phone number under mine, and now my phone was in the Gulf of Mexico.

The other e-mail emptied my head of blood and possibly of

brain, if brain had a pipe to slide down. It was a group e-mail with no addresses hidden. It came from Charles in California, and the first cc was to Ginger, the liaison at the high school, whose name I had learned over the years of such correspondence. The subject line was, "Forget the Year, Remember the Years." This was going to be sentimental, and I was going to be upset. Seeing these people exhibit what they thought were feelings was like watching Dick Cheney speak softly on television.

Charles hadn't learned to write much better than Joan, but at least he made no pretense of writing books. Charles rambled on and off, and I figured out that what he was trying to say was that, even though this was not a reunion year, he felt that the thoughts about mortality we all surely had had during the storm —no matter where we were—made it essential that we have a reunion before our forty-fifth or fiftieth. The school had said it was a great idea as long as not every class decided to do it, so he was ready to get this thing going.

He got right down to all the details. Dates. Costs. Venues. Lists. Contacts.

Alyce's subject line had been, "See you there."

Next to "See you there" I had written in my return subject line, "Clearly you are not the class psychic."

Alyce enjoyed what she thought was my general rage, because it was a familiar sort of rage, the special cynical kind that New Orleanians grew up with, the kind that could make me spot a local among newcomers in a checkout line after a minute of conversation. Of course, newcomers had no rage; they even had no cynicism. Neither did people in Mississippi, though that was when I lived there. Possibly now things were different, but I had a feeling humor wasn't in the mix. Oh, choosing a place to live was going to take some time. At least I knew nine hundred thousand dollars would buy me nothing in

Manhattan. That was where I always had thought I would fit. That was where my father should have gone. Well, maybe Queens before Manhattan, but he'd have delivered me to Manhattan eventually. I'd have sold Grammy's boulevard house for a one-bedroom and worked myself up by now.

\*\*\*

That was when the barrage of e-mails started.

At my school, anyone who attended for a full school year was considered an alumnus. I supposed it was considered some badge of honor to claim the place, and a lot of people gave money and went to reunions and stayed in touch with one another even though they didn't have the simple mental capabilities to get past, say, eighth grade. That had no meaning for me except that the e-mail list was much larger than the graduating class, and it didn't include the entire graduating class. I, for instance, was not on it. Nor were four women I could think of who had gone on to cerebral lives and saw no reason to look back with pride on a school whose most noted alumni were pro-football players.

Each person who wrote had no idea that cleverness did not lie in poorly covered up bragging. "I'm trying to schedule a speech in China sometime in March," Joan wrote. "I might not be able to make that date." And where are your psychic powers? I wrote back to Alyce. Louise Silverman Whatever wrote that the Japanese magnolias that bordered the back of her property would be gorgeous that time of year, so maybe she and Charles could work out one of the parties. She was sure she could keep it under a hundred dollars a person; that was what one of her daughter's debutante parties had run. Since when did Jewish girls make their debuts?

I phoned Alyce. She was a busy woman, but she always

took my calls. She claimed I was entertaining, and it had to be true. I had a fat little portfolio, but she was up there with the Board of Trade, so I was more of a talisman than anything.

"I was just going to call you," she said. "You need to sell some stocks and get more into the Endowment Fund."

"Well, I'm calling you to tell you these high-school people are making me crazy."

"I don't get you," she said.

With Alyce, it was difficult to know if she meant it. Sometimes she really didn't understand because she was such a conciliatory kind of person, but sometimes I actually baffled her. "You know I stay away from that past," I said. "I even lived across the state line to do it. I've been trying all this time for a way to find peace of mind over those people. Doesn't that say I'm serious?"

"What about living well as the best revenge?"

I wasn't in the mood to debunk Alyce's textbook definition of living well. She needed a better definition than what we learned from schooldays: a certain kind of haircut, a certain neighborhood, a certain synagogue or Episcopal church. I could top the *New York Times* bestseller list and be on a first-name basis with a number of enduring talents, but that made me someone to whisper about. "I was in Darby's novel," Alyce reported one woman had said at an early reunion. It was as if one of the men had said he caught an STD from me, I said, but Alyce said she was bragging. Of course the woman who said she was in my novel hadn't crossed my mind since graduation.

But the girls who had written that evil note on my German grandmother's frantic letter had not had even a reprimand. On the other hand, the only way I had been able to complete high school was by perfecting an I-dare-you stare—and only after the school had been threatened by media exposure. Both they and I had learned some kind of lesson from the school, and I'd been thinking ever since that I was going to unteach it. So far I hadn't figured out how. Alyce hadn't been an up-close witness. After time, I'd hoped that wouldn't have made a difference. She'd lost her father to slow emphysema when she was past forty, and I thought even gradual loss would explain something. I'd have blamed the tobacco company.

Alyce suggested that maybe after this much time had passed those girls-now-women might have had some insight and realized that they owed me an apology.

"Did you hear what word you just used?" I said.

Alyce was the same age as I was, and sometimes she backtracked slowly. We were getting to that marijuana stage in life, of memory dropping off as we moved forward, except that our heads didn't buzz.

"Apology?"

"Insight."

She thought about it for a moment, then said she had to agree with me. Women who stayed in their zip codes all their lives, women who always had housekeepers and no financial worries, women who always had someone, parent or husband, who told them how to vote: these were not people who found thinking necessary. They preferred to look for weakness and talk about it. They were good at it, because they'd done it all their lives. Schadenfreude was fun.

"Know what's funny about you?" she said. "You've written in first person as a black man. You've told a story from the point of view of a bisexual woman. Oh, remember that book about a thirteen-year-old boy? Why can you empathize so absolutely completely with every kind of person you'll never be, and you can't get inside the kind of a head that could have been yours? I mean, they were all around you."

I ached for her to feel like me.

"Inside me there's some of each of those characters I've created," I said.

Alyce was quiet, surely going down the list of three.

"Look," I said, "I *could* write a book using one of those women's voices. I just wouldn't understand her when I was finished."

"That's why you don't know they're scared shitless of you."

It didn't seem as though Louise Silverman Whatever was shy and reticent the day she accosted me outside Marino's.

"And to think I trust you with my money," I said.

"Nothing more objective than money."

"Oh, bullshit," I said happily.

As she had every five years for as long as I could remember, Alyce begged me to show up to see all the people I had no reason to see, the ones who weren't among Louise's friends. Reunions made no sense to me. Not in big groups, not one on one. On the other hand, if someone was relegated to the past until I found a way to triumph over her damage, that was her slot. When Louise Silverman Whatever broke out of the space-time continuum, all I needed to do was call Security.

"I can't see any reason why my mind would change," I said.

"Everything's changed lately," Alyce said. "Do some thinking."

"By the way, I'm probably an orphan, definitely a mother-in-law, and with my luck a grandmother," I said.

"What?"

"Talk to you soon," I chirped, and I hung up.

# Chapter Eight

As someone who considered it a big public philosophical statement that a woman should consider a man an emotional risk when she gets pregnant, I was going against myself a lot. At least that's the way it seemed when I hung up from talking to Alyce. The orphan part stood to the side, but the mother-in-law and grandmother parts seemed to be connected. So I thought a woman got married because she was pregnant. Or because she wanted to have a baby and went along with social norms and grabbed the first man who crossed her path. Either or neither could apply to what Honor had said. "If you have a kid by yourself, you're messing up the kid bad." That could have been her rationale for marrying Sciutto, to show me how to make a family. Or it could have been a chance to put space between her and me, marrying such an odd boy and doing so in such haste. Really. To punish me for not giving her a father, for having set up her father to reject her by making him stay away. When Honor came home from school on Father's Visiting Day in third grade, she said I had ruined her life, and I better never tell her again that all she needed was loving each other.

I watched shows like *Maury* with fascination, wondering where my own belief in eugenics came from. For someone whose life was so twisted by Aryan supremacy, I had gone to considerable lengths to engineer myself a certain child. I hadn't gone to a sperm bank and checked out IQ and height and mental health and European origins and overlap among all of those traits, but I had chosen a man with eyes so green that they could not be genetically recessive. Honor had her father's green eyes and good pieces of my mother's attitude, and I realized that some things slipped past the chromosomes, while others didn't, so what could I learn from Maury? After all, on his show I'd see two people who looked like greased hogs produce delicate, angelic three-year-olds, and I thought maybe the choice of partner didn't matter at all. If that was true, maybe Honor wasn't going to bring me Baby Huey in a christening gown after all.

I was regretting a little that I'd told her and Sciutto not to be in touch until his father came through with the five hundred dollars I'd paid to bond him out of jail. I never had punished Honor. Never. Before she was two, of course, consequences meant removal of something, child or possession, hers or mine. When she briefly went to nursery school in New Orleans, the first long phrase she learned was Child Protective Services. I didn't know why. I didn't know how. Possibly she learned it from Letty, but I doubted it. All I knew was that when I threatened time out, she invoked Child Protective Services. Not even the acronym, but the whole title, perfectly uttered, each syllable, each consonant. I laughed with love the first time she used it, even the second and third. After that, I saw hollering and leaving the room as my only options. Eventually reason became possible, and it worked remarkably often.

Now she was punished, in her first time out. I knew I was deluded in thinking that being cut off from me was a form of deprivation to Honor, but I was trying to look strong in front of Sciutto. They had to come up with money. Honor had income of her own from her graduate assistantship and a nice little trust, enough to live on because she didn't need to pay for housing. I hoped she wouldn't want to protect Sciutto from his family badly enough to take five hundred dollars from her own earnings. Surely this boy or man, or whatever he was, was wealthy beyond what was right, if he was Sciutto Gotti. I'd never let that "if" come to my conscious mind before. Being Kevin or Evan or Devin Morrow seemed a long way from being any kind of Italian heir apparent. But Devin Morrow sounded like a made-up name, too. I didn't want to think about it. I would have to go back to thinking about my Baby Huey, which might not be even a tiny duck egg yet. Or at all. I wanted Sciutto to be a Gotti, with endless cash waiting to be wired.

I wished I were the praying sort. In particular the praying sort of the birthday-candle wishing bent. I'd ask for Honor to call me. She was the only close family I had besides dead Letty, and I needed to have someone around who had an interest in my choices. Not an interest of the openly caring kind, which I'd given up on long ago, but an interest of the vested kind, wanting good outcomes for me because they affected her. Honor would inherit everything from me unless I willed it away to suffering animals, and I'd considered doing so more than once. But I didn't want to leave behind a woman who not only would rage against me, but also would rage against dogs.

The only wormhole I had into Honor's life was what I left in her dining room. All of my treasures, treasures as Honor would see them, were in that room. She might wait a few days and pawn my fifty-thousand-dollar Rodrigue painting for five hundred dollars then give me the cash. I needed to tell her I was coming over to retrieve my belongings because they weren't safe there.

PATTY FRIEDMANN

I didn't want to go to her with the tone it would take. I
didn't like the tone of my thoughts. I was contorting everyone I
knew into fantastical shapes, but those shapes were dark and
grotesque. I was having nightmares in my simple day thoughts.
All I needed to do was phone her and ask for the money. She
would tell me a check was on its way to me. I'd never punished
her before. She didn't need me to start now.

I called her cell phone, and it took four rings, one short of
voice mail answering. Messy air was followed by her non-hello,
"Hey, I thought you weren't talking to us 'til we paid you that
money." I could feel Sciutto in the messy air.

I was ready, much to my surprise. "I said not to call *me*
unless you had the money," I said. "Does your silence mean
you don't?"

"You're pretty good," she said, and the messy air organized
itself into dead air that meant the mouthpiece was covered. I
called out so she could hear me over whatever she was
whispering to Sciutto. "Let me talk to him," I said. "Unless you
just want to put me on speaker."

"Hey," he said after a few more seconds of dead air.

"Hey, yourself."

"What you need?"

"Good morning," I said.

"Good morning."

I told him I didn't *need* anything; I wanted something.

"If you're talking about that half a grand, you know that's
chump change to my dad," he said. "I didn't even bother him
with it." I didn't know whether to translate that to mean that he
was sparing his father the reason. "I just called his office, and
they put in a requisition. It might take a billing cycle."

"Bail bondsmen don't wait a billing cycle," I said. "I came
up with the cash in about an *hour.*"

The next thing I knew, Honor was on the phone. "Do you

94

realize Sciutto's my husband? Why are you treating him like that? This is a man who takes care of me."

Honor came by that tactic honestly, but this was the first time she'd used it. My father always had said the best defense was a good offense, and I'd heard it often and liked it but never used it. It was one of the few legacies I had from him, and I'd quoted it to Honor.

What surprised me was this *husband* business. It was as if she'd been waiting since third grade to throw that word at me. The taking-care was a nice touch. Maybe it was true. There was more in the world than money. I'd told her that.

"Come on," I said. "Don't you think I've earned a little familiarity picking him up from jail in the middle of the night?"

She had to give me a little giggle for that one.

"Listen," I said. "This isn't a time for antagonism." I stopped. Honor and I always had been polysyllabic with each other. That's what probably had sent the girl into graduate school. But I had a feeling Sciutto was listening, and I had a feeling he didn't like abstractions. "I mean, we're right now in the part of the country where everybody's in a fucking mess together, and you need to knock yourself out trying to get along." The murder rate was down to levels unseen since my childhood. Traffic deaths surely were down. Probably infant mortality was closing in on zero because New Orleans seemed remarkably free of children. If the city was in so much pain that no one could hurt anyone else, then we were part of that pain.

"I don't know why you're on my case," Honor said.

I apologized to her. I told her I loved her. I told her my house was in the Gulf of Mexico, and my mother surely was dead.

"You don't like Letty," she said.

"I guess I love Letty," I said. "Hey, see? Talking to you helps me figure stuff out."

95

PATTY FRIEDMANN

"She doesn't like her mother, but she loves her mother," Honor said to Sciutto.

"Makes sense," I heard him say in the background, and for some reason I knew absolutely that they weren't extrapolating to Honor and me, not thinking Honor loved me but didn't like me.

"Look, no matter if you hate Letty, you've got to find out what happened to her, right?" Honor said. "I mean, I'm cool with her, but even if I weren't, I'd damn well want to know where she is, especially if she's, like, dead. You call the FBI? You know, there's websites for missing people. At least there were during the hurricane."

I'd put Letty on that website when the National Guard came by right after the storm. Now it was impossible to log onto the computer without being led there. Thousands of people were listed, and if they were found, they probably weren't taken down. Thank goodness it was the worldwide web, so someone dumped unceremoniously in a small town in the west could go into an internet café and see his name and see the contact number to report himself alive and report in. And maybe someone with space in New Orleans would send fare to get him back, but probably not. Letty on that list was pointless. Letty was almost completely computer illiterate. Well, not illiterate, but deliberately computer-ignorant. Her first act upon finding herself would not be to log on and find out if she was in fact lost. And the odds against her being spotted by viewers of the website were astronomical.

Still, I had looked. And she was on there with her own phone number. She could leave herself a message saying she was alive.

I also had tried all government agencies, local, state, and federal. Lines were busy during all business hours, and recordings after hours did not allow for messages; they said to try back during business hours. I decided, just as Honor did, that the FBI was where my best chance was. Letty was not going to disappear locally. She would have been found noisily. Anything bad washed up quickly in New Orleans. It was impossible to throw evidence in water or bury it somewhere shallow, because the place was too wet, and someone would find the trove. People burrowed and poked and floated all over the city too much, and a body with or within a Chanel bag would have been news.

Letty definitely had to have crossed a state line, because Letty did not believe anything except New Orleans existed in Louisiana. I supposed that meant that I still believed that Letty had abducted herself, refusing to go to, say, Shreveport because she didn't believe in it. So Letty was FBI-eligible, and I narrowed my phoning down to their number, but hitting "redial" every ten seconds did me no good.

"You can't just call the FBI," I told Honor. "Their line is always busy."

"So use your connections."

I heard Sciutto in the background saying, "What?" and Honor whispering, "She can't get through to the FBI," and I wondered what he would say. Was he under surveillance? Could Honor just walk out her front door and talk to whoever was sitting in a car across the street?

Honor told me to hold on, and the phone went to dead air so I couldn't hear the telltale conversation. Finally she said, "Sciutto says that we're nuts. Half the people in New Orleans are missing, so the FBI has bigger problems than Letty. A *lot* bigger problems than Letty. He thinks you need a P.I."

I didn't know what that was. I was sure I'd heard it before, with all of the reality television I'd watched, but I couldn't work out the acronym. All I could think of was public defender.

"Private Investigator," Honor said when I hadn't reacted. She said it like she hadn't just learned it one minute ago.

I liked the idea. I liked Sciutto right then. We were all in this together, and they were my family. Sciutto knew all about family, even if right now he was telling me that his family was accessible only through a requisition slip. Maybe money was something different from loyalty and commitment. Maybe Sciutto was going to be good for Honor in the right ways. Maybe Honor was right, that he was her big man, tending her.

"So you two can find one for me?" I said. "I'm sure search-ing the Internet is easier than going through the phone book."

"Are you nuts?" Honor said. "Please don't go all solipsistic on me, Darby. You haven't even noticed that Tulane's closed, and if I want to do next semester, I'm going to have to leave town. You're not the only one with problems."

"Oh?" I said. "A problem?"

I was waiting for Honor to admit she was pregnant, and that sounded like a possible opening. Though being pregnant did not seem like something she would present as a problem. Right then I was not going to come out and ask her about it again. When Honor was in her mid-teens I had learned that sometimes asking direct questions was the direct route to direct silence. When I really wanted to know something, the only way to get information out of her was to feign indifference. That was not the same as ignorance. And making sure she knew which one showed was an art I'd perfected over the years.

"Problems, plural," was all she said before we hung up.

\*\*\*

I was of the age that used the Yellow Pages. I looked under private investigators, which referred me to services like collection agencies that I didn't need. There were about a half dozen, and I could tell from the brief listings that most were like what I'd seen on *Cheaters*, doing surveillance in contentious divorces. There was so much nastiness in this business. Were these detectives ever gentle enough to want to reunite families like Troy Dunn on *The Locator*? Too bad Letty hadn't been missing for decades. I could have called Troy Dunn. That was another reality show that justified my cable bill as a tax deduction.

I googled one of them, found his website was called cheatertracker.com. Another had a long list of information he could find, all about assets and patent infringement and workers comp fraud. That one listed missing persons along with runaway teenagers. He required everything you ever knew about the person, which included the names and addresses of everyone she knew and all of her hobbies and Internet history. If I had that, I'd do it myself. As far as I could tell, hiring a private investigator only made sense if I found myself too alone. Though that was a distinct possibility.

# Chapter Nine

When I lived in Mississippi, I had a well-defined life. At least after Honor was grown and didn't dictate the parameters of my days. I went to bed very late so I could sleep very late, in effect living in a time zone that had little overlap with that of those around me. The only person terribly inconvenienced by my schedule was Shoshana because she was on the east coast, where it was an hour later, but she was just as absolute in her refusal to squeeze into predictability as I was, so for the most part she and I relied on email, and when we caught each other, we caught each other. With the hours I kept, I could roll out of bed and write until mid-afternoon and consider myself complete for the day each day. After that, anything meaningless was all right. I could scrub or shop or watch terrible foolishness on television, and it was productive time or it was not. I could be plotting as I scrubbed or collecting funny names as I watched television, or I simply could be laughing at Paris Hilton and Nicole Richie being brilliantly stupid. I enjoyed the rich silence of my own company. No one complimented me, but no one criticized me, and I loved that balance above any interaction. If I needed a companion, I went to fantasy, fleshed him out, quirked her up, created a story, started writing.

I was as happy as a sleeping baby every day all day in my Mississippi life. If a phone call intruded, or I had to leave to visit New Orleans, I became unhappy, but I took on a little frisson of extra happiness as soon as I was on my way back. I needed to recreate that life. I didn't need the grand Mississippi house that was big enough for Jefferson Davis—or, rather, for those who imitated him, at least architecturally. I needed a space where the neighbors didn't intrude, and the walls didn't scream at me to behave or Letty would know. I could stay free where I was, but I had to get out. I even had figured out what to do about Letty's phone number. It was the contact I'd posted for her to call in the unlikely event that she found herself. I thought I'd have to have it transferred to wherever I moved. Then I realized that all I had to do was change the message on her answering machine to say callers could reach me at a new number. I hated to speak over what might be the last recording of my mother's voice, but I might have to. "Just buy another machine," Charlotte said. "They're cheap now, I'm sure."

Charlotte was helping me find a place to live, and she'd probably helped me too well. The house she found tested me. My first reaction, oddly, was not *no*. "Arthur came home and told me about it two days ago," she said. "You can't ignore that kind of coincidence."

I told Charlotte I was going to drive by. She asked if I wanted her to go with me, and I said no, I wanted to see what it felt like to drive up all by myself. I imagined her shrugging through the phone line. The front of a house was the front of a house. It might have had what was called a New Orleans paint job, which was an application of paint to the front because no one can see from the front what the sides and back of a shotgun look like. But basically it was going to be the exact same house. There was no way to explain that the person driving up was not the exact same me.

When I pulled up in front, I felt as if I'd come home after a long imprisonment. This was where I'd lived with three pieces of furniture before Honor was born. Everything after that, not just Honor by any stretch, was a responsibility that took away from me. Yes, I remembered living there and being in the shower with a headful of shampoo when Letty phoned to read me her poetry, and that had been an encumbrance, but it had been my only one. Letty was my worry again, and maybe she could be reduced back to my single worry in this house.

I sat parked with no fear of what I assumed still was not a good neighborhood. I sometimes played that game I made up in which I'd half-close my eyes and pretend it was a year in the far past, and I hadn't experienced certain things, that I didn't yet know certain people or inventions. If I did it in a car, I couldn't look at the dashboard because there was FM radio and a CD player; I'd look up through the windshield. *I'm here in front of my house, home from work and Honor is in the back in her car seat.* It lasted as long as it took for me to see the fresh yellow paint and shutters that were a reminder that New Orleans was cleaning up from a historic storm. With the storm came all the other recent facts.

I wrote down the name and phone number of the agent.

***

The agent named Ladette gave me the tour of the house. It was too small a place to be staged with furnishings to make it attractive to buyers. Instead it was bare-bones empty, not far different from when I'd first lived there, before Letty had married Eddie and tossed me his old furniture that had a vague scent of uncaring middle-aged man. "It's a perfect place for a woman living alone," Ladette was saying. "And since the storm this is a very hot neighborhood. There was no flooding."

I told her I lived in this exact house thirty years ago.

"Were you nuts?" she said, and we both burst out laughing.

She let me roam. Any other buyer could have seen the whole house in two minutes. I took it one room at a time, able to see every change. I knew when a light switch had been replaced, of course when a wall had been painted. Improvements were good to see, but I was amused by what was kept, especially what I had done myself. I had put in a splashguard in the kitchen that reflected my childlike lack of talent, slightly dancy rows of half-inch tiles that made a primitive image of the house and the ones on either side of it. It seemed to me that traces of myself meant scrimping, yet for me they were comfort.

"I haven't been exorcised out of here," I told Ladette.

She gave me a look I knew well. It was the *I know you're Jewish* look. I'd seen it all the time when I went to my almost half-Jewish school.

"I just mean the house still has traces of me," I said.

"That's a good thing, right?"

"If I ignore the fact that it means they saved money on replacing stuff I did a long time ago, yes."

Ladette just smiled. She'd been in the business a long time, and she wasn't one to push, especially on a house under three hundred thousand. Ladette had listings worth more than quadruple this one. The owner must have been a childhood friend who had too many rentals in her portfolio and decided to unload in the post-storm market. Everything was priced to gouge after the storm, especially close to the river, where it had stayed dry.

We were in the room where I'd put Honor's crib and then her big-girl bed, and I was looking at the walls and remembering the whimsy that Honor had loved greedily, and Ladette probably knew she had me.

She handed me her business card. "If you're interested, just call," she said. She had the good sense not to look dead certain.

\*\*\*

Like anything bureaucratic in shut-down New Orleans, real estate was wobbly and slow. I had called Ladette that day and as soon as we had agreed on a price I had said I wanted to move in the next day. In a wobbly, slow city, rules were made for bending to the limit, and the owner let me rent until the act of sale. She had nothing but my sincerity to protect her, but that was a valuable commodity in those weeks.

I bought only three pieces of furniture for my old new house. This was not in any way an act of PTSD, the way articles were saying such behaviors indicated. Fear of loss. That made sense, of course. Though my counter would have been that losing everything and surviving would mean that loading up again would be easy, knowing that things were just that, things, easily forgotten. New things, that is. A mattress and box spring, set on nothing but a metal frame, did not do for me what the canopied tester bed from Letty's childhood had done. That bed hadn't made me feel like royalty or even like Letty. But it had made me feel in place. That bed had been too heavy to move. I didn't know why the storm hadn't left it where it stood, a scrap of floor under it, everything else gone.

I was gambling on this house because I was putting my treasures in it.

Honor didn't know what I'd been doing because Honor evidently was too busy justifying a semester in New Orleans doing nothing with Sciutto instead of a semester at any college in the country, even the Ivies; this was the generosity of the world to New Orleans. Honor would have found my house business boring. I was holding onto the Mississippi property until I knew I was fully awake, and in the interim Alyce let me pay cash for the little New Orleans house. If Honor had been in the mix, she would have insisted on going to Hurwitz-Mintz and buying decorator furnishings for each of the tiny rooms. She would have no memory of the house at all, would see it as adorable, free of meaning. Each sofa and throw rug would have to color coordinate with the art stashed at her house.

I phoned Honor to tell her I was coming to get my stuff. I called it stuff.

"You realize what kind of so-called 'stuff' you've got over here?" she said.

"I didn't half break my back loading it into my car to haul it out of Mississippi for no reason," I said.

"Like that George Rodrigue is worth a shitload all by itself."

I wondered what had prompted her to inventory all of my property. She never before had had an interest in my collection. It had been wallpaper to her.

I also had works that were either signed and numbered or originals by Rouault, Toulouse-Lautrec, Clementine Hunter, Walter Anderson, Hogarth, and a bunch of my friends other than George who also weren't dead. The Walter Anderson itself had skyrocketed in value since his studio had been blasted in the hurricane. The reason I had so much good stuff was that Letty had decided that good art was strictly representational, the truer to life the better. (The Lautrec and Hogarth came close to meeting her standards, but she preferred color.) She acted as if my taking that ugly so-called art off her hands was a favor. Honor in many ways was like her grandmother: the only art she liked was photography. Color photography. It looked odd in the boulevard house, but it was her house. I wasn't sure what I'd do about my collection, such as it was, when I died. I realized I could just leave it for Honor to dump, but I didn't like the idea of contempt at the gone stage of my life.

I thought about saying that one day Honor would not be my only descendant, that maybe she would have children who would share my taste in art. But I checked myself. It would take her off on a tangent.

"That stuff can't be replaced," I said.

"That's probably why it's worth so much," Honor said.

"You mean money."

"Well, yeah," she said.

"Well, I don't."

"I know *you* don't. I always know *you* don't. You write this one book, which weighs, what, maybe two pounds, and it takes you about six months to do, and you get, what, a million dollars or something, so how are you supposed to give a shit about money?"

This was a new Honor. Money always had mattered to Honor, but not to the point of thinking hard about it.

I told her I wanted her to come see my new old, old new house. Why? Because then she would see that I was not the one who had something to show.

"How's Letty going to find you?"

"I'll leave a message."

# Chapter Ten

I forgot this was the address on her birth certificate.

Naturally Honor had driven past this house a number of times in her life without bothering to mention it to me. So when she pulled up behind me, her car less loaded than mine, but still full of paintings and other treasures, she leapt out as soon as she'd shifted into park and ran over to me. "This is extremely cool!" she said. "How did you find this?"

I asked her if she knew what house this was, and this was when I learned that since she first saw her birth certificate because she needed it for her driver's license, she'd been checking out this house whenever she was in New Orleans. Seeing the front of a shotgun hadn't told her much, and yet it had told much of what she needed to know. I hadn't been reticent about giving her the history of her creation, which was a sight easier than explaining the Book of Genesis that all of her little friends were getting in their regular Mississippi Bible lives. I lived on a nice little street with nice little houses, and a very nice man lived in a big building on a funny street named Tchoupitoulas. She loved learning to say Tchoupitoulas. He helped me make her, I said, and she said, "Did he put the head on?" That was a good shared story for a long time, no matter how angry she later became because he never came into her life.

I hesitated, knowing her reaction. The man on Tchoupitoulas Street found it, I told her. He didn't tell me; he told Arthur.

"Well, fuck," she said. "*Now* he shows his face. *Now* when he's made me feel like crap all my life."

"You know I made him stay away."

"He could've found me if he wanted," she said. "I give him just as much blame. He's no better than a father who'd have lived in the house and rejected me."

When she was about twenty, she told me Amanda came to her and said she should track him down and get it over with. Amanda even had done the easy detective work: she looked in the library in the old Yellow Pages for a photographer on Tchoupitoulas Street. Honor had ranted at Amanda for a good week or so. "It's not my place to love him first," she had said.

I wanted this moment to be as if I were bringing baby Honor to the house. As if we were a sweet twosome. I would pretend inside myself so she wouldn't know.

I told her to lock the car. Though nobody in this neighborhood, thirty years ago or now, would look through the windows and see paintings and bother to break in. Trying to run up the street with a framed piece of art and then to unload it made no sense. I needed Honor to walk into the house to see three pieces of furniture.

She could hear her footsteps echo on the hardwood floors as she walked slowly from front to back. The first room had a sofa. The second room had a table. And the third room had a bed. The fourth room was empty. The last room was a fully redesigned kitchen with the only vestige of my life there the splashback I'd put in. The bathroom was next to the kitchen, just like a real shotgun. "I swear I remember that," she said, pointing at the splashback. Before she knew what she was doing, Honor hugged me.

I walked into the fourth room, now empty. "This was your room," I told her, trying not to let too much love leak out. "I decorated it in Winnie the Pooh characters. The real ones, not the Disney ones."

"No wonder I'm getting my doctorate in English," she said.

I was tempted to put my arm around her shoulder and give her a squeeze, but I knew better.

\*\*\*

Only after we had carried in the paintings did I remember that maybe Honor was pregnant. I had given her all the small ones because she was doing me a favor, loading and unloading, and I thanked myself. Though I wondered why I wanted this possible pregnancy to hold. I supposed because no one ever wished for a tiny preventable death. I knew she wouldn't offer to help me do the hanging, pregnant or not, because large pictures on walls usually were mounted by the magic of male strength.

I didn't want Honor to leave. I had a lot to do. But I wanted us to be the two of us for as long as we could. We could picnic on the floor. Maybe Lucille was still in business. Lucille would be as old as Letty now. Lucille's corner grocery-sweet shop was my home and sanctuary and source of sandwiches when I lived alone. I was sure Lucille was still working because she wasn't like Letty, waiting for nothing to do. I was sure Lucille was still alive.

"You ate a lot of food from Lucille's on Tchoupitoulas when you were little. You want to go have a Proustian exper-ience?" I said.

She said she found it hard to believe anyone was still in the same place with the same ingredients after all this time. I asked her where she was from. She said that was a very good question.

"Are you serious?"

"Do you recall that you dragged me kicking and screaming across the state line to wring all my bad New Orleans ways out of me when I was three?" she said. "Why shouldn't I tell people I'm from Mississippi?"

"Because you're not. If you had the privilege of being born here you better claim it. Especially now. Have you seen how many people are coming here and acting like they discovered New Orleans for the first time and saying they're staying here forever? Whatever sense of humor you picked up, you better wave it around like you're something special, because it makes you local, and being local isn't something you can just claim."

She looked at me as if to ask me if I realized what I was saying.

"Yes, you do, too, have a cynical sense of humor you can't get anywhere else. You just need to use it more."

She was quiet, as if I'd just told her she was beautiful for the first time. I'd been going at her wrong, evidently.

"I'll bet you five dollars you can't find anything familiar at Lucille's," she said. "And that includes the building."

"Oh, let me hug you," I said, and when I did it, she hugged me back.

\*\*\*

Honor lost her bet. Though I didn't tell her the reason, we went around the corner the back way, using an old trick of mine to stay out of her father's line of sight, and we saw immediately that Lucille's was open for business. It used to be R&R; now it was R&R&R. It was like so much of New Orleans. A person could ride past and say, "Oh, dear, so much devastation," and then say, "Oh, my, that's how it looked before the storm."

The weatherboards were a different color than the faded off-yellow they had been when I lived there; now they were a faded blue-gray. I'd say that meant one paint job. A stranger from the north could drive by and think this was wind damage, but I knew better. There was little point in painting a wooden structure in New Orleans when humidity would undo the effort within the year. Things would be different now. When this building was painted next, the red X-mark from the National Guard would disappear, and passersby could say, *Definitely been painted since '05.*

I was nervous walking into the shop. My last visit had been as a young, foolish woman whom Lucille enjoyed like crazy because she could call me out on my mistakes.

Two women were behind the counter. An old Lucille and a fairly good copy of the Lucille I'd seen last. Probably that third R. "Well, look what the cat done drag in," the old Lucille said as soon as I'd cleared the threshold. I'd never been behind the counter before, but I broke all the rules and scurried back there to give her a hug. Honor and the copy of Lucille looked at each other as if they'd been through this before. Lucille pulled back, looked at Honor. "This got to be the baby," she said. "You look just the same. I know you don't remember your old Auntie Lucille."

Honor told her no, but from what she'd heard, she had Lucille to thank for her existence. Lucille had been the go-between with Honor's father, who went in there for cooking oil and toothpaste and bleach. She wouldn't carry messages, but she would carry phone numbers. And she would sometimes tell me what he said.

I expected Lucille to cast her eyes down and demur, but

113

Lucille said, "You sure do, baby, you sure do. I just stood here and carried messages like a pigeon."

Lucille introduced me to her granddaughter Cecelia. "It's nothing like it was back in the day, no," Lucille said. "She just here checking up on me. I give her this business, she take, what you call it?" The granddaughter told her "equity." "She take the equity and get herself a dress shop on Magazine, pretty soon she got three shops, all over town, only one flooded. Couldn't've done that thirty years ago, no."

All I could think about was that I still had Lucille.

"You still run this place?" I said.

"Aw, no, baby," Lucille said. "I got staff."

"I *told* you," Honor said.

What.

Honor spoke straight to Cecelia, as if the two of us didn't exist. "I made a bet with my mother that if we came in here, the food was not going to taste exactly the same as the last time she ate here."

"You going to lose that bet," Lucille said to Honor. Then to me she said, "You want a couple of roast-beef po-boys dressed to go? I may not do the business and stock the shelves, but I sure do all the cooking."

***

Lucille had known to give us several sheets of butcher paper. She had followed my career in the *Times-Picayune*, but when I told her I'd moved back into my old house she told Honor and Cecelia she knew for a fact without looking that I didn't have "ary chair" for sitting on even if I had a table. She had visited my house once, and that had been all it had taken for her to tell me there was no point in coming back. Even after Letty had dumped all of Eddie's man furniture on me, and Lucille could have sat on a genuine lightly stained leather sofa.

Honor and I sat cross-legged on the floor with dripping sandwiches and Barq's. "I've never been away from Sciutto this long," she said. "I need to get back."

"What's he going to do in New Orleans if you're all he's got?" I said. I loaded my words with concern. Inflection wasn't something I could use in print, but I could create it in tone.

"You don't think taking care of me is a full-time job?" she said, smiling with just a touch of irony in her expression. "But really, he's got plenty to do, I assure you. Don't forget, his dad is, like, a major businessman, so all he has to do is make connections, and he'll be really busy. Especially now when there's so much going on, you know?"

There was caffeine in the root beer. I was feeling bubbly in my arteries. "So have you offered to connect him to your dad's partners in Cooper Transportation?" I said.

She looked up at me under hooded eyes, her mouth working at that sandwich. I wasn't exactly someone whom she could tell that her family really did own a trucking conglomerate. "All I said was that if we were going to have a good relationship, we shouldn't mix love and business. He agreed."

Honor was a sharp girl. Not sharp in the way I dreamed of when I mixed visual and make-believe genes, but sharp in a self-reliant way that made her different from Letty. Sometimes she was so similar to her grandmother that I remembered that Jules Feiffer cartoon about the woman who tried to do the opposite of her mother as a parent only to find she'd reared a daughter just like her mother. But Letty was a foot-stamper, while Honor seemed more willing to expend the energy to connive. And yet if I dared to allow myself to think of all the men our distaff line had bedded, while all but Honor's father and my daddy had been slightly repellent, my grandfather for his drunken uselessness, Eddie for his terrible sense of humor and love of garlic, only Sciutto was truly shocking. Honor was a glorious girl. Men stopped to look at Honor. If women stopped to look at Sciutto, it surely was to wonder what she was thinking.

"I guess you're not going to do next semester at some other school," I said.

"Now how can I ask a man, who only wants to look out for me, to move to a strange city and then leave him?"

"I thought you said he had plenty to do."

"We're *married*, Darby. I mean, I just love sitting on his lap; I don't need to do anything else."

"Clearly something I know nothing about," I said, giving her what she wanted.

She put down her sandwich, which was only about one-third finished. I knew one thing about my daughter, that she could pack away limitless amounts of food, never exercise on purpose, and still stay slim in a non-threatening way. Honor was a whole-po-boy with fries kind of girl. "I really need to get back to my husband," she said.

"You look kind of queasy," I said.

"You trying to hint at something?"

"I'm actually not," I said. It was true. I was thinking about her eating habits. "But as long as we're at it, I'd rather ask you straight up." I'd been restraining myself too long about pregnancy, using my old rule that had applied to long-ago secrets, like confessions about losing toys or taking a few puffs of marijuana. A baby was a different matter.

"I'm a grown woman now," she said. "You have to respect my boundaries. What you're thinking is awfully sensitive. You wouldn't make that kind of suggestion to anyone else, so don't make it to me. If I told you, Sciutto would be really upset. He wants us to have a very private life."

"Doesn't my being your mother count for anything?"

"Does Letty being your mother ever matter?" she said. "Sciutto says if I let you cross one line, you'll cross them all. And I won't exist as a separate entity anymore."

I wanted to ask her if one Mrs. Sciutto Gotti was still a separate entity.

I controlled myself.

"Just wait 'til you think I'm dead," I said. "Just wait."

# Chapter Eleven

I created my prison fantasy easily. My prison fantasy was everything about solitude and nothing about external control. I made my cell, I gave myself an excuse not to leave, but no one told me when to get out of bed or when to turn off the lights, and certainly no one chose what I would eat. I left a sign on the door that said, *If I'm not expecting you, go the fuck away*, and I turned off the ringer on my phone, checking for messages if I bored myself. A living Letty was a punitive Letty and so had lost the right to make me neurotic. I had taught myself how to create a small shell in Mississippi, and I had used probably a hundred square feet out of about three thousand. Now I was wasting a much larger percentage of space. What I was wasting could not disappear, in fact had waited for me, and for all I knew one day the Mississippi house would wash back up onto the beach, intact. But I still wouldn't use most of it.

I spent most of the day on the sofa in the front room. I'd chosen a sofa with wide seat cushions so I could surround myself with pillows and place my laptop in front of myself on a cushion, my legs bowing around it. Whoever named the laptop was nuts: ten minutes with the computer on my lap, and I began to feel as if I was going to sustain first-degree burns. Sometimes I sat cross-legged with it perched on a pillow on my ankles, but I felt that if I stayed hunched over, I'd get stuck that way.

The novel about Letty was going more slowly than the one about my father because I had more chronology about her. It was fiction, but the fiction was filigreed and contorted history, as was all fiction in varying degrees. So I had all of Letty's life to play with, while I'd had only the years between 1939 and my father's death in the previous book. Daddy had given that oral history in which he refused to talk about any time before his coming to America. He called it America, not the United States. I decided when I wrote the novel to respect his decision. It was easier for me because he wasn't here to answer my questions about his younger years, questions he hadn't answered when I was a child, either. There was probably a lot of sadness in those years, of being born in Germany in 1916 and maturing straight into evil.

With Letty, I had adequate witness and documentation all the way back to her birth. When I started writing, she brought out photographs to our first few interviews, as if I were doing a long-overdue biography. Very quickly I told her that I thought I had enough; all I needed was to get a sense of what her house and school had been like. Before she could volunteer to hold forth, I assured her that poking around at Honor's and steeling myself to visit the school archives would suffice. I could build a lot of story looking at photos of rows of girls on sports teams. I couldn't bear hours of all the wrong details delivered while Letty drank black coffee and became more and more excited.

Now I didn't have Letty around. I didn't need to question her, but I needed to know I could. I needed to have her nearby so I could have perspective—even though Shoshana had said that for the novel to work I had to find my perspective, think it through, and alter it considerably, or no one would want to read all of my complaining. Letty's absence was altering my perspective considerably. I wasn't the type to make bargains with God—*oh, please, just bring Letty back, and I'll never again have an angry thought*—but I was the type to make bargains with myself: *oh, Self, please remember when you were small, and Letty was sad and gentle and willing to live in an apartment smaller than this house because she loved your daddy.*

I was at the point in the novel where Letty was in high school. She and I had gone to the same school, a school that never changed. I had a friend or two who had moved to New Orleans and had not known any better and had sent her children there. We had tried to sort out why the ethos was set in stone; where did it come from? When Letty went, it was half Jewish orphans and half rich children like her; was that where it had started? "It" was meanness, in the headmaster, the principals, the teachers, the students, the parents. Did the school start out making sure the rich children stayed and felt comfortable in their superiority? But Letty hadn't been a mean girl. She'd been fat, with a huge mass of unkempt curls, and Grammy had had little use for her. Was the start of meanness in the rich mothers? Oh, in the rich fathers, too. The school would have fostered that meanness, to keep things going.

And in my years? I wasn't mean. And Letty wasn't mean. But I was just one girl. Besides, Grammy paid my tuition until she was tired of letting my father hold his head up, then she forced me onto scholarship. There was her injection of my quotient of meanness. When the meanest girls in my class wrote on the letters from my grandmother who died in the camps —"Hitler didn't kill your mother. You killed your mother"— the deepest cruelty to come from that school showed up in my living room.

I was going to make young Letty into an amalgam of herself

and me. I was going to explain for the first time the culture of meanness in our school. I knew readers all over the world would relate to the viciousness of young girls, but I was going to open up the lens to take in the entire little society of this one particularly heavily Jewish school in this one particularly heavily Catholic southern city. It didn't matter if it was the 1930s or present day; all that had changed at that institution were a few brown faces and a few more debutantes.

I had heard the story of my parents' meeting so many times that two names stood out, Shirley and Ted. Both would be in their eighties, like Letty. Both went to what was then called Manual Training, Ted, Letty's wealthy neighbor; Shirley, a girl of eastern European Jewish extraction whose parents scraped by to pay her tuition. Of course Shirley was scoffed at by the rich girls, and left out by the girls who lived together in the orphanage. Did I need to find Shirley for stories?

Then it came to me that, for all I knew, Shirley was still alive and still in touch with Letty and was living somewhere in Louisiana or Mississippi or Texas and sheltering Letty. Ted, too. Though Ted was not the type to leave New Orleans. But Shirley, definitely Shirley. It was a long shot, because Letty didn't take her car, but otherwise, why not?

I clicked down the Word file, pulled out the photocopy I'd made over at school of the class photo. Shirley Kleinfeldt. There could only be one Shirley Kleinfeldt, it seemed to me. I brought up Google, put in Shirley Kleinfeldt. I couldn't believe it. Even when I put her name in quotation marks, she had over six thousand citations. Shirley was an MD, and in addition to running a full-time pediatric practice, she had a research operation that did studies for GlaxoSmithKline and a couple of other pharmaceutical companies I'd never heard of.

I kept scrolling down, long after I knew Letty couldn't be with her. Not because Shirley was a busy woman. Shirley was clearly a woman past eighty who slowed down for nothing and gave her time and money for everything. She served on boards, yes, but she also went to Honduras and Guatemala two weeks every year and worked with sick children. Shirley would have driven to New Orleans to pick up Letty, refusing no as an answer. But Shirley lived in Seattle.

I *needed* to know Shirley. I went to Anywho.com and found her phone number. It was an office number, and I was apologetic for calling during working hours. "Could you just tell her it's Darby Cooper from New Orleans, and my mother's Letty, and she can call me back whenever it's convenient?" I said.

"You're in New Orleans?" the woman said, sounding as if she were saying, *You're on fire?* "Hold one minute."

In a matter of seconds, a voice with a never-shed New Orleans accent came on. "This is Darby?" she said.

"Hi," I said. I was actually shy.

"Oh, wait, you're not calling to tell me you've lost your mother, are you?"

Lost. Oh she meant, as in Letty died. "Not as far as I know," I said. "I mean she's kind of missing since the storm, which is why I googled you, and when I found you, I just had to call you, because, see, I thought maybe she'd left with you or something, but then I saw you live in Seattle, and she left without her car, and I'm sure you're very kind, but you wouldn't have driven all the way down here to get her."

Shirley laughed, and I calmed down. There had to have been a good reason why the young good Letty had chosen her for a friend. I was going to make her glorious in the book.

"I've read a lot about you," she said.

"Are you serious?"

"You're pretty famous. I didn't have to google *you*."

That felt pretty terrific, because Shirley was the kind of person I wanted to know about me.

"I bet Letty told you about me," I said.

"Oh, honey, I lost Letty when we lost your daddy."

I wanted to fly up to Seattle.

"I wish I knew you," I said.

"I think we've been friends for a long time. We just didn't do anything about it." I began to cry, silently. I didn't think she could know. "Hey, we've probably both got longevity genes. Give me your e-mail. We'll make up for lost time."

I sucked in a long sniff. "You're in the next novel," I said. "You better be nice to me."

"I read your last book," she said. "I'm not afraid. I've been a good girl."

*** 

I had to admit that Shirley was right, that my father's death had been the flash point at which Letty lost allegiance to all that mattered to him. Dead was dead. He wouldn't know if she betrayed him. He wouldn't know if Grammy took back her soul that he had held so delicately in his scarred hands, scarred from years of so much repressed pain that they broke out in blisters and bled. Letty had been a loyal wife, living in small houses because that was all Daddy could afford. He took salaries he had to take because Grammy sabotaged him. As soon as he died, Grammy threw money at her so she could live like a rich woman once more. The message was that all the years with my father had been one big mistake; look how good life was now.

And as soon as Daddy was dead, Letty chose the friends Grammy approved of. So many were the mothers of the mean girls, even the mean girls who had written on my German grandmother's letters. These were the women who could dedicate an entire day to shopping, with a nibbly lunch in the middle of the late day. They would talk about one another, then switch places. There was no room for a Shirley in such a circle, but then Shirley long ago had been too smart to stay, going off instead to Stanford first and many graduate schools after, dressing too much in white coats to need to do much shopping.

It would take incontrovertible evidence to make me call one of Letty's New Orleans friends. I would need fingerprints and DNA before I would phone one of those women to ask whether she knew Letty's whereabouts. It made some sense that Letty would have thrown her Chanel bag into the trunk of one of her widow friends' Mercedes and carpooled up to the mountains in North Carolina, but I wasn't going to be the one to find out. I could just see Letty calling up Louise Silverman Whatever's mother and saying, "Can you believe that that rotten Darby wouldn't even let me be with her during the storm? Well, I'll show her," and Mrs. Silverman would say, "Hey, let's go on a vacation; grab your cash." Of course Letty would have had a few thousand lying around. I assumed cash-hoarding was Letty's style. She would have picked it up after Daddy died. "Hmph," Letty would have said, "Bernie's life would have been completely different if his mother had kept a money stash."

\*\*\*

When I wrote, I needed complete order. I couldn't have a dirty dish or unbrushed teeth. Now that I had started this little search for Letty, I had to finish my thoughts. Ted was my other thought. Ted Kern. He grew up two houses down from Honor, but I'd been on the boulevard often enough to know his house now was owned by a couple with two little girls. That only meant Ted had found a similar house elsewhere in New

Orleans. Ted had been a good guy. My father loved saying that
about him. Ted had been in the Army with my father and had
lured him out of the barracks to the bar where he met Letty.
Ted may have been a rich kid who went to my school when it
was called Manual Training, but he was a good guy. It was
possible to go to my school and be a good guy. You just had to
be a guy. That school produced quite a number of decent men.
I didn't mind looking for Ted. He was the type who might have
looked after Letty.

He was in the phone book. I had a phone book because the
only two stipulations I'd made for my arrangement with the
seller was that she get me telephone and cable service. That
would have been foolish at any other time, but after the storm
getting such utilities was not a given. So I had a phone book,
and there he was, an address in the 100 block of Broadway.
That was Lambeth House. That did no good. If he was in
Lambeth House, someone was taking care of him; he wasn't
running around taking care of other people. Poor Ted. Maybe I
would go see him sometime. It was a straight shot up the river.

I needed to stop imagining Letty in her present spoiled and
annoying incarnation, or I was never going to finish the novel
and sustain my motivation to keep looking for her: I needed to
think of the young, sweet Letty that I would care about.
Searching for Letty, for story, for finding in real life, had to start
in fantasy. I would have to do that with nothing else on my
mind. I got out the photocopy of her high-school class again. I
stared at her photo and Shirley's. Each was in a sepia oval. Each
girl looked so hopeless. I propped the composite up on the
back of the sofa. I would keep myself in the 1930s, never mind
the technology. I shut off the phone. I put on my white noise
machine. The highest setting.

# Chapter Twelve

I was writing four pages a day, good pages, clean pages. I was honest with myself: the free time I gave myself as a reward wasn't tax deductible. I watched foolish reality television that I would have flipped off if anyone had walked into the room. But there was the freedom: no one would walk into the room. I answered to no one. My family in the worst or best possible case was four generations of women, Letty, me, Honor, and the unborn child I thought of as Katrina Fema. The baby was a girl, if she existed at all, because then she would be one of us Coopers, not a gawky duckling. But Honor had no time to give me, or take from me, and Letty and Katrina Fema weren't showing up anytime soon. I could be my most true self. And I liked my most true self, wanting no one else.

But toward the end of the day I checked my messages, and Shoshana was there. I couldn't write without behaving like a writer. My next book only would see the brightest lights if I remembered to nurture my last one, and the excitement over *Werner Weiss* hadn't died down at all. It especially hadn't died down because people were curious about my being in the zone where Katrina hit. I phoned her back.

"Could I play the sympathy card?" I said.

"Nice try," Shoshana said.

We had to negotiate, and it was easy because we were more or less on the same side. Both of us wanted to sell the hell out of the *Werner Weiss* book, but we were poles apart on where I needed to be when that happened. Shoshana's agency had enough inquiries for me to do a second national tour, going from big city to college town to state capital, sitting in bookshops and showing up at television stations at six in the morning. The theme was perfect, Shoshana said, the comparison between the Holocaust and Katrina. "I think that's a disgusting comparison," I said.

"And people outside of New Orleans will love you for saying that," Shoshana said.

I felt myself breaking down on the phone.

Shoshana could hear me breaking down on the phone, though I didn't cry.

"Writers aren't cut out for that kind of life," I said. Or tried to say.

Shoshana told me she already had an alternate plan. She'd had a feeling I wasn't in as good shape as I'd been, say, before the storm. She also said she'd had a feeling I'd be the last to know.

I couldn't imagine a plan. I'd once taped a video of myself in a downtown studio in New Orleans, coming all the way in from Mississippi to do it, but small operations like that surely were dead now.

Shoshana's plan was for me to come to New York, and an intern in her office would make a video of me for something new called YouTube, and Shoshana could send it out to everyone who'd asked for an appearance. It would be just like having me there. I'd do a few appearances, but Shoshana would be with me. I would have no responsibility except keeping my wits, and while she realized that wasn't a given, she thought it was a strong possibility when I was being so well tended. And what about a signing? She reminded me that I'd signed pages before. I could do it in her office. Or I could have books sent to my house for individual inscriptions. "I'll pay," I said. Postage was a small cost for freedom.

I considered asking her whether I could find a young person in New Orleans to do this YouTube, but I was pressing my luck. People always said, "Don't forget, your agent and your editor are working for you," but they were stupid. My agent and my editor had complete power over me. Shoshana might have been a friend, but in truth I was all business to her, and she could have dropped me on a whim, sending me official papers and never speaking to me again. I never pushed my luck with Shoshana. Respect figured in there somewhere, and from time to time I thought we had an ideal relationship in the greater world, but then I decided, no, I wanted her to stick with me no matter what, no matter if I slipped.

I told her I'd be there as soon as I could get a reasonable flight. She told me Monday would be good, to hell with cheap flights. I forgot Shoshana knew that frugality was silly for me in most situations.

Before I called the airline, I called Alyce to ask her if I could use her apartment. She was in New York so often that she kept a *pied à terre* in the East Village that definitely cost more than hotel rooms in dollars but considerably less in aggravation. I always offered to pay her, and she always told me to forget it. When I began to feel guilty and stayed near Times Square once, she found out, and she fussed at me, telling me I was wasting my money when I had free accommodations in the city.

"I'm flying in on Monday, too," she said. Her tone was one of excitement. The apartment had two bedrooms. Anyone else would have told me she was sorry, no, but Alyce saw this as a chance for adventure. She didn't say why. I told her I planned to get a flight out late afternoon on Tuesday, so keep that in mind. "Works for me," she said.

\*\*\*

By four in the afternoon on Monday, Shoshana had gotten my money's worth out of the trip. We had done four different YouTube interviews, with Shoshana the voice behind the camera asking me provocative and heart-rending questions. I prompted her in advance to ask about Letty, and I told the world she was missing. "Apologize to her," Shoshana said between tapings, and I found a way to say I was sorry I hadn't shared space with her during the storm. "You didn't sound very sincere," Shoshana told me, and I tried harder in the next taping. Shoshana was going to send these interviews to television and radio stations all over the country just by attaching them to e-mails, and it would be almost the same as if I were packing and unpacking in identical hotels and cabbing to identical airports. I put out my Letty bulletin even when Shoshana took me to do an interview on something called *The Daily Show*. I'd never heard of it, but then I was almost strictly a reality-show devotee. I liked the host, and I liked the show, and I thought I would watch when I got home. This Jon Stewart was the first Jewish man I'd ever found sexy, and I'd known Jewish men at every place in my life. He was hilarious and helped me do my Letty pitch in a way that, for the first time, didn't make me feel as if I was prostrating myself in front of my mother. I told all this to Shoshana as we ate lunch in her office while I signed title pages. I could daydream about Jon Stewart. I told Shoshana that I hoped she knew she was enabling me to stay home forever.

"Who's the old one here?" she said.

"Definitely me," I said. Shoshana didn't look as close to seventy as she was. And if knowledge of technology was a measure of age, she was somewhere in her thirties.

"That's why I can't retire," she said. "You need someone to poke at you."

I reminded her I was writing a book. She reminded me back that without her I'd be simmering in sour juices and coming up with a manifesto for the truly grumpy.

It was a wonderful lunch. I didn't spill one drop.

I took a cab to be as much on time as possible at Alyce's apartment. I'd gone straight from the airport to Shoshana's office, so I had my overnight backpack with me. I felt as if I could pass for a New Yorker, and that pleased me, and I wondered, not for the first time, what would have happened if Letty had broken away from her mother and let my father take us to New York and succeed in his business. I'd have been a girl who ran these streets with sure knowledge. Of course, I wouldn't have had all the southern unhappiness that enriches fiction.

Alyce was already at the apartment, stretched out on the sofa, reading the *New York Times*. Her BlackBerry was on the coffee table, and I knew that within about thirty seconds it would go off, and the newspaper would be folded down onto her stomach, and she would look at the phone, go back to reading. As soon as she'd finish the section of the paper, she'd put it down, clack at the keys with her thumbs, then go back to reading. Really, Alyce could live in prison the same way I could. The difference was that Alyce loved people.

She leapt up when I let myself in with the key she'd left with the doorman, gave me a hug, plopped back down on the sofa, tossed the newspaper aside. "Sit!"

Alyce grilled me, as if every second of my day were a thousand dollars I had invested. I found myself becoming enthusiastic, forgetting that I'd come with trepidation because Alyce said we had an adventure.

I told her I'd have to introduce her to Shoshana one day. I imagined they'd do well planning my funeral, but I didn't say that.

"You ready to go out?" she said.

"Oh, crap."

"Have I ever done anything to harm you?" she said.

"There's always a first time."

She assured me that we were just going to do a little shopping, then go to dinner, then come back and have an early bedtime. I began to wonder what I was going to do with my free day tomorrow. But I'd be happy to think of something, because it surely meant recovering from my adventure tonight.

We had dinner reservations way up on the Upper West Side. I asked her why, and she said it was because there was a restaurant she adored. It would mean we could shop in midtown and be halfway there in time for seven. It seemed to me that sitting down to eat at seven ruled out an early bedtime, but then I told myself I was going to stay on Central Standard Time.

The crowds were thick on Fifth Avenue even at that time of day. Having come from Mississippi via New Orleans, I had the habit of looking for familiar people in crowds. I was looking straight ahead as Alyce and I worked our way to a light that probably wasn't going to last long enough to let us cross, and I saw her. "Holy shit, that's Letty," I said.

I broke into a run. I didn't pay attention to whether Alyce followed me or not. I kept my eye on Letty. Same hair from the back. Same height. Same stride, compromised just a bit by age. The crowd was so thick ahead of me, and people were slowing down, knowing they weren't going to be able to cross. I screamed, "Letty!" It was too noisy on the street. I couldn't even hear my own voice. I kept pushing and running, feeling like a nasty New Yorker, not caring. I could see her making it across the street. I was twenty feet from the corner. I pushed. The light changed. Ten feet. Everyone was stopped. I could barely see her. Cars were passing in front of me. I stepped off the curb. A car honked, rushed by. I stepped back onto the curb, looked, saw another car coming, a little more slowly, stepped into its path, it honked, sped up, I screamed, "Letty!" I couldn't see her anymore. I was back up on the curb, and Alyce had caught up with me. "Maybe she went into Bergdorf's," she said.

I ran into Bergdorf's. I was out of breath. That was not a store to run into and run through, no matter how old or dignified I was, and I was more old than dignified. I went farther and faster than Letty could have, not needing to range far, while Alyce waited at the entrance. She was explaining to a salesman what my problem was when I returned. "You could have just asked, it turns out," she said as we were leaving, Letty-less. "They notice everybody who comes in. They'll definitely remember you."

"So you think that was Letty? I'm pretty sure it was Letty," I said.

"Depends on how many times you see her again."

"Here?"

"Anywhere."

\*\*\*

"You're going to spring somebody on me," I said when we walked into a restaurant that looked like several hundred other restaurants in Manhattan, many of which were walking distance from Alyce's apartment.

"But I promise it'll be all right," she said. "In a bad way

that'll be a very good way." She gave her name to the maître d' and said, "Reservation for three." I hoped she was going to be on my side, whoever this was. At least she didn't say she had a reservation for a half dozen.

He led us to a table where a dumpy old woman already was seated. Her hair was gray and curly, but curly in a natural way, as if she washed it and let it dry, and cut it when it occurred to her that it was about time. I wasn't ready to like her just because she didn't look like most of the women I shared with Alyce. I'd have liked to think she was a stranger, but I knew better. "Darby!" she said, trying to get out of her seat and not doing well at it.

I recognized her as soon as I got close, because it was impossible not to recognize anyone you'd known in childhood. Joni Joan. So this was what a psychic was supposed to look like. It made sense. Poets and painters and people who transcended reason were supposed to let themselves go because they had more important things to think about. I considered myself to be one of those people, and I always made an effort to blend in because I thought sloppiness was show-offy.

I let her hug me. She had that funny popcorn smell of fat people. Joni wasn't one of the mean girls at school, but her cousin Linda was, and Joni was rich and liked herself quite a lot. She applied to Seven Sisters colleges with no chance of getting in, then went off to one of those private universities out west that were like Tulane, catering to moderately dumb kids whose parents had limitless funds and no clue about mind-altering substances.

I ordered a double vodka and tonic. I made a point of saying I didn't care what brand. Joni asked for Grey Goose on the rocks. Alyce asked for Chardonnay. I intended to put a packet of Splenda into my drink. Or maybe two packets of sugar.

I watched Alyce and Joni talk about traffic on Broadway until my drink came, then I dumped three packets of Splenda into it, stirred, and took two big sweet gulps. We might have chosen this restaurant for Joni's convenience, but I liked it for how heavy-handed the bartender was. The vodka hit me right away. "So what is this all about?" I said.

Before Alyce could get words out of her open mouth, Joni said, "I hope you both understand that I'm on the clock."

Alyce just looked at her.

Joni let out a *we're-old-friends* chuckle. "Oh, this happens all the time," she said. "I guess it's the price of fame."

I tried to catch Alyce's eye, but she was having none of it.

"It's hard to explain to regular people," Joni said. "But when you're in the limelight, everybody wants a piece of you. And given what I do, people come out of the woodwork, thinking I'll give them a free reading or something. So I have to tell them up front, I'm on the clock. Even old friends. If you want just to visit, great. But if you want me because of my powers, I'll have to charge you like everyone else."

Alyce was speechless. I was halfway through my drink.

"I have zero clue why we're here," I said. "But I have serious doubts that Alyce wants parlor tricks."

I took another sip. I thought I might order another drink. That was the great thing about being in New York. No car.

"Parlor tricks?" Joni said.

"Poor choice of words," I said. "I'm not good with words."

"Do you know who Darby is?" Alyce said.

"Hush," I said.

"I read about her in the *IN News*," Joni said. "I never give anything to the *IN News*."

"Neither does Darby," Alyce said. "They get her information from the *New York Times.*"

"I'm walking out of here," I told Alyce.

Joni reached across the table and put her balloon hand on mine. It was surprisingly soft, but that made it disgusting instead of sweet. I wanted to pull away. I made my mind send numbness to my hand. "I apologize for not knowing about you," she said. "I'm just a very busy person. Being in demand 24/7 is exhausting at this age, if you can imagine." Then she brightened. "Hey, I've written a couple of books, too. It's a lot of work, huh."

I turned to Alyce, my hand still caught in a trap. "Why don't you tell us both why you brought us together tonight?" I was slurry, but I was cheery. Truly slurry, not truly cheery.

"I thought a small reunion would show you how easy it'd be to show up at the big one," she said to me. "People change after all this time."

"So wrong," I said. "So wrong." I got up and walked out.

# Chapter Thirteen

I needed Alyce more than she needed me, but she always swore she didn't see it that way; when a person saw money in seven and eight figures, she had to fill her life with intangibles. And whatever I had, it wasn't quantifiable. "I'm your magical bouncing decimal point," I would tell her.

"See?" she would say.

We were back in our right places, Chicago and New Orleans, talking long distance. After dinner that night, she had found me at the apartment, and we had let the wine and the vodka do all the talking. I lay supine on the sofa, as if she were my psychoanalyst, my eyes closed, and tried once again to explain why I wasn't yet ready to see schoolmates.

"But Joni wasn't one of the girls who ruined your father," Alyce said.

"Don't you see how ruinous she is anyway?"

"I think she's hilarious," Alyce said. "You really pulled a good one when you called what she does parlor tricks."

I had to think about that one. Was my plan going to be taking all these people down to the fool level? Would I finally calm down if I could make them all know—absolutely know—

that they all were buffoons and not worth my time? The message would have to be that I had survived their destruction because they were a waste of the earth's resources, breathing its air and drinking its water and eating its food. No.

"People like her think they are entitled to look down on people like me because they have money," I said. "Nothing I say would make a bit of difference."

"Oh, Jesus," said Alyce who went to Jewish Sunday school with the lot of them. "You have more money than all of them put together." I started to say something, and she interrupted me. "And no, I'm not Joni's broker. I just know without asking that you're the big success in the class, money and otherwise."

"They all have husbands."

"Which you don't want." Alyce got up to get herself another glass of wine. "Want some?" she said. I shook my head, no.

I tried to tell her that I needed a plan to get peace about my father's death at the hands of those girls in our class. Until I did, anything related to school was just going to open old hurts.

"I watched you tonight," Alyce said. "If you'd let me throw the *New York Times* and the sales of your book and your TV appearance last night at Joni, you'd have shut her up."

"There has to be a better way," was all I said.

We let the rest of the evening fill up with jokes about prescience, none of which would have been funny cold sober. I said nothing about the popcorn smell. Sometimes it was too easy to have evolved into a girl from our school.

\*\*\*

Now Alyce wanted my permission to give out my phone number. This was the first time I didn't have the comeback that I was in the phone book. But I had the comeback that I was usually in the phone book. Did I want to know who was looking for me? "I can think of a lot of people you wouldn't want to talk to," she said.

I asked if this was one.

She pointed out that probably half of our class of sixty-two were boys, and she could think of only two truly mean boys. "Oh, but time changes people," I said. "Remember?"

I reminded her of a story I'd reported to her a few years back. One of my books had launched in New Orleans, getting me the full top of the front of the Living section of the paper, complete with a color photo. It was hard to miss, even if you were someone who went straight for the Sports section. Anyone who claimed a basic level of literacy would have known I had a launch party. I was mortified by it, white-faced with terror from the time I got out of bed that morning until the last straggler left the party well after ten at night. The next day I was still in New Orleans, and I had gone to Walgreens to buy extra-strength Tylenol. I had bumped into Joseph Jungfrau, whom I had not seen since high-school graduation. Joseph had been a hanger-on because he wasn't Jewish, not by a long shot, and he also didn't have one of those French names that went back centuries in local society. He had no academic or athletic skills to speak of, so he was the sort of boy people looked at funny when we came to twentieth-century history and otherwise ignored. In those narrow aisles, we couldn't avoid each other, and in truth seeing him was easy after having faced so many strangers the night before.

I surprised him. "Joseph!" He was hoping not to be caught. I surprised myself. My headache was close to suspicion-of-brain-tumor level.

"Hey, Darby." Like in the hallway.

I told him I'd had a book launch the night before, and it'd have been great to have seen his face there. I actually meant it.

139

"Hey," he said, "I'm a litigator. I don't see you coming into the courtroom to watch me do my work."

Alyce assured me it was not Joseph Jungfrau looking for me. I told her I was sure it wasn't.

\*\*\*

It was another classmate on the phone, not an hour after I hung up with Alyce. It wasn't one of the girls. It was one of the good boys. Jon Hershfield. Jon had been the right kind of boy. Basketball, not football. Honors English but not honors math. Latin, not French. He was the kind of person I would vote for if he ran for class office. But I found my walls falling away with all of this exposure to schoolmates. I was sure Alyce was trying to teach me something. As if she had been in the world longer than I had.

Jon had an offer he didn't think I could refuse.

"You don't sound like the Jon I remember," I said. Jon could put the word out that I had no more patience.

He apologized. He said he could see where he sounded a little over the top. His sister had sent him clippings about me, and he figured I was used to high-pressure types.

"You obviously didn't read the clippings," I said.

"I thought I did."

Jon had been in Mrs. Grout's honors English class with me twice, so I knew he had fine-tuned reading comprehension skills that only senile dementia could take away. Without mercy Mrs. Grout had taught three generations to watch every punctuation mark and think through every thought. She also had wrung out every drop of pleasure from literature. But Jon and I and hundreds of lawyers and doctors were difficult to dupe with the written word—if we looked at it. Most of us did not, if I could judge by how baffled most were by me.

"If I see pushiness coming in my direction, I freeze," I said.

"Would asking you to meet me for coffee be pushy?"

"Not if I get to choose where," I said.

I phoned Alyce after we hung up. "What are you trying to do?"

"All I'm doing is, I'm running this committee to pull together this reunion," she said. "Let's face it, if I can drag your butt in, they'll all be impressed." I took a big gulp of breath, ready to drag Alyce straight back to second grade. "Hold on, hold on," she said. "You're not a trophy, at least not to me. But you've got to admit, they probably think you hate them, so if I can get you to show up, they'll be knocked out."

"That makes me a goddamn trophy."

She said she could see that. "Really, the truth is that you need to go back for your own sake."

I asked her whether she'd ever heard of relegating something to the past because it wasn't fixable. Certainly my father had wanted to relegate his mother's death to the past. He hadn't wanted to know where or how his mother died. When Grammy dragged me to Bergen-Belsen and got the record that his mother died of typhus at Auschwitz, she violated everything my father had chosen to do. School wasn't Nazi Germany, but girls in our class had used Nazi Germany to destroy my father. They needed to stay in the past until I found a way to change history in my mind.

"You're in New Orleans. Nothing gets relegated to the past there," she said. "If it does, the past is just sitting there looking right at you, so there was no point."

"I can't stay here, can I," I said.

Alyce reminded me that I was in limbo and needed to stay in limbo. It was too soon after the storm to know what to do about my Mississippi house. Besides, Mississippi was in so many ways a distant suburb of New Orleans, and she was sure that Letty would be back before it was all over, which meant I'd be going back and forth as much as ever if I chose to rebuild. So an escape from seeing Louise Silverman Whatever in Marino's meant considering more than my two current options. Or, Alyce said, I could get ready to go to the reunion and face all the demons at once and free myself.

I didn't know what other effect she had, but at least seeing Jon Hershfield wasn't sounding so dreadful anymore. I asked her if Jon had said why he was looking for me. "All he told me was that he'd been in New Orleans since the storm, and now he wanted to be in touch with you."

"Oh, shit," I said.

What.

"What if he wants to go out with me?"

"Well, it's a lot better than Internet dating. You know his real name and where he's from, and you definitely know how old he is."

"You have to be insane. Dating a man from our class would be like dating my brother."

"You don't have a brother."

Thank God, I thought. If my parents had had a son, he would have been a total pussy. "It's disgusting," I said.

Alyce was silent for a moment. She knew that junior year I'd had a crush for a few months on her brother, who was two years younger than we were. Her brother looked nothing like her: her parents had all possible color combinations, and she'd taken the light ones while he'd taken the dark ones. I'd made her admit he was adorable, but we were sixteen, and she had protected him fiercely. Not that I'd have known what to do with him if I caught him. "I have taboos," she said. "But I still want to hug and kiss him."

"It's all about personality, I guess." I was picturing my hypothetical brother, who wasn't tall but bought expensive clothes, who was lazy and had a lousy sense of humor. That was my way of creating a taboo, I supposed, making the worst version of a male Letty. Maybe I would add such a brother to the novel. I would make him fat and give him Letty's curls. Such a character pulled me back to my old writing ways, when the only thing autobiographical about my fiction was ideology. I could have so much fun with him, knowing Letty would read the book, certain that Letty would chafe over having a fat son. I caught myself. Dead Letty was going to read this book. And Shoshana was going to say I could write a book that didn't jibe with the *Werner Weiss* story. I could see where academics might enjoy the forensics of literature. Oh, she put him in to annoy her mother. Oh, how can two novels about the same characters have plot lines that disagree?

"Give Jon a kiss for me," Alyce said.

\*\*\*

Jon was a good-looking man. He shaved his head shiny, a choice I ordinarily found unpleasant, reminding me too much of Mayor Nagin's blockhead. Women who frolicked in the 'sixties liked hair, as long as it didn't connote a heroin habit. (Sciutto definitely had a lot of hair, and I didn't know what it connoted except a bad attitude.) Not being one to have thick locks, Jon chose to have none, so I had to notice his face, and what stood out were his blue eyes. He probably had the exact same eyes in high school, but he didn't use them. He was a new person. I could give him a chance.

He was seated at one of the back tables in Rue de la Course when I walked in. He already had a big paper cup and a bagel in front of him, along with a laptop and a black bag with several sheets of paper poking out. Rue de la Course was the kind of place where a man could leave a computer but a woman wouldn't leave her purse, and he came over to me in the pick-up line, squeezed me around the shoulder, and said it was his treat. That was all right with me. I was having herbal tea. I could use double vodka to handle Joni, but caffeine was not going to work with Jon—or anyone else for that matter. I'd had the idle thought that caffeine should have been outlawed in New Orleans after the storm. No one needed extra reason to tremble. But of course that was a private joke with myself. New Orleans couldn't even enforce serious laws.

Jon had been living in Atlanta since college—until recently. I wasn't going to judge him for that. I let him do all the talking. People always talked nonstop to me. He'd been back in New Orleans since before the city opened up after the storm. I nodded. He had known he needed press credentials because the only other way to come in was to be military, and a person his age couldn't pull that one off. He expected me to smile conspir-atorially. He came in and had free run of the empty streets for several weeks. As he saw it, the storm was all his.

"So you're the exact person I wanted to see," he said, once he had established his bona fides as something of a hero.

My heart was not stirring.

"We've known each other a long time, right?"

"Well, not continuously," I said. A person could serve a full sentence for murder in the time since I last saw him.

"Look, I trust you."

"Okay."

Men didn't care about trust when it came to women. I took a happy swig of tea. This was not going to be romantic.

He swiveled his laptop around, not respecting what looked to me like a pretty terrific bagel. I reached over to save it, put it on my side of the table. He didn't notice. He had something to show me.

Jon had a lot of computer savvy for a person our age. Or he

had mastered one trick. He had a slide show, and he angled the screen so I could see each frame with no glare. These were black and white photos, much like photos I would see if I bought a copy of the newspaper. The *Times-Picayune* wasn't trying to move on and strive for normalcy; it was enjoying its ability to capture images and stories that could win a Pulitzer Prize because everything lying around was freakish. I had seen Ernie K-Doe's dead piano. I had seen women crying and holding babies. I had seen cars on top of houses. What Jon had most of, though, were photos of black children. Black children showing every possible form of deprivation. Standing in destroyed churches with daylight streaming in from open roofs. Playing in the dirt because they didn't have toys. Never mind that they probably once had had electronic gadgets just like any kids anywhere in the country. He had shots of little black girls whose wild, thick hair wasn't brushed. But I knew a lot of little girls looked that way if they got up in the morning before their mamas. Anybody who lived in New Orleans knew that. Really, anybody who had a girl knew that.

"These are good," I said. And they were, from what little I knew of photography. The composition pleased my eye, and the contrast seemed sharp. Though I could take sharp pictures: cameras were so advanced that a subject would have to move for the image not to be sharp, as far as I knew.

"They really are," Jon said.

Oh, God. Even he had gone out into the world liking himself.

"I guess you're glad you came in and documented what happened back where you grew up," I said. I started to comment that I was too close to it to pay attention, but I didn't have the impression that he cared about knowing.

"That's what I want to talk to you about," he said.

"I was here," I decided to say.

145

"That's terrific!"

Oh.

"Listen," he said, "I've got a proposition for you. I thought it out carefully before I called you. Talked to my lawyer and everything. You like my photos, right?"

Sure.

And then I found out why Jon had looked me up. Jon knew I was a writer. Since he was a financial planner, his definition of a writer, I figured, was someone who could have gotten an A from Mrs. Grout—now. Good grammar, good punctuation, good structure, all of that. He'd looked me up on Amazon and read the excerpts from reviews. He was a busy man, making his plans, and he didn't have time to read books. The reviews told him that a lot of my books were set in New Orleans, and I captured the local dialect and mores. He didn't need to know anything besides that about my skills.

He spared me no details. He wanted to see if I was a professional. That meant that, even though I could do the writing, I also needed to be enough of what he called a bigwig. At that, I stood up.

"I don't know where you're going with this, but I can see being judged a mile off, and I don't need it," I said. I grabbed my purse. I had my eye on the bagel, but I decided I could get my own bagel on the way out if it meant that much.

"Wait, wait," he said, standing up. "I knew I'd mess this up. Please wait. Give me a minute."

I sat, happy to be angry.

"I just googled you to see if you had writing connections because I want to do a book together, and it'd be good if you know people in New York."

I knew Shoshana and my editor cross-pollinated with me all the time in the media. I also knew they would protect me from foolishness.

A book?

Jon rifled in his black bag and pulled out what looked like a document.

What he thought would be a guaranteed bestseller would be a book of his photos with a made-up quote on the page facing each one. I would write in the voice of each person he had photographed. I could use dialect "out the wazoo" is the way he put it. He had a contract drawn up and everything.

I asked him if he knew these were actual human beings. Well, sure, he said. "I mean, I don't think you can publish a photograph of someone without permission," I said, "and you sure as hell can't make up quotes and attribute them to him."

"Even if it's just a kid?"

"What'd your lawyer say?"

"My lawyer drew up our contract."

His lawyer knew nothing about the content of the book. That became clear when he showed me the contract. I'd been willing to keep talking because it was possible that he had more photos that weren't going to violate rights, and it also was possible that this could be a book in which I could write essays that said things no one else had said. So far I hadn't read a lot of honesty anywhere.

Jon was offering me a flat fee of five hundred dollars and no royalties.

"What is this?"

He said his lawyer drew it up. I asked whether his lawyer dealt in intellectual property. No, but he was sure he'd consulted someone who did.

I knew it would lose my negotiating power, so I didn't ask for his bagel. I went up and got one for myself. I cut it up, slowly spread cream cheese on one piece, took a bite, felt pleased, felt capable of thinking. Exploitation.

"You've got me confused with someone else," I said finally.

"You want to make a counter-offer?" he said. "This was the lawyer's idea. I'm clearly not in the book business, and you are."

"I don't think we'd work well together," I said.

"You're going to steal my idea, aren't you."

"Try to remember that you said you trusted me," I said.

The bagel came in a little white paper bag. I closed up the plastic cup of cream cheese, slipped it and the plastic knife in with the bagel, threw the bag in my purse, and walked out. As soon as I got to my car, I opened it up, covered a full quarter of the bagel with cream cheese, and stuffed it into my mouth. I chewed, swallowed, and hiccupped all the way home.

# Chapter Fourteen

Honor was waiting on my front steps. "Why weren't you here?" she said, her face red, more with misery than petulance. I felt apologetic, not that anyone could expect me to be home, but that Honor for once had needed me. "Hey, come in, sweetie," I said. I took her shoulder, and her shrug was small and not sincere at all.

"I think I need to stay with you, probably just tonight," she said.

Sure.

Close on the sofa, I waited for her to speak, but she said nothing for quite a while.

"I'd go to Amanda's, but, like, she moved back in with her parents. And most of my friends are away. The idiots thought there was something good about going to school out of town. I mean, Emory? What the fuck is Emory?"

She folded her arms on her knees and put her head down.

"I said you could stay here," I told her.

"You're going to judge us," she wailed. I said nothing. "Oh, God, I didn't know I was going to make him so fucking angry."

"He hit you?"

"He said you were going to ask. He told me not to come here. No, he didn't hit me. He just screamed at me and scared me to death. He's so big."

I scooted a few inches away from her on the sofa. I had experience.

"How was I supposed to know his dad took away his black card? He got a DUI out in California or something, and his dad got pissed, so he took away his black card, and now he's got to get it together. You know what a black card even is?"

I nodded. I didn't tell her that most of my information of that nature came from reality television. I also didn't tell her that I watched a show called *Growing up Gotti*. I'd watched it before Sciutto came to town. It met all my criteria for tax-deductible viewing. Especially now.

"So he needs cash, but how am I supposed to know that I have to give it to him without him asking? He says that makes him look like shit, and when he looks like shit, he feels like shit, so I tell him, hey, I thought you were on such good terms with your dad, where's my mother's five hundred dollars you promised?"

I asked her what kind of answer he had to that.

"That's when he started hollering at me," she said. "He told me I was really ungrateful, after all he gave up to be here with me. You know, looking out for me, taking care of me, so now I'm trying to make him feel like shit. I mean, he was screaming so loud I thought he *might* hit me, even though he never would. He was just really, like, up in my face."

So what did she do? I hated to think. I'd seen this almost word for word on *Dr. Phil*.

She told him she was sorry, and that made him really furious. Of course it did.

"You swear he didn't hit you?"

"If you're going to keep casting aspersions on my husband,

150

I'm walking right out of here," she said. "He's a good man. And we have a close relationship. But if I piss him off, he has nowhere to go, and I've got here. At least I *think* I do."

I was not particularly in the mood to become someone's villain when I was aching so hard to go back to my room to call Alyce and tell her what a villain she had sent to me. And Honor had been turning me into bad mother for every stage of development since she learned the word *no*.

"Stay here to cool off," I said, getting up to go into the back room, laptop in tow.

"Are you fucking serious?"

I nodded. Any words would be trouble.

"I'll try not to *bother* you."

\*\*\*

This was the house where two-year-old Honor would play quietly until I had a fully formed paragraph in my head, and no sooner would I begin typing it than she would walk into the room and announce she was hungry. I would try typing at more words per minute than she could speak, but I never succeeded in saving more than maybe six. A fragment of a sentence never did me any good. Honor would have those times in her marrow.

I remembered that since Honor was two, the Internet had come into existence. There was an icon for saving a draft of an e-mail if I was interrupted. A paragraph or even a sentence could be lost, but at least Alyce wouldn't know it. Alyce didn't have time to waste on covered mouthpieces. And she surely didn't have much tolerance for fools who thought their petty grievances meant more than a phone call in progress. I'd figured that out a long time ago when Letty had beeped in on Call Waiting.

Honor and I were separated by the table room. If she wanted, we could stay that way for days, though she'd have to pass through my room for the bathroom, and I'd have to pass through the sofa room to leave.

The subject line was, "Another Lousy Specimen."

So, Alyce,

Romantic intentions would have been so much easier to stomach. And trust me, Jon is nobody's prince. I mean, he's bald. [I didn't write fucking bald because this was a company e-mail, and it had censors. I could get thrown right out of her address book.] He wanted to exploit me. I'll spare you the details, but he wanted to get a book published, and he'd taken a bunch of lousy photos and wanted me to write all the text—I mean all the text—and he'd pay me $500 and no royalties. Oh, and he wanted me to get my agent to sell it. Plus, he didn't get permissions from his subjects. Oh, oh, and to top it all off, his subjects were mostly little black kids, and he thought it'd be good if I used dialect to put words in their mouths. Okay, I guess I gave you details. So you can draw your own conclusions. The guy is a dirtbag. Which is why I'm telling you all this. First you get me to meet a woman who thinks she's the center of the universe because she pretends to be a Magic 8 Ball, and then you connect me with this guy who thinks he can buy me for $500. Now our class had, what, 62 people in it, and that's only about three percent, and you and I are equally three percent, I know, I know, but forget numbers. Jon and Joni, well, Joan so they don't have to sound so gosh-darn cute, represent the benign part of the class. The ones I'd give a chance. Why are you doing this? I guess I still haven't said no because I think you're exploring memory, and maybe I'm exploring memory, too, so I'm trying to keep an open mind. But, good grief, Alyce, those two meetings took me back to feeling like I was in high school again, and I'm here to tell you that feels like you-know-what.

I wrote the e-mail in three minutes, as fast as I could have spoken it, it seemed. Though in a conversation, Alyce would have had something to say.

I went back to work on my novel, looking for clues as I composed, and I was so engrossed in thinking about Letty that I didn't hear Honor walk into the room. She stood over me. The same Honor, but no longer three feet tall. Silent, giving me a few seconds to stop what I was doing before she fussed at me.

I did the save and patted the bed for her to sit.

Honor crawled right up to the head and gathered both pillows to herself.

"I want to talk."

"If you want," I said. "I respect the fact that you're married." She gave me a small smile. She couldn't tell I was lying.

"So I'm not very happy right now." She was facing down but looking up at me through her lashes.

"Okay," I said.

"You're not going to throw it in my face?"

Honor was the tar baby. I wasn't putting my fist into that one.

"You and Sciutto are going to get together again tomorrow," I said. "What will my getting all involved do?"

"It'll show you care."

"All right," I said. "If you have any doubts." She gave me a smile that said, *Don't push your luck.*

153

"I think now you know you didn't know him very well when you married him," I said.

"How would you know?"

I wanted to be using e-mail with her. I wanted time to think. I couldn't think. I couldn't protect both her and me.

As always, I chose to protect Honor. "I just know a guy who gets angry because you don't give him money isn't worth shit."

"Don't be so mean. You're always so mean. I don't know why I talk to you."

I raised one eyebrow. I could do that.

"You have zero clue what goes on in a marriage," she said. "It's give and take. We depend on each other."

"You depend on him to tell you what to do, and he depends on you to pay for everything."

"Aw, crap, you twist everything until it makes no sense," she said.

I shrugged. "I'm sorry," I said.

***

Sciutto didn't ring the doorbell until almost dark. Honor and I had stayed in separate rooms. Self-consciousness from the presence of another person made me productive. I thought about starting to write in a coffee shop, but decided productivity wasn't worth much. I knew Honor had nothing but her cell phone and my television to get her through time, and the timbre of the voice I could hear seemed consistent, with no music, no sound effects. I knew somehow that she wasn't talking to Sciutto. Honor had remarkable self-control. When she used the bathroom, she walked through on me as if I weren't there.

I went to the front when the bell rang. "It's for me," Honor said when both Sciutto and I were standing in the sofa room.

"I know," I said, but I didn't leave the room.

Sciutto had a fistful of flowers. They looked sorry in his square fingers. They had no rubber band or decorative paper. In New Orleans after the storm, they did not look fresh. But they did look like a television cliché. And more easily acquired than jewelry.

Honor seemed to start to melt. I thought I'd trained Honor not to melt. Or, rather, Honor had taught herself not to melt because she didn't want me to see her do it.

Sciutto apologized. He said he was wrong. He said he didn't know what came over him. He said he'd never done anything like that before. He promised he'd never go that crazy again.

I pretended to yawn. "What," Honor said. She stifled a yawn herself because it was physiologically impossible not to.

I told her I wasn't saying anything.

"You should've sent her back home," Sciutto said to me.

"Excuse me?"

"She's a married woman," he said. "You don't get in between a man and his woman." It might have been my imagination, but Sciutto seemed to me to be getting larger, the way some animals did in the wild, only they were covered with hair or feathers.

I looked to Honor, but I knew there was no point. She was easing her body up to his, making her edges line up a little at a time.

"I have just one thing to say. The media are all over this place. It seems to me that if *you* make one slip-up, mister, your daddy's going to find out when they knock on his door."

Sciutto didn't get angry at me. "I'm not one bit worried," he said.

***

I had put a lot of words onto pages during the day, so after they left I tried to cleanse my mind by seeing whether I'd made any sense. Being productive because I might be watched at the keyboard wasn't an experience I wanted to repeat, but I was curious. For all I knew, I'd written gibberish. I went back to where I started in the morning. I couldn't read. I had ADD. Acute ADD. It would go away. But the words were just strings of characters on the screen, meaning nothing. The day belonged to Honor. Possibly with progress for me, but I wouldn't know that night. The night belonged to Honor, too.

For a few moments here and there, I had been her mommy. When she was small and muscle-tough, she had called me Mommy. But if I called my mother Letty, she called me Darby, and only fear of complete change let her slip. The move to Mississippi had squeezed a "Mommy, do you love me?" out of her every few miles. For a few seconds today she had let me see her in pain. That was all I needed.

It seemed to me that this Junior Gotti, *especially* this Junior Gotti, whose family was so thick, would be a daddy, a kill-for-my-child daddy. I wasn't sure how it would play out when his child was out of control, but if Honor were out of control I'd go running in and grab her by the collar. At least I thought I would. By out of control I meant go-to-prison out-of-control.

I was considering contacting him. That's what I did when Honor was small, and she and a schoolmate were heading for trouble. We lived in a small coastal city, and everyone still had a land phone, and everybody still had a phone book, and besides, usually I had the numbers of Honor's friends, even if I didn't know their mothers. *Our girls are picking on Elizabeth, and I thought it'd be best if we talked to them together,* I would say, or, *Listen, they're buying beer, and we need to deal with it together.* Honor always thought of me as a very uncool traitor, but I'd always tell her I could have been a lot worse.

It seemed to me that a husband and wife were more connected than school friends. In most cases, parents of couples met each other at extravagant weddings, in fact grew to resent each other over matters of cost and taste. But Honor and Sciutto had spent their own seventy dollars, and for all I knew Gotti didn't even know they were married. I wondered what it would take to get an annulment.

I decided to google *annulment*.

I found a lot I could throw at Junior Gotti. I figured he was Catholic, and annulment was a very Catholic trick. But that was just for starters. In Louisiana there were so many grounds, some of which I knew probably wouldn't work—bigamy, incest, mental retardation, underage—and a few I could see as possible: coercion, fraud, duress, intoxication. What tripped me up was the process. The price was good—a little over double what it cost to get married—but the person who filed was supposed to be one of the spouses. It would do no good to get Sciutto's father to drag himself down to the courthouse with me to demand an annulment when neither of the newlyweds wanted one. Especially when courthouses were few and far between in New Orleans right then. Even the name Gotti wouldn't scare a small bureaucrat who was showing up to work in a city where everyone either was taking life too seriously or not taking it seriously at all. When everything was trash, it was hard to care about treasure.

Maybe I could contact him and tell him that the deceased Mr. Cooper had worked as a manager of a grocery store and surely never had heard of Cooper Transportation. That would be grounds for nullification. Not that Honor had perpetrated a fraud. But that Sciutto had brought someone useless into the family.

I started looking for his father online. I found many photos of Gottis, of course, many news stories. His father, I learned, had given up a life of racketeering for the past seven years and was staying out of jail. I was confused, though, because this man only had been married since 1990, and he had six children. I did the math. Sciutto wasn't born after 1990 unless he was some kind of gigantic prodigy, and I knew that was not the case. I stared closely at the photos of Junior Gotti. As one who'd been shameless in creating my own daughter, I was sensitive about eugenics. I knew faces. I did not see Sciutto in Junior Gotti.

# Chapter Fifteen

I was alone. I dared anyone to touch me. It was a safe way to live, but at that point being alone was not good. It didn't translate into loneliness, but it did leave me relying on limited resources. Usually that was good because I trusted no one as much as I trusted myself. I wasn't arrogant; no one knew I felt that way. But I wrote books, and that meant needing empathy for the world. How could I write if I didn't know how anyone and everyone felt?

Now I wasn't enough. I could lie back with my eyes closed and pretend to be Letty or Honor and imagine what each was thinking. I figured that way I'd know what to do. Weeks ago I'd given up on Letty because I didn't know where Letty had taken her head; at least I thought she had packed it up and taken it herself. But I was trying now to be Honor.

Honor was in love with a boy—yes, a boy, not a sixteen-year-old boy if he was going to fit the Gotti biography, but a boy—and he promised to take care of her, to do her thinking for her so she never had to worry. As if she were a small child. But instead that boy screamed at her and terrified her. I thought girls only went after men who abused them when they'd been

PATTY FRIEDMANN

abused themselves. I hadn't abused her. Maybe total absence was abusive. Her father's absence was cruel, the way she saw it. I thought it simplified life. She never would have the pain I had when I lost mine.

Oh, but abuse was so appealing, it seemed to me. Pull and push. Menace her, make her think she's going to be hit, then offer delicate flowers. Those flowers Sciutto brought looked stolen. To me they seemed shoddy, to her they probably had a sweet, gentle, broken quality. Honor was not going to believe anything I told her about this boy.

And she certainly wasn't going to explain to me why Sciutto had no resemblance to Junior Gotti. *Oh, he looks like his mother*, she might say. But I've seen photos of his wife, I'd say back. *His current wife*, she'd say back.

Whoever Sciutto's father was, he had not made life simple for this boy.

I wanted to have another self to talk to. To have Honor to talk to about Letty or Letty to talk to about Honor sometimes had worked before the storm, I realized, because all of us were related, and I couldn't be ashamed because each of them would have to be ashamed, too. I tried to think of whom I could call to help me figure this out. But I had respect between me and each of my friends. It was a barrier. If they knew about my foolishness, we wouldn't be friends. I didn't tell almost anyone that I watched reality television. My CPA had to know, but I told him with an I-dare-you tone and a good laugh, and he was too busy questioning whether the IRS would believe me. I couldn't call Shoshana and tell her my daughter married a boy claiming to be the son of Junior Gotti even though Shoshana loved nothing better than an unexpected narrative flip. If it wasn't going into the current manuscript, she would think it was a distraction that would make me too crazy to stay on track.

160

Alyce was clinging to me as one of the few people from her past who wasn't stupid. Charlotte already thought I *was* stupid.

I watched *Growing up Gotti* on DVR, looking for ideas, all by myself. Nothing came but the passage of time. And a feeling that I liked that Carmine all right.

\*\*\*

For a week I pretended that solitude was good, that this was what I wanted, no tethers, the ability to write with no other thoughts. I didn't need to go to a coffee shop. I didn't have a lot of strangers walking past me, judging me if I wasn't typing, but with no interruptions, I typed quite enough.

Honor phoned after a week. "Sciutto says we need to forgive you," she said with no preliminaries.

Oh?

"Yeah, he says family is the most important thing, and you're pretty much all I've got, so I've got to learn how to get along with you."

I thought that made sense. I waited.

"You didn't call to apologize, but maybe if I called, you'd feel like it?"

I moved the mouthpiece away and took in a deep breath, exhaled. "Would you like to tell me exactly what it is you think I did wrong?"

"Hey, you came in between me and my husband," she said. "I don't know much about psychology like you do, but I think that's some kind of golden rule."

Every now and then I wondered what would have happened if I'd reared her Jewish and sent her to Jewish Sunday school. At least she'd have learned the golden rule, which had nothing to do with being married to a fake mobster.

"I have nothing to say to that."

"Just admit you fucked up."

"Look, you came to *my* house. You complained to *me*. I was just sitting here minding my own business."

"You heard what Sciutto said. You should've sent me home. Did you? No. What'd you do instead? You threatened him."

I remembered Sciutto puffing up like a giant adder, half filling the room. It had not been a conscious process. I did not remember threatening him. Even if I had had a knife. I could barely have reached a fatal entry point. And if I'd had a gun, I couldn't have imagined a bullet penetrating deep enough to do harm. "I'm too small to hurt him," I said softly. "So are you."

"You didn't say you'd attack him physically," she said. Her tone was peevish, and I could tell she was looking at Sciutto with an expression that said, *You sure you want me to do this?*

I remembered. I'd hinted that if he really harmed Honor the media would pick it up. "Oh," I said. "You think I was going to call the newspaper. All I was saying was that if he is who he says he is, if he commits a felony, the national media are all over New Orleans and will pick right up on it."

Silence.

Then, whispered, "What do you mean, if he is who he says he is? I'm in the other room."

I told her I had doubts about his identity, but I already was in trouble with her, and I wasn't going to get into any more fights. As long as she was clinging to this marriage, I was not her closest ally, so anything I said made me the enemy.

"You already fucking said it!"

She had a point.

I figured it was better to give her specifics than to let her go running to Sciutto with more reasons I was evil. So I told her I'd bonded him from jail with another name, and I'd looked up

Junior Gotti, and learned he got married in 1990 and had six young kids, and what more did I need?

Honor laughed. "Oh, God, Darby, why don't you just come out and ask when you have questions?"

Right. "You want to tell me how those questions can have an answer I can live with?" I said.

"Listen," she said. "Men like his dad have mistresses all the time. Goomars. His mother was, like, his goomar for fifteen years. He took care of her and everything. And he sure as shit takes care of Sciutto. Sciutto just goes by his mother's last name. And Sciutto is the nickname Junior gave him. He was going to get made in the Gambino family and everything, but his dad quit the mob. So he's going to have, like, a regular life. We'll probably live here, with the house and all."

"His dad mean to his mother?"

"I think it was a big romance," she said. "You know, long distance most of the time. You don't get caught up in fighting when you only see each other every now and then, and it's all secretive and everything."

"So being a big brute is all right if it's a marriage," I said.

"He came at me *once*."

"If a man terrorized me once, I'd walk away," I said.

The air sounds changed around her voice. She was in a different room. Playing to an audience of one again.

"That's why you're all by your-fucking-self."

"When you want to have a civilized conversation, give me a call," I said. I needed Honor, but I had limits.

"Okay," she said. "You'll be sorry when I'm pregnant." Then she hung up.

***

I wondered what Letty would think. Not about the impending great-grandchild, but about claiming Gottis. Letty was a fame hog, what Honor would call a star-fucker. Letty would go to a thousand-dollar-a-plate dinner just for a chance to have her photo taken with Bill Clinton, long after he was out of office. She went to the Bacchus parade to wave at Nicholas Cage. What was respectable fame? Bill Clinton was pure and clean in my opinion, but not in others'. Nicholas Cage worked hard, but his image was dark. Did Junior Gotti get a pass because he straightened up? Did Sciutto choose a good name? Letty could not brag about a Gotti.

I needed to find out that Sciutto was a Morrow.

With no one to help me, I had to plot carefully. Plotting didn't come easily to me. I got a pencil and paper.

Contact Gottis
No trouble with Gottis
Use internet
Disguise self on internet
Facebook/password/computer
Carmine

What I had to do was go to the library. Going to the library wasn't a given after the storm because some couldn't open. Nix Branch was lucky. It was on Carrollton Avenue, and it was possible now to drive on Carrollton Avenue and map out the topography by looking at the trees. If the magnolias were dead, it meant the salt water had come that far and flooded. If they were alive, the elevation had been high enough. Nix was at Willow Street, and Nix also was a good six feet off the ground, so Nix's books and operation were in good shape.

Usually I was uncomfortable walking into libraries uptown. Librarians knew me on sight, and I was sure they thought I was coming in to check whether they had my books prominently displayed or, preferably, checked out. They also would look at what I took home with me, and I felt as if I had to walk out looking intelligent, even though I was a reality-television kind of person and longed to pile up the nonfiction instead of the Faulkner. Today I knew I'd look strange using their computer, because they knew I relied on a computer at home and didn't need a public one unless I was up to no good.

But it didn't matter. As in almost every other sweet place in the city, walking in meant a reunion and a catch-up, everyone coming around the desk for hugs and shared adventures. One of the librarians had lived in the East and lost her house, and that was worse than my losing my house for some reason, so I didn't mention it.

I logged on carefully. I created a gmail account, carefully. I still had a lot of the Spanish from college and decided I'd use my Spanish. My screen name was BuscandoMentira@gmail. That sounded like a pretty robust kind of guy to me. "Looking for a Lie at gmail." I went all over Facebook and found a few pages for Carmine Agnello, who was also Carmine Gotti. That made Sciutto's story possible. Carmine was using both his father's and his mother's names. All right. I was learning something without asking questions. I found an e-mail address. This was so easy it was making me shaky. I reminded myself I was in the public library, and I was safe. No one, especially Sciutto, was going to check on me in the public library.

I wrote Carmine an e-mail. I told him there was this guy whose name was Devin Morrow. He was from Tampa, and he said he was Carmine's cousin, son of John Gotti, Junior. I asked him if they were in touch or if they'd been friends as kids. I thanked him for answering me, please. And then I sent it.

I waited a week because Carmine seemed like a busy kind of guy if I could judge from the television show. Besides, the people at the library would notice my coming two days in a row. I brought my little camera, just in case.

I couldn't believe it. Carmine had answered back within ten minutes of my having sent the note. "Never heard of him," he had written.

I pulled out my camera and took a few shots of the screen, complete with my letter, his answer, and both of our addresses. I'd go by a Walgreens and get prints. I didn't know what I'd do with them, but I planned to keep them in their cardboard envelope in my purse. I wanted to forward the e-mail to myself, but I didn't. After I got into the car, I realized there would have been no harm, but I didn't feel like going back.

# Chapter Sixteen

I was at the point where the Letty character was twenty in
my novel. This was going to be tricky.

I'd done well with her growing up. She and Grammy had
succeeded over my father's protests in replicating her life in
mine, so I had a lot of the raw material—the school, the
houses, the social attitudes around her. Letty had made it to
twenty with decency surrounded by shamelessness. Now I had
to frame her marriage to my father in a believable way. It was
not going to be easy, because even I found it hard to believe
that she had stayed in Grammy's thrall when she had such a
good man.

My parents, each in a different way, had told me about the
first months together. No matter whose point of view I had, the
marriage made no sense—at least not the way they lived it.
Letty was sad and shy and in truth was willing to marry the first
boy who asked. Never mind that he was too Jewish and too
foreign for her parents' taste. My father was sure he had fallen
in love with Letty for her sadness and shyness, but he had no
family left, and it seemed to me that he wanted to get married
as quickly as possible so he would be part of a real American

family. When I heard his story and figured that out, I was reading about Dick and Jane, who were real Americans, and I wondered where Grammy got the idea that she was so much more the genuine article than Daddy, but I never asked. I just saw him try and fail to be a good, rich businessman, and I saw my grandfather cut off all his customers. The issue, though, was why Letty didn't love him enough to make him leave New Orleans. He could have gone to Baton Rouge or New York City, but evidently she needed Grammy's approval more than his.

My job was to draw Jewish New Orleans to make her choice believable. Since I never had believed it, I didn't have the picture in front of me.

I needed someone to interview, well, to chat aimlessly with until Letty made sense. Letty might very well have been the ideal person to talk to, but probably not. I decided I would call Shirley. Since she was a busy person, busier probably than Carmine Gotti, I sent her an e-mail asking when she might be free to talk, and my phone rang about two minutes after I hit send.

"I can tell if you want to talk that you're not bearing good news about Letty," she said. "But I don't think you've got bad news, either."

I told her I had no news, but I was writing my book, waiting for news, killing time by writing, and I needed perspective. Could she remember being twenty? Could she remember Letty clinging to her mother when she should have clung to her husband?

"It's kind of a New Orleans syndrome," she said.

"Oh, please, no," I said.

"I didn't say it was a pandemic!"

I laughed.

"Look, I can pick it apart clinically, but for your money you ought to talk to Ted."

I told her Ted was in Lambeth House. She made me explain exactly what Lambeth House was, and when I did, I realized that it warehoused a lot of broken bodies with good heads on top. "If he's in the phone book, he probably has a reason," she said.

*** 

People expected unexpected phone calls in New Orleans to be announcements about deaths. That probably always had been true, but more so since the storm, when there was no newspaper delivery, and reading the obituaries couldn't be a form of recreation. When I said I was Darby Cooper, Ted said, "It's Letty, isn't it." I heard condolences in his voice but not any measure of grief.

"I don't have a clue if she's alive or dead," I said, "but I assume she's alive."

"Good, good." He sounded relieved.

As a single man in Lambeth House, Ted wasn't lonesome, but, he said, a visit from me would be excellent. That was his word, excellent. A few of the ladies would know who I was, and that would make him quite a catch, having a visitor who not only was young enough to be his daughter, but also was terribly pretty, and to top that off was famous. "Though I think living long and being smart don't have much to do with each other," he said on the phone. "You don't hear a lot of debate about Nietzsche around here."

I thought I was going to his apartment.

Yes, he said, but what was the point if he couldn't walk me out?

He was ambulatory, so I brought him a plant. Before I

phoned I'd thought about flowers or cookies or candy, but then I had been picturing him in a wheelchair with a breathing tube. Ted deserved a twice-a-week reminder of me. A *damn-gotta-water-it-again* reminder of me. He had been a schoolmate of Letty, but he had been my father's friend.

When he saw me in his doorway, he squeezed my face as if I were ten and he were fifty, and he gave me a sloppy, truly wonderful old-man kiss half an inch from my mouth. He was the kind of old man I could tell once was very angular and good-looking, but probably hadn't traded on it. "Do you know about bromeliads?" he said happily.

"I know you probably have a balcony and probably can't kill it," I said, going in behind him. He moved more slowly than Letty, and he wasn't very steady, but he didn't hold onto anything as he walked. I saw the balcony doors ahead of us. Lambeth House had views of the levee, which weren't spectacular, but they were better than most, and surely cheaper than the multi-million-dollar ones where the river hit downtown.

Ted told me that bromeliads were related to pineapples, and Christopher Columbus had found pineapples in the Americas, and he went on until he got to the point that pineapples meant hospitality, so he would keep his pineapple cousin on his table and if he liked a visitor, he would tell her about it. Yes, it was always a her. What would a man be doing in his apartment?

He sat me down at his newly pineappled table and shuffled over to his kitchen, brought back a plate of Gianna-brand hand-decorated cookies from Whole Foods, asked me if I wanted coffee. He had decaf. I was in the mood for ice water, I honestly was, and he could make that from his brand-new LG refrigerator. He'd had to replace his old refrigerator after the storm, but he was not going to complain, not at all.

He sat across from me and stared. I smiled and stared back. "I'm looking for them in you," he said. I told him I figured that.

That was why I was smiling; I was giving my daddy his best shot. Letty wasn't a smiler; smiling made wrinkles. Smiling probably also compromised her position, but she didn't say that.

Ted had grown up with Letty, a couple of houses up the boulevard, never carpooling to school because Letty had a driver until Letty had a car. When the war broke out, Ted enlisted, and he was stationed in New Orleans until he was deployed. He and Letty and Shirley and a couple of others were planning to go out in the Quarter one night, and he asked his barracks buddy Bernie to meet up with them. This was part of family lore, how poor Bernie, who struggled with English and didn't know New Orleans, found the bar where they were drinking. How Bernie had very little money. No one knew Bernie was saving his money to try to save his mother back in Germany. Ted had treated him to a Schlitz beer, and Bernie had asked Letty to dance. That was how the romance that created Darby began. If you had asked Letty's parents, the marriage was Ted's fault. If you had asked Letty and Bernie, the marriage was Ted's gift.

"So, young lady, what brings you to old Uncle Teddy?"

I giggled. "I'm writing a book."

He interrupted me. "The book you wrote about Bernie, well, disguising Bernie but really about Bernie, was a great tribute," he said. "I really should have contacted you, but I thought you probably had thousands of people contacting you. Anyway, you did his memory proud. I loved that man."

Images of my young sad father filled my head. I wondered where Ted had been when Grammy was torturing him. They had been young men, so I wasn't going to ask now. I knew about being young and lost. Ted probably had been off getting an MBA or something that had nothing to do with his nature. "The book was easy to write," I said. "I mean, with honesty."

"So what's left to write about?"

"Letty."

He whooped so loudly that he set off a long, phlegmy bout of coughing that made me decide I was going for the phone if it didn't stop in about three more seconds. He was bright red. The coughing stopped, and he reached for a paper napkin on the table, wiped his eyes, let out a few bouncy small coughs. He pulled it together to look me in the eye. "You're not joking, are you," he said, and then he started laughing, not caring that he kept making himself cough.

"Let's just say that I'm versatile," I said.

He laughed some more.

"Hey, if you were friends with both of them, I'd say you're pretty versatile, too."

He stopped to think about that one. "Interesting," he said.

I told him why I was there. I was stuck at exactly the point in the book where he introduced Letty to my father, and I was under a strict mandate from my agent to make Letty a sympathetic character.

"You don't need me," he said. "You write fiction."

"Aw, come on," I said. "Seems to me she was kind of pitiful all the way until Daddy died."

"You forget," Ted said. "I grew up on the boulevard just like she did. I knew her mother and all the other bitches that lived along there. Letty might've been beaten down by all of that, and she did marry Bernie, but having sympathy for her is hard."

"Try."

So Ted stuffed mostly chocolate cookies into himself, then got up and made a cup of caffeinated coffee, and he talked nonstop about our shared mythical princess named Letty. Mythical Letty was twenty years old during the war, and she was pudgy and unkempt. That was a sorry state with a demanding mother, but it was a sorrier state at Newcomb College when all the Tulane boys were enlisted. I could imagine it. Princess Letty went to work at Higgins building landing vessels for Normandy, which enraged her well-manicured mother. Was this true? This was true, and Ted helped me care.

Ted took me forward, through the wedding. Only he and the household help were the witnesses to the sorriest ceremony he'd ever seen. So much anger, and so much fear on Bernie's part. But as for Letty, as this was about Letty, well, her mother thought she looked dreadful, and her father offered her money if she got a divorce within a certain amount of time; Ted forgot, but this was fiction. Make it a year. Did he have to keep going? He had seen their apartment, a shame for a young couple with an infant. Diapers hung on a line across the living room. Unnecessary when her parents could have helped. I knew that, I told Ted, but what about Letty? "You're going to have to imagine her pride," Ted said. "You have the facts, you always had the facts. Now get inside the mind of a woman who's too proud to beg or get angry. She's really no different from you."

Was this a man talking? Where were men like this when I was thinking about looking? "You ever been married?" I said.

"Yep, twice," he said. He grinned. "Divorced twice, too." He winked at me.

I didn't remember any of his kids at my school. No, he said, his first wife considered not sending them there grounds for divorce.

What?

"Look, I could have bought my way onto the board of directors, but there was no way I was going to turn my kids into rotten little assholes. My wife thought if she *didn't* have kids there she was a social failure."

I told him I didn't remember his having any kids there. The

school ran from kindergarten through twelfth grade, so it was possible to know people in a twenty-five-year age range.

"My money, my choice," he said. "Franklin was open by then. Couple of PhDs, which doesn't matter as much as a couple of decent people. My ex still thinks they're a pair of losers."

I told him my class was having a reunion, and a friend was pressing me to go.

"Now that's a whole other thing," he said. "You should go."

"I thought you were my friend."

"It's your tough luck that your memories are full of lousy people, but, honey girl, they're your memories. You need to go back and get a refill."

I didn't tell him that the part about my father's death in the book was true. Ted didn't need a bad new memory.

# Chapter Seventeen

The one subject where we made no headway was the missing Letty. Ted's take was that Letty was off on a toot, very much alive, and I should search as well as I could, but try not to worry. I could go back to my little house, mire myself in sad, loving feelings about a young, mythical girl who concocted reasons to marry my daddy. They would be right reasons, having nothing to do with her mother.

I thought about seeing Ted again, maybe taking him out for lunch. Not exactly dating him, though surely at his age he would know that it would have nothing to do with romance. Then I realized that I preferred solitude, and especially solitude that meant no entanglement with men. I wondered a little about myself, whether I was crazy in an unfortunate way, but I remembered that comfortable crazy was fine. I did no harm. And I wrote books.

Ted had said, though, that I should go to my reunion. The thought never had bothered me much, because at that point I was pretty sure I could not do it. I'd say no. No discomfort in a no. The only reason it wasn't an absolute no was that I thought I'd shown Alyce or Alyce had shown me something about vindication, and I thought maybe I needed vindication. Now Ted was pushing me to go back. Ted had the luxury of a full generation of years. Not Letty-generation years, but Ted-generation years, years accumulating wisdom.

Alyce phoned me before I could phone her. She was going to be in New Orleans in five days. When she came to town, she always planned to meet to update me on my portfolio, but this time she had a separate plan, and she was calling to ask if I was interested. A long shot, she said. Possibly not so long, I said back.

As she trusted I remembered, she said, she was running the planning committee for the class reunion. Did I want to go to a meeting?

"Good God," I said, "that's like my almost being willing to get a flu shot, then you tell me I'm going to be lined up against a wall and blasted by a shotgun."

"So you'd come?"

I told her I was *starting* to consider exploring the idea of *maybe* showing up to *one* of the events at the reunion. Jumping in with the most crazed members in the class, probably all sitting down in one room, didn't leave me much chance of hiding in the bathroom.

Then it occurred to me that I'd read in a group e-mail that Louise Silverman Whatever had offered her house as a venue. She definitely would be on the committee. Or at least present at the meeting to make sure the plans didn't involve food that would stain her priceless rugs. "Louise Silverman will be there," I said.

"Why not get her over with while you have me and Zachary to protect you?" Zachary Homer had been the kind of nice boy who could not possibly have changed. Zachary stayed on the periphery and got elected to absolutely everything. He was the only person I knew from school who came to any of my book signings. Naturally Zachary would say yes to a reunion. He probably even would co-chair the committee with Alyce— because he knew he was the class Switzerland.

I told her I'd already done my full-grown encounter with Louise outside Marino's, and at the time I'd considered it over with. I could go to that one place, and Security would protect me from Louise, not with a baton or taser but with sarcasm. She was powerless to buy the fine foods that women like her *needed* from Marino's. Since Louise was coming to this meeting offering a backyard lined with Japanese magnolias that hadn't been killed by the flood of salt water, she had power.

"I'm going to do for you what you won't do for yourself," Alyce said.

"This is a lot riskier than investing," I said.

That night I had a peculiar dream, mostly peculiar because I remembered so much of it, and I carried its peace around all of the next day. I dreamed I had a book signing down at Faulkner House, and my daddy was there. He was older than he ever became, and he stood next to me the whole time I was speaking to a crowd that filled the second floor of the Cabildo. Before the Q&A, he took the microphone from me. "I can know everything," he told the crowd. "My mother can know everything. It's only fair. Just remember that. It's only fair."

\*\*\*

Alyce insisted that she and I meet for coffee before going together to Louise's house. *That* was where the meeting was. She had her briefcase with a sheaf of papers for me, none of which I understood, but she said that's what she was there for; let the left side of my brain shrivel if I wanted. All I needed to know before the meeting was that I was a multi-millionaire and could buy and sell Louise if I chose, and I should walk into her house and look around like I was a buyer who didn't see what she wanted.

I had a feeling Louise was her client. But it didn't matter.

I was not about money, remember? I tapped the left side of my head. "Raisin," I said.

Louise's house was what I would have called lovely. That was a middle of the range word in New Orleans. Most surviving houses in New Orleans were lovely. The little house I was living in was lovely. It was old, wood frame, turn-of-the-twentieth-century. Hers was two-story, painted a tasteful shade of the palest yellow with trim and shutters in a green and blood red that probably were chosen by Louis Aubert; he was the colorist to all the uptown ladies who had no sense of what they wanted. Lovely, but not a landmark.

A black woman in a uniform answered the door. "Aw, no," I said to the woman. She looked at me incredulously but said nothing. "I'm sorry," I said. "I don't know the lady you work for." I turned to Alyce. "Let's get out of here." Alyce took my elbow and firmly pushed me through the door. The woman kept looking at me, and something clicked; she understood what I meant.

"Come on in, ladies," she said. I heard a touch of irony in her voice, and I thought maybe she'd go home that night a little less disgusted.

Louise had taken a perfectly lovely, lovely house and made it an eyesore. The walls were pink. Not an almost-white pink, and to her credit not a Pepto-Bismol pink, either, but the kind of pink Kay Thompson had thought was terrific for Eloise's apartment in the 1950s. Frames of art work were gold and ornate, but the art looked one point better than what she could have bought on Jackson Square. A lot of cityscapes, New Orleans, yes, but also Montmartre, the canals of Venice, Parliament in the fog. Even if her furniture had been genuine antiques it would have been too heavy for the small rooms that came with that kind of house. We were ushered into a room filled with overstuffed chairs and sofas, just off the living room. This was supposed to mean we were going to have a casual meeting. The food was casual, covering a coffee table as big as my bathroom. Nothing from Marino's, surely.

The room was full of old men and ageless women, and no one got up when we walked in. The only place left to sit was a loveseat that did not look comfortable at all. It was too high off the floor for us to be able to sit back without our feet dangling, and it was too narrow for us to have natural space between us. Alyce and I had no choice. I sat down, kicked off my shoes, dared anyone to notice. My feet were clean. I'd wait a few minutes, cross my legs, wrap my arms around my knees, give Alyce space, dare anyone to notice. I didn't speak.

"In case you don't recognize them, this is Alyce and Darby," Zachary said. "Do you two need introductions to everybody?"

He was making me have to look at them all. I had the ability to recognize anyone I ever knew in childhood, so that wasn't my problem. My problem was having to look at them. I saw challenge on their faces, as if each was daring me to have forgotten. All except Louise, of course.

It was equally divided among men and women, five of each. Not including me and Alyce. And of the women, three had been at the sleepover party that destroyed my family. I felt nauseated.

"I don't want to do this," I whispered to Alyce.

"Hey, no whispering," Linda said. Linda was one of the three women.

"She said she doesn't want to do this," Alyce said. I heard annoyance toward Linda in her voice. Either Linda wasn't her client, or she was keeping her promise to me, or both.

PATTY FRIEDMANN

"Hey, we were just kids, last time we all saw each other," Linda said.

*One another*, I wanted to say. You don't even speak good English.

"If you're smart, you'll try to show that you're not a kid anymore," Alyce said.

"Aw, come on," Louise said, "one of the reasons we're getting together is to recapture what we had together when we were kids."

"So, Darby, does that make sense to you?" Alyce said.

I could see her plan. She wasn't going to talk for me. She was going to put her hand in my neck and make her puppet speak.

"I can see going to a reunion to look for memories, and reliving them is logical," I said. "But I don't think war veterans go back to Normandy or My Lai to re-experience death and destruction. Seeing the landscape is enough."

I looked straight at Linda.

"I have no clue what you're talking about," Linda said. She clearly was accustomed to enjoying the camaraderie found in ignorance. She looked around the room and found a few giggles. She also found a few scowls.

"Of course you don't," I said. I was being too cryptic. But no matter what I did, this was not going to be the night when the girls who destroyed my father were going to say, *Oh, I ruined Darby for life; I owe her an apology.*

"Why are you here tonight?" Louise said like a gentle hostess.

"I invited her," Alyce said.

"And I don't think I'm going to do anything productive," I said. I slowly leaned into Alyce so I could press my elbow against her arm in a way no one could see. I wanted to be sure she knew what I meant by "productive."

180

Zachary tried to take over.

"Playing basketball brings back fun from high school," he said. "We've already reserved the gym. Show you're still good. But other stuff? I don't think you want to go back to those games."

"God, I had so much fun in high school," Linda said.

"Have you changed?" Alyce said.

"Sure."

"Well, this is your chance to show it, don't you think?"

Linda looked to Louise for support.

"All we're saying is that we want a reunion where we can feel like we're seventeen again," Louise said.

"Louise—" Alyce said, like a patient mother.

"What." Louise honestly did not understand.

Alyce looked at me. I could not resist. "I'd ask you all if you knew what parallax views were, but I don't think anybody's in the mood to get all academic, you know?" I said. I looked around, because it was a pretty good joke for a school-reunion meeting, but no one cracked a smile. "We've got parallax views of school, all right? That's two Ls in parallax if you feel like looking it up later. It would be a good thing, really."

Silence that seemed to hold more bafflement than anger took over until Zachary spoke. Zachary was the platonic ideal for reunions. He had been good as a boy, and time's only change had been to mature that goodness. The people in our class hadn't had any collective sense, but we had recognized that Zachary knew how to lead, and with age he had honed that skill. He also had the ability to know that he wasn't going to parlay his character into any sort of top-dog role in life. He wasn't a boss or a politician. This was my private thought process, nothing I shared. Zachary was a primary care physician. He could pull order out of mess, he could control without power.

Zachary called the meeting back to minutiae, though in that crowd money oozed right back to emotion. If Louise was going to hostess—hostess, not host—one of the gatherings, she would have to charge a hundred dollars a person. She passed around a paper detailing a menu, a list of hired personnel and their hourly fees, a list of rentals of linens and china and glassware. Louise gave a little speech about how there was a slight flexibility in the costs, depending on how many people showed up.

Sarah, who had not been at the sleepover, said, "Hey, Zachary, didn't you give a brunch last time and pay for everything?"

Zachary nodded. He looked embarrassed.

"So why don't we try to find somebody who wants to foot the bill?" Sarah said. "Or maybe have it at a restaurant? We wouldn't have to worry about the weather."

"God, I better rent a tent," Louise said.

Zachary said we would put out an e-mail notice asking if anyone wanted to host a reunion party. After all, we had an entire weekend.

I thought Alyce and I would leave as soon as all of the business was settled, but Alyce had no such intentions. We had arrived in my car, but that made no difference whatsoever to Alyce. "Come on, you're going to practice standing up," she whispered to me.

"No whispering," Linda said goodnaturedly.

"Are there some rules posted on the wall?" Alyce said.

Linda leaned over and gave me a hug. "Good to see you," she said. She hesitated a fraction of a second, gave Alyce a hug, too.

I didn't say anything. Now Linda, Alyce, and I were in one of those cocktail-party chat triangles that is impossible to escape. I assumed Linda had a rich Jewish husband, so maybe she had enough money to become one of Alyce's clients. I'd try to behave.

"How've you girls been?" she said to both of us.

"Fine," I said.

"Great," Alyce said, "I don't live here."

"Oh, I know what you mean," Linda said, which meant that any response was an invitation for her to hold forth on her own life. With anyone else in New Orleans, it was all right for life to mean only the time since August 29, but Linda's was downright solipsistic. Katrina had blown straight at her house, well, her zip code, 70125, and the flood had washed straight towards her door, well, towards enough of her zip code to make it unpleasant to live there. And naturally they had no mortgage, so they saw no need for flood insurance, and this was an event that was all flood and no wind. Thank goodness they had the money for repairs, though they'd had to bring in a team from Texas and put them up in a hotel; you know how that goes, or maybe you don't. No answer was required.

"Darby's entire house floated away," Alyce said before I could stop her.

Linda looked at me as if she'd never met me before and wanted to see whether she'd missed something. "You were living down in the Lower Ninth Ward?" she said. "What in God's name made you do that?"

There probably hadn't been more than a few white people in the Lower Ninth Ward. I could have picked up my little shotgun house and put it down there and fit it in—before the storm. But I'd still have been just about the only white person. The only difference between me and everyone else was they went out every day to go to work.

Alyce looked at me, waiting for me to say something. I refused.

"Darby had a huge house just like Beauvoir on the beach in

Mississippi," Alyce said. "That's where the storm came in. Not one stick left. It all went into the Gulf."

"Sorry," Linda said, sorry only for herself. "I can't keep track of people. I have no idea of anything that's been going on with you since school."

Before Alyce could say a word, I tried to grab her arm and lead her to the door. Alyce pulled back. "You need to google her," Alyce said. "She's only the most successful person in the history of the school. We're talking fame *and* fortune."

"I thought I saw her picture in the paper," Linda said. "But we're a lot older now, you know?"

When we got to the car, I said, "So, did fame and fortune make her sorry she destroyed me?"

"Hard to tell with those women," Alyce said. "Hard to tell."

# Chapter Eighteen

I could not write for three days. I didn't leave the house except to get a sandwich from R&R&R, didn't answer the phone. In anyone else, that would be depression. I didn't consider it depression. I considered it a disconnect from my work. For a writer, that's dangerous, because it's possible to be following a thread through the story and to drop that thread and not be able to pick it up again. A writer might have that happen and not know it, go right back in and keep on with a narrative, but the voice would change, the characters would flatten out, and before she knew it the reviewers would say, *This seems to have been written by two different people.*

There I was, the daughter of a spoiled woman, trying to tell her life history in a loving way, and I just had exposed myself to a room spattered with her doppelgangers. I lay on the sofa in my sofa room, so different from Louise's overstuffed room, staring at the ceiling, eyes closed, trying to take advantage of that evening. Ted had told me to go get a refill on my memories. It seemed to me that Ted was too sharp to mean that I should stand around and talk to people who also were in the girls' room the day Kennedy was shot. Or even those who

185

remembered reading Tennessee Williams in Mr. Garland's English class and who also took too long to figure out why he lived in the French Quarter and gave special consideration to a really cute blond kid named Stephen Norris.

I struggled to think.

I tried to imagine young Letty. Ted had given me young Letty. But my head was full of mean-girl tricks, and now I knew that mean-girl tricks didn't dissolve over time. They simply became more refined; a woman could deny having used them because they came in fractions of seconds and never in straight-up words or actions. I knew the Letty of my lifetime. I best remembered the Letty from after my father died. A mean girl. The girls from the other night made it hard to believe that Letty hadn't always been this way.

The days went by imperceptibly slowly when all I could do was think. I slept fitfully during the day, not at all at night. I couldn't read. Reality television was obscenely slow, I realized for the first time. If Maury Povich interviewed a couple, he let each one scream incomprehensibly over and over, jumping up and down, running back and forth, so he could stretch out a contested paternity a good seven minutes when it should have taken thirty seconds. I left the TV off, narrowed myself down to nothing but my own creations.

When I finally began to fear my bowels would turn to rocks if I ate one more sandwich from Lucille's, I told myself I needed to reread what I'd been writing and try to jump back in as it flowed past. I discovered I had been just at the point where Letty was going to the synagogue with her parents on Yom Kippur and seeing my father there. He'd been wearing a yarmulke, probably the only one in the entire city. Oh, was I lucky. I'd only been in a synagogue twice in my life, both times with Jewish classmates who'd brought me along to Sunday school. The same Sunday school where Louise and Linda went. I could let my imagination go.

So when the phone rang, I felt rich enough to answer.

"I want to come over, but I get to do all the talking."

Honor.

"I'm really happy to hear from you."

"Never mind." She hung up.

I waited a full minute before calling her back. I had to be careful under Sciutto rules.

I told her I'd like her to come over, and I'd do my best. "You really have to," she said. She wasn't huffy at all.

I thought I saw why when she came to the door. Honor had what was practically a big red handprint on her left cheek. Her eye was swollen from the injury. She wasn't using any kind of makeup to cover it up. She didn't seem bothered by it, almost as if she had an injury sustained by climbing a vertical surface no one else could master.

Honor's eye. My little girl's eyes. They were that beautiful sea green that I wanted, and they were that beautiful sea green that had given her a lot of permissions out in the wide world that she hadn't always earned. To me they were simply the same eyes that once had had a certain innocence, even when her sweet mouth was shrilling, "I want chocolate!" Honor was two now, and someone had hurt her badly enough for me to want to raise a ruckus to whoever had been in charge in my absence.

I said nothing, but my eyes were narrowed, and my lips were pressed tight. This was what I had to do.

"Don't act all pissed," she said as she walked into the sofa room. "I tried to get him first."

"I told you I'd do my best."

"Yeah, I know."

She flung herself back, tears rolling down that same little angry face I knew so well; she stared at the ceiling.

"All I want is a solution," she said. "And I don't want you to give me one, okay? I just want you to listen 'til I come up with one, okay?"

"May I tell you stuff?"

"I know what you're going to tell me," she said, "and it's, like, totally useless. Anything you've learned in your life has nothing to do with my life. I don't want to turn out like you." To make her point, she waved her hand around the room that was empty of furniture other than what we were sitting on.

I told her that she needed to give me a little credit, that I sometimes got her messages, that I had something to show her.

"You're supposed to just listen," she said.

"Fair deal," I said, knowing she wasn't leaving my house without seeing my photo of the computer screen from the library. Though then she'd need to start over.

She took in a deep breath and said, "Okay, so this is the guy who's supposed to be able to be in charge of everything so I don't have to get all upset about responsibilities. Well, I catch him adjusting the thermostat. I mean pushing the heat up to eighty. Now you know I've always done what you always did— but only because it's the right thing—and I keep it on sixty-eight in the winter."

I kept my expression neutral. I hoped she had mentioned me, but knew she hadn't.

"So I walk right up and push it back down to sixty-eight, and he asks me what the fuck I'm doing. Well, here's where I figure I started the whole fight because I said, Look, it's *my* house, and *I* pay the Entergy bill, and *I* say where we keep the temperature, and besides, *I* believe in global warming." She gave me a slightly guilty look, as if she had let slip the only salient piece of information, that Sciutto did not believe in global warming. If anything, I was surprised that the subject had come up.

"Let me guess," I said.

She nodded. "He pushed it up, I pushed it down, he pushed it up, and I tried to knee him in the 'nads. But damn is he tall. He called me every name in the book, not just cunt but Jew. And that's when he smacked me.

"I started the whole mess, and now I've blown everything."

I felt sick. I never had used corporal punishment on my child. Not even when she was pre-verbal and could have been deterred from danger by the tiny shock of a pop to the diaper. Where was all this coming from?

"So getting hit in the face really sucks. And he says I started it, so he better get out for the night or he'll fucking kill me."

"A woman a third his size swinging and missing is nothing more provocative than a little kid," I said. "You just grab her and hold tight. He was wrong." As soon as the words were out of my mouth I realized I'd broken the rules.

"You have *got* to chill."

I folded my arms in front of myself, crossed my knees, ached to take it back.

I wanted to ask when Junior Gotti was going to give him money so he could pay the bills, but that was not even a fact-finding question.

I nodded.

"Aren't you going to say anything?" she said.

"Do you want me to be your mother or a piece of furniture?"

She shrugged, and I said nothing.

"You are so fucking frustrating!" she said.

I smiled in spite of myself, and that made her look angrier. I took in a deep breath, knowing I had to talk nonstop or she'd interrupt me. "What's going on? Huh, Honor? Look at things from my point of view. Since you got married, I've been in this classic double bind; I can't win for losing. Maybe you came over

189

here so you can blow up at somebody. Lord knows you set it up
just perfectly. You and Sciutto probably play that game a lot.
Maybe you want me to be the good guy. How am I supposed to
know?"

I didn't give her a chance to interrupt. I'd not heard my
own voice in recent days, but it seemed to work.

"Look, I'm just not in the mood. It so happens that I have a
life, and I just hit my stride on my work, and I get tired of
wasting my time getting set up and knocked down all day by the
one person I love the most."

Her expression went from trumped up rage to something
close to contrition. Not contrition for what she'd done exactly,
more like regret for coming very close to losing a chance to talk
to someone who gave a damn.

"Okay, I want you to know I respect your work," she said.

Honor was getting her PhD in English. She had read a huge
body of work. She never had read one book I'd written. Not
even when I had offered to pay her to proofread an early
manuscript.

She also had developed a habit of interrupting me when I
was writing. I'd created card files, then online files, for book
collectors to support her when she was small. Nothing I ever
did, especially sitting at a computer writing books, ever had
struck Honor as work.

"That's not the issue here," I said.

"So what *is* the issue?"

"If you have a problem, and all you want to hear is the
sound of your own voice, don't bother having another person
in the room," I said. "That's kind of my credo."

"I *knew* you'd bring your own life into this!"

"I'm trying to tell you the opposite."

"Oh."

She had to process that for a moment.

"You want an actual dialogue," she said.

"Well, if you're going to sit on my stupid sofa and talk, yes."

"So, talk."

Questions could do no harm, as long as I didn't load them with cruelty. And I thought my knowledge would make cruelty easy. I asked her where Sciutto was.

She shrugged, a disingenuous shrug. He had no cash for beer, and no friends to speak of in New Orleans, so she assumed he slept last night in his car. She was pretty sure she saw his foot in the back side-window when she was leaving. She made a point of slamming her car door so he'd hear her, in case he was in the mood to go inside and take a shower. Sciutto didn't smell too good without a daily shower, she whispered.

I imagined that salty, hammy smell of big people. Or the acrid and fishy smells of body odor. Or both. Even the sweet olive on the boulevard couldn't mask the fishy pig smells in my imagination. I didn't even like Sciutto from a distance.

"Don't ever say I told you that," she said.

What next? What about going back to the house? She needed to get him out of the house. Either he would kill her or he would have worked his way up the boulevard picking flowers for her. She was a hundred percent sure it would be flowers. I was ninety percent sure he would kill her.

So why was she talking to me? Why didn't she just come over and blow a little time so Sciutto could freshen up and make a bouquet? She even could have put on a big hat and gone to a movie or Walmart, anywhere in Jefferson Parish where no one would look at her face funny.

"Because we, like, obviously, fight too much."

"So you come to the one person who's had zero exper-ience," I said, doing her a favor.

"Touché," she said. "But, hey, Letty's not here. I know *she*

191

had lots of experience. She had two husbands. I figured you maybe watched."

"Well, I'm here to tell you my father never laid a hand on her," I said. "And from what I can see, Eddie was something of a saint himself. He put up with things that I'd have slugged her for."

"How can you talk about a lady who's probably lying murdered somewhere?"

"Letty's not dead," I said.

"I hope you're right, because I sure miss her," Honor said. "I wonder what she'd tell me to do."

"She'd tell you to throw the bum out," I said.

Honor stood up. "I don't need to put up with that kind of crap."

"I was just directly quoting your grandmother."

"I swear if she's dead, you're going to be really sorry," Honor said.

I gave her a wide-eyed look, as if to say, *Who isn't sorry when her mother dies, and I dare you to say you might not be.*

"You know what I'm talking about."

I told her that all she had to rely on at that very moment was her own mother. And her own mother had just one thing to say. You need to throw Sciutto out.

"He's broke in a strange city."

"So you move in with me."

She cast her eyes around the room.

I told her I'd sleep on the sofa until I bought a bed for her old room.

"Look, I'm not going to run away from anything, let alone my own husband," she said. "He and I just have to quit getting so pissed off."

"The only way to do that is to see a shrink," I said. "This absolute very second."

"You think anybody in his family ever sees a shrink?" Honor said.

I told her she might be surprised. Though today was not going to be the day when his pedigree was coming up.

The only problem, as I saw it, was that the entire city of New Orleans was one big lunatic asylum after the hurricane. Every medical doctor worth his degree was referring his patients to a therapist. Bellyache? Psychiatrist. Headaches? Psychologist. Anorexia? Social worker. From what I knew, there was not one single person living inside Orleans Parish who did not qualify for antidepressants, anti-anxiety medication, and sleep-aids.

If Honor and Sciutto wanted professional help for an old-fashioned, antediluvian problem like homicidal abuse and rage, they would have to take a number.

As soon as she marched out the front door, I began to cry. I felt the same way I did the first time I dropped her off at nursery school. She hadn't looked back that time, either.

# Chapter Nineteen

Alyce was too conservative an advisor to be calling me out of the blue with money news. So it had to be personal.

She was offering me an invitation to appear at a book group in Houston. There would be a small honorarium. "You're in charge of my finances," I said. "You want to tell me where it makes sense to take a minimum of twelve hours to speak to maybe twelve people, half of whom will have checked the book out of the library?" I thought for a second. "Unless it's your client."

"Cut it out," she said. "You keep accusing me of having these clients all over the place. I don't take on anybody who doesn't have at least half a million."

Oh, that meant Louise and Linda in New Orleans didn't have half a million. At least not of their own money. Maybe their husbands had many millions, but they weren't giving very much to them to play with. They were the type who'd sign up with Alyce to impress her. Though Alyce never was impressed by money. Unless it was philanthropic money in astounding amounts.

I told her to ditch this gig, knowing that I was on a roll with a new book and didn't want to break stride even for my own family. Surely anyone living in Houston who was idle enough to have a book group was a Bush Republican. I would want to show up with a torch and a pitchfork.

"You remember Linda R.?"

"Are you insane?"

"People change," she said.

"That's your little scientific hypothesis, and so far it's not working," I said. "Can't you find another lab rat?"

"God, I love you," she said.

Control over my money wasn't Alyce's source of power. I wasn't sure what it was. I thought maybe it went back many years, to her ability to play with anyone and everyone. She had a way of talking to mean girls and cheerleaders and mean cheerleaders and still sit with brooders like me at lunchtime without making anyone angry. She wasn't like Zachary, probably only because of gender. In matters of gender, being nice was not a good idea if you were a girl.

I told her she must have had some reason not to tell Linda R. to go to hell on my behalf. Or at least to have said something pessimistic like, *I doubt Darby would consider such an offer.* Did she do that? No, she said, she wouldn't even do that with a mutual fund.

"Look, this will make you feel good," she said. "Linda called me up because Louise told her she saw you the other night."

She was still friends with Louise. I did not feel good.

"Don't you get it?"

I said that so far all I could see was that the clique was still intact, and they still were finding ways to hurt me.

Alyce processed that for a moment. "Yeah, I guess I didn't tell it right."

"Good luck."

"Linda called because she wants to apologize for what she did when we were kids. She figures that reading the *Werner Weiss* book with her book group, then admitting her role in it would be the most honest way."

"Holy fuck." I couldn't see anything hurtful in that—other than having to relive the worst day of my life. Which I did fairly often in my dreams anyway. This could be my first moment of getting better.

"I think that means those bitches the other night know good and well who you are," Alyce said. "They were trying to act like they hadn't paid any attention to anything you've done since high school, but they have seen every goddamn piece of news about you since you first got published. Sour, sour grapes."

"Holy fuck." Ordinarily I didn't let fame affect me. I could go into a bookshop in Seattle and meet people who'd read all of my work and would talk to me as if they knew me personally. I could be on television and pretend for ten minutes that I was on a first-name basis with Jon Stewart. But the life I had now, the life I'd fantasized about as a child, had nothing to do with me. I was still the Jewish girl at a fancy private school who didn't go to reform Sunday school and wound up on scholarship because her rich grandmother quit paying tuition. I still was Letty's unfashionable daughter, the one who'd brought shame on the family by deliberately having a baby out of wedlock. Now I truly was still the Jewish-by-matrilinearity woman living in a tiny house with no furniture. It did not matter that I had written many books, one of which absolutely would survive in Holocaust archives.

No, I had to admit that fame only mattered if it could annoy people who had nothing to show for their lives yet looked down on me.

\*\*\*

I could tell this Linda was scared to phone me. I recognized her voice after so much time. Voices were a lot like faces; know one in childhood, and time can't eradicate what makes it distinctive. Her sentences were short and disconnected, and I let her go on for probably far too long before I put her at ease.

"Hey, Alyce is my financial advisor, and she said I should come there, so this must be a valuable meeting," I said. She probably never in her life had heard me so jolly.

"Right, we're giving a hundred dollars for about two days' work, including travel time," she said, jolly, too.

I wanted to ask if I was going to have to pass around the hors d'oeuvres, but that opened up all kinds of racism. One of the worst parts of my worst night had been the mean girls sending black taxi companies' cabs to other girls' houses. It was supposed to trick their victims, but when I pointed out that it affected the black cab drivers, who were called Negroes back then, I'd been told they were out anyway. Linda had been part of that. I didn't think lack of empathy just dissolved over time. Or maybe it did. But probably not in Houston, Texas. Linda surely had Hispanic household help anyway.

The travel time I could handle, I told her. I didn't think it would take two days unless I drove, and frankly I didn't have time to drive. I didn't mention that driving might be a good idea, because I could keep the radio off and think, come up with ideas for the Letty book, though only one way. I'd have to dictate them into some kind of player, because I wasn't going to pull over on I-10. I knew I wasn't going to have productive thoughts driving back. I was going to have regretful thoughts. I had regretful thoughts whenever I did a promotion for the *Werner Weiss* book.

"Oh, we'll pay for a plane ticket," Linda said. "I just thought since we'd run late that you'd want to spend the night."

"Good God, no," I said before I could censor myself.

She was silent. She must have had a glorious home that anyone would have loved to sleep in.

"Katrina has turned me into something of a homebody," I said. "It's nothing personal. You had to be here."

"I know a few people there," she said.

"I know," I said.

***

When the taxi pulled up to Linda's house, I was amused. As a girl I had believed that one of the few things I needed to fit in at school was a two-story brick house. Now two-story brick houses in New Orleans were fifty years old and had a nice patina to them, but they still were symmetrical and unimaginative.

Linda had chosen the security of symmetry without the patina of age. Her house was twice as large as any house in New Orleans because lots in Houston could be twice as large. The landscaping was nail-scissors precise, no flower or shrub untended. "I had no clue this is where I was going," I said to the cab driver, apologizing, tipping him a dollar over twenty percent.

But Linda was changed. She had gained about thirty pounds, and she no longer colored her hair. She had a good haircut, and her clothes were cotton, but she gave a message in the way she looked. "Hey," I said, and I hugged her at the door. She had opened her own door.

She reached for my backpack. I wasn't staying overnight, was catching an eleven p.m. flight, but I was carrying a few books and notes. I thought about Letty's Chanel when I packed, felt even a little pretentious to have L.L. Bean. But L.L. Bean that I'd owned for twenty years seemed all right to me. I told her thanks, but I wasn't carrying a purse. I liked her for her offer. I bet she wouldn't have reached for Chanel.

No household help was in sight. This house was too big for one person to keep up. If I owned this house, I would pay someone to help me. Or closed off most of the extraneous rooms, declaring it a museum of mediocrity. It was a house for rearing safe children. Her children could come back with their own children and walk around with no complaints.

But Linda led me through as many rooms of indeterminate reason as Louise had in New Orleans, only these were bigger. And just as clean. Maybe she had a service of independent white women come in once a month. "I mostly entertain in the kitchen," she said. "Well, I mostly don't entertain."

It was early afternoon, and for lunch she did not bring out tiny deli sandwiches or hand-cut vegetables. "Soup?" she said, and she let me peer into a Mason jar of thick vegetables with a few teaspoons of liquid. We had homemade bread and cold stick butter and iced tea, and I was wondering how she was going to pull off a book group in a matter of hours.

"I know, my fridge is bare," she said. "The deal is, the book group keeps me because, unlike the rest of them, I actually read. They know I hate having company, and they let me slide. But when I said I went to school with you, a couple of them said, 'Okay, Linda, you get her to your house, we'll bring the food.' So I said, 'I am strictly not putting out linen napkins and china and shit,' and they said, 'We'll bring paper.'"

I told her flat-out that I knew she was the same person I knew when I was sixteen, but she wasn't the same *person*.

"I escaped," she said.

Houston and a two-story brick house did not strike me as an escape. After all, when rich people in New Orleans scurried out of town to avoid Katrina, they hit the I-10 straight for Houston. In the past month or so I had seen bumper stickers on Lexus SUVs that read, "Thanks Houston."

I told her Houston was New Orleans West.

"If you go anywhere but Newcomb, you escape," she said.

"I went to Rice and grew the hell up."

"You look like it."

She looked down at herself, straight at the slight mound of belly fat that at our age was a sign of cardiac danger and the loss of youthful arrogance.

"I mean the way you act," I said.

"I've lived most of my life in Houston," she said. "But I'm still a Democrat."

I didn't ask why she knew that was all right to say. Most of the class had had Mr. Ralph for Civics in ninth grade and had become Kennedy fanatics. The few people I still liked had taken Mr. Ralph's lectures on government to heart and never swayed. The rest, like Joseph Jungfrau, had not.

"So why do you still talk to Louise?" I said.

She crossed her eyes, rolled them up in her head. "My daughter went to Newcomb," Linda said. "You can kind of do that when you don't come from New Orleans. Of all people, she meets Louise's son. They got married straight out of college despite all my pleading and warning. Two kids later they got divorced. We're co-grandmothers, which to me should be the square root of nothing. But not to Louise.

"Louise talks to *me*."

# Chapter Twenty

I saw no flaws. No facial lines or lesions, no clothing wrinkles, no scuffs on shoes, every hair in place. These were, it seemed to me, simply Texas women with nothing else to do. In New Orleans, there were women like this, but never a complete roomful. Some kind of crisis, usually with people who disappointed them, would make several in a rich New Orleans crowd come in apologizing for why they had a bit of dishevelment. Even Linda did not look frayed.

I sensed no meanness. By six o'clock more than twenty had showed up, and they didn't break up into groups. No one whispered. I was never alone. Each came up to me and gave me her name, and each said she knew I couldn't possibly remember everybody, but she wanted to say hello anyway. I was astonished that Linda had accumulated so many friends since I last knew her. I had maybe a half dozen, and they lived in different cities and didn't know one another. "How do you all know one another?" I said when I found myself in a little circle.

"Why wouldn't we know each other?" one woman said, and the rest laughed. It occurred to me right then that most of them were Jewish. It was possible, despite streaked hair and plastic surgery, to recognize Jewish physiognomy if a person went to our school. But these were nice Jewish women. I didn't understand. I wasn't going to ask outright. Not outright. The food was flawless, Southern Jewish food. Not the Kosher Cajun food people up north would expect, but a liberal use of ham and seafood laid out in meticulously cut sandwiches and hors d'oeuvres. The synagogues in New Orleans raised money throwing crawfish boils. I always wondered what my father would have said about that. I'd been reared with no religion whatsoever, but that had been because my mother's world had to be their world. He had come from an observant family in Germany, but the unspoken understanding was that, since they had been obliterated, they had no say.

With chairs brought in from the dining room, Linda's family room accommodated the whole group almost comfortably. Not comfortably to the point of sinking into pillows the way Louise's house had been, but comfortable enough for no one to have to squeeze up against anyone else. I always got a hardback chair set cheese-stands-alone at these kinds of gatherings. It kept me from drifting off.

Linda stood up first and gave a speech. It was not the usual bio that made me grimace.

"Thanks, everybody, for putting up with all my idiosyn-crasies so we can have Darby Cooper with us tonight. You're all really kind to make this a beautiful occasion, and I promise Darby knows that I am not the hostess who made all this happen."

An appreciative laugh. I smiled.

She went on. "I wanted to have her here for two reasons tonight. First, of course, this is an incredible book. I don't need my judgment to tell you that. *The New York Times* and *Publishers Weekly* and every other reviewer has raved about it. It's perfect for us to discuss.

"But it's also a very important book for me. It's personal. Um, see, I went to high school with Darby, and I know really well about her father's death. And, uh, I want to talk about it. I know we'll talk about it in a literary way and all, but I want to say some things about it from my point of view."

"Aw, Linda, please don't," I said. I wanted to leave the room.

"This won't be bad," she said.

I looked around the room, and I got the impression that everyone there was promising it wouldn't be bad. They didn't know what *it* was, but they would fix it themselves.

I gave her a nod.

"Darby tells a story about some mean girls whose horrid behavior led to her father's death," she said. "I know this is a novel, but as we all know it's got a lot of truth behind it, and this part is true." She took in a deep breath. "I was one of those mean girls. I wasn't part of the trick where they wrote on her dead grandmother's letters, but when you're associated with killers, you're as bad as they are.

"I've heard from those women over all this time, and I've mentioned what happened a lot of times. They refuse to talk about it. Even when I say I feel guilty. So I'm here right now to tell Darby I'm beyond sorry. It won't do any good, but I'm saying it. I'm so sorry."

I couldn't burst into tears in front of so many strangers, but I felt myself turning shock-pale, and tears began to run down my face. Finally I smiled and said, "If I mess up tonight, you'll all know why."

Linda got up and came over to give me a hug. I held on for a little bit longer than a usual hug.

\*\*\*

205

I deserved the pronoun *you*. I even got it from seasoned interviewers. It happened whenever I had first-person narrators. And here it happened because someone based on myself was in the story. No one wanted to talk about the writing process, the creation of the narrative, the construction of the characters, even the process of spinning fiction from fact. They all wanted to probe my personal life. That happened most of the time in book groups. I'd never been in a book group, but I'd heard jokes about them. Book groups had little to do with literary criticism and a lot with drinking wine and spilling personal connections to the story at hand.

In this case, everyone wanted to ask me questions so she could talk about her own life. The Jewish fretting came up first and fast. That was the essence of the book, but no one noticed that. They just wanted a forum for talking about not fitting in when they were among the only Jewish children in public school or private school. I tried to say that being the only second-generation Jew among sixth-generation Jews was a little tricky, but no one was sixth-generation anything in Texas, so it didn't count. Trying to explain a book theme of being some-thing and yet not wasn't what we were there for.

Marriage was a rich lode. My parents' marriage had not been a pleasure to study, then twist into fiction. It had been the vessel for that Jewish identity issue, but it also had raised that question that was so difficult to answer. What about Letty's loyalties? I was working on that right now in the new novel, and I had to tread carefully, not wanting to affect my own thoughts. I felt they were unassailable, set out in the *Werner Weiss* book. The only person who could say anything that might set me back would be Letty, and she not only wasn't present, she wasn't all that credible.

"Why didn't the mother leave home?" one woman asked.

"I'm trying to show an overlay here," I said, wanting to

keep this a book study. "This is about two loyalties, new family, old family. You know, like how she was reared and how her husband was reared."

"If she'd left New Orleans, her mother wouldn't know what the hell she was doing in her own house," one woman said. "Huh, Linda."

"Oh, for Chrissakes," Linda said, knowing all her friends in the room, except me, were in on the joke. She turned to me. "You remember my mother?" I shook my head, no. I'd been asked to her house to help her with math a couple of times, but her mother had left us with the housekeeper. "Hah!" Linda said to the room. "Speaks for itself. My mother was never around, see?"

I wasn't going to challenge her. I was sure Louise and Linda B. and the rest who came over for longer stretches than an hour of geometry had met her mother.

"When I left for Rice instead of staying to live in her house and pledge AEPhi, she just threw up her hands, like I was an alien life form," she said. "If you leave New Orleans, you can do whatever you want."

I considered that. I wondered if geography played a role. If Houston was far enough, if the Mississippi coast was just a suburb of New Orleans. "I moved away," I said, before I could remember that this was supposed to be a discussion about the book.

"But I found you in New Orleans," Linda said. "I don't think moving away counts if you move back."

I said that I would explain my own situation, but we really weren't here to talk about my life. Then I told them that I was one of the very few people who had evacuated *to* New Orleans for Hurricane Katrina. "Hey," I said, "that might tie in thematically with the book. Or maybe with my next book." Refuge in hell. Then, before someone could be polite and ask about the next book, I went on and explained how my house at the Mississippi Gulf beach had washed away, really, honestly, washed away, not leaving one stick—and it had had a brick chimney, too.

I thought that gave them all the information they needed. I had escaped, yes. I had crossed a state line. It was now up to them to decide if I'd done as well as Linda. It seemed to me that rearing a child in Mississippi public schools, which was implicit in my story, was better than a two-story brick house that was too big for any New Orleans lot available after the year 1920.

These were polite women. They were born to express concern. Was I all right? Did I find a place in New Orleans? My daughter? My mother? I gave them short answers; yes, my mother was alive, as far as I knew. No, neither of their houses sustained any damage. But back to the book. All right, back to the book. I brought up the question again, because I was curious. "What was your feeling about the mother clinging to her parents who really were cruel people? I get a lot of negative feedback on that."

"I think people who don't live in small towns like New Orleans don't get it," Linda said.

"New Orleans is hardly a small town," someone said. "Not even now, when half of its criminals are living here." The person next to her gave her the obligatory dirty look. Maybe they weren't all Republicans. But I still thought their husbands were.

"New Orleans is a small town, but only the people there know it," Linda said. "Anyway, forget I said that city. I just mean that when you live where everybody knows your business, you can't escape your parents. And the mother, what's her name, Lily, is kind of paralyzed trying to prove to them that she's good enough."

That was a point I'd been trying to make.

"Well, she's never going to do that," the woman next to Linda said. "All they want is for her to be really wealthy."

Linda said, "I'd imagine that having a kid like Darby might make some points."

I was embarrassed. Linda wasn't pandering to me. She actually meant it. She remembered failing geometry. And she had no way of knowing I'd gone on scholarship because my grandmother had set my father up to knock him down: when she quit paying tuition, he had to reveal his income to the school, and I had to make good grades, and together we knew we had no fussing power.

"If I got paid a lot of money for grades, my grandmother would have been impressed," I said. "I mean the Darby character."

"Hey, if this is all about defeating the father who's not good enough for their daughter, why didn't Lily leave town when he died?" the woman next to Linda said.

"You have no idea what you've just asked," I said.

They were about to hear about the process of writing a book, about how unclean it was.

\*\*\*

I belabored what for me was the obvious, for anyone else just terms in *New Yorker* articles. I had an agent named Shoshana. I had an editor named Julie. I'd connected with Shoshana decades ago when she read a short story of mine in a literary journal and had contacted me. It was her job, at no charge to me, to read my work, if she liked it, to send it out to editors who might buy it. The editor with whom I'd had my great successes was Julie. I got escalating royalties from the house

where Julie worked, and usually that was fifteen percent of
retail; Shoshana took fifteen percent of that.

The women were sitting slightly forward in their seats. This
was boring information, but I knew they were doing arithmetic
in their heads. I wasn't going to do any for them.

"What you need to know mostly is that a book has to go
through my agent first, really at this point as a courtesy, though
she *can* veto it, and then the editor is going to pick it apart until
she thinks it's ready to publish. Assuming, of course, that she
wants it at all."

"Did they both like it?" one woman blurted out.

Oh, I was a good storyteller, wasn't I?

I smiled, as if I were about to tell everyone that Hansel and
Gretel were walking up to the gingerbread house. "Liking a
book sometimes is a yes or no matter," I said. "But with this
book, it got interesting."

Everything had worked with *Werner Weiss*—right up to the
ending. I had ended the book with a truth, a make-them-throw-
up ending. The note from the mean girls had, in effect, killed
my father. The end, so there, how do you like that? Julie loved
my writing, my language, yes, but more than that, my empathy
with my characters. This pre-dated a purely autobiographical
book. Still, Julie could not hold her job if she didn't have
commercial brains. She had to look at every acquisition for
what it would earn the corporation. Shoshana knew this.
Shoshana was a businesswoman, too. Shoshana had aesthetic
sensibilities, but aesthetic had to be salable.

Shoshana and Julie wanted an ending that felt better. I had
made the reader ache for this Werner; there was some
unwritten rule that I couldn't kill him off.

"I'd said, 'So what the hell am I supposed to do with him
then?'" I told the group.

I did several three-way debates with Shoshana and Julie, and in each one they tried shaming me, reminding me that I was a fiction writer, not a memoirist, that surely I could find a sweeter fate for Werner. "But the whole book builds to his tragic end," I argued, and eventually found no comeback.

So, as everyone in the room knew, I'd compromised by letting the mother character and the me character move beyond the death.

I wrote an epilogue that let the reader walk away in peace. And that was how fiction worked sometimes, I told the book group. It had nothing to do with what the writer felt.

*** 

I had to leave for my flight before everyone else was ready to stop eating and drinking and talking. Linda walked me to the door when the cab honked.

"If I'd known you were going to change my life, I might have stayed overnight," I said to her.

"Might have?" she said, smiling.

"Nah."

"Probably smart," she said. "Don't make too much of it. I'm the only one who grew up to understand."

"You just might be enough," I said, hugging her, and I ran for the taxi because I was forever sorry for those cab drivers back in 1962.

# Chapter Twenty-One

B eing a passenger in a night taxi in Texas was like being on a low mix of nitrous oxide, getting just the right sensory deprivation to ride deep and right. I wasn't worried about offending the driver by not speaking. When I got in I apologized by telling him that something too amazing for words just had happened to me. He was Hispanic, but I could tell from his reaction that he thought he knew what I was talking about. He'd seen the house.

I wasn't going to backtrack over the evening. I never replayed such experiences, at least not the personal parts, looking for the joys or gaffes that I might rethink and rethink until they were slivers of soap. In my jacket pocket was my honorarium for the event, mostly fives. They had been organized for sandwiches, but not to pull together a fresh bank check for me. It was funny, nothing about me. I would think about my new book.

I leaned back with my eyes closed and started to think. When I was at the dentist, I often did my best book-working this way, and his assistant knew to have a pen ready so I could write on my hand. It seemed to me that I'd gotten surer about

Letty-Lily tonight, but something new was floating around. I'd said flat-out as always that Letty-Lily could not leave because she had something to prove. And why couldn't she leave after Bernie-Werner died? Because she still had something to prove.

But it wasn't that simple in the epilogue, and that was because I'd been forced by Shoshana and Julie to remember what actually happened. Only Letty and I knew, and surely Letty had forgotten by the time the book was published. She certainly never said anything to me, but then Letty never let me know that she'd read a single word of it. She'd been that way with everything I'd ever had published. "It has nothing to do with you," she would say. "It's just that I was a psych major."

When Daddy died, Axel, his one deep-down friend in America, had come to New Orleans to see whether he could be of any help. Axel and Daddy had been boyhood friends in Stuttgart, always planning to go into business together, and in Axel's mind nothing happened to change that. Not even the war that made Axel 4-F and successful in New York, while the U.S. military sent Daddy to New Orleans and all that entailed. My New Orleans grandfather fought Axel's help every step of the way, even when Axel bought the building Daddy was renting from my grandfather. Axel had done his best, then eventually had been someone on the phone every few months. He would have paid my tuition, I knew. He would have set up a trust fund for me, I knew. But Letty had something to prove. No more Axel help because that would prove nothing to Grammy.

What I put into the Epilogue was true. Axel came down to New Orleans and said to Letty, "You owe it to Bernie. You move to New York, I'll set you up. You work a little in the office, you live great. The kid goes to the best public schools in the country. You see what he wanted for you."

In the book, Letty had told him yes.

In real life, Letty had told my grandmother she wanted to do it, and my grandmother had offered her an allowance and said she would give up the money my grandfather had put in trust until my father died.

Letty was too lazy to pack. Letty said, thank you, but I'll pass, to Axel.

We were pulling up onto the Departures ramp when it came to me.

Of course.

Axel.

***

Searching my mind for information I didn't have put me to sleep on the plane. I wanted Axel's last name. Or the name of his business. This was different from looking for story lines. This required specificity of memory, and with time and use of other parts of my brain, my memory was weakening. I'd bought a t-shirt to sleep in that read, "I don't need my memory/ I have an imagination," and that was true until I hit a terrible moment of aphasia. When I needed a precise word and had no access to it, I was ruined for that writing session; if it was important enough, I would stop or look for contexts where it might appear.

But Axel had been an adult in my young life, and no one had told me to call him Mister. Mr. What? I went through the alphabet, limited myself to German names, came up with nothing, and in the darkened cabin of the plane I fell asleep on the short flight to New Orleans. I woke up with no *oh, right!* recollection, and I decided I probably never knew his last name anyway.

It was the middle of the night. I could do nothing until daylight. I mean, I could go over to Letty's and poke around for

an address book, but not at that hour. Danger had come back
to the streets. No longer was New Orleans an exclusive place,
where its only residents were die-hards who needed to be here
so badly that they would go without electricity. Everyone had
been so polite. All the rotten people were back now, the spoiled
rich and the angry criminal, and I might encounter either in
Letty's neighborhood at one a.m.

I sat up, waited for good daylight, planned what I would
say. I had little doubt. I wasn't going to be accusatory, though I
had a right to be. What if I was wrong? This was a good man,
though Daddy always had joked about how his mother had said
Axel was *nichtsnutz*. "She always said it with affection," Daddy
said, explaining why a goodhearted man who was so successful
had seemed that way to this grandmother I never knew. He
didn't want his mother to seem to have poor judgment.
"Remember, she knew Axel when he was very young and
chasing women."

"Now he's not so young and still chasing women," Letty
would say, with amusement.

"*Nichtsnutz*, huh," I'd say. My accent was flawless because
my father was teaching me German secretly.

"Hey, you really sound German," Letty said.

"They always pick up the accent they hear," my father said.

No matter what, I would enjoy hearing Axel's voice.

\*\*\*

I tiptoed into Letty's house as if the information I would find
there would surprise me before I was ready. I knew her well,
knew there were only about three places she would keep an
address book. I didn't know why I tried the two less probable
places first. As I expected, it was in the large kitchen drawer
that could hold both phone books and one smaller item. It was

sandwiched between the phone books, the White Pages drooping down over it, as if she rotated the three directories according to need.

This was the same address book Letty had had since long before my father died. It was twice as fat as it was originally, stuffed with slips of paper, business cards, corners torn off envelopes. Entries were in many shades of ink, lined through if an address or phone number changed. No e-mail addresses were listed. I flipped through, saw no dead people were crossed out, as far as I could tell. I turned to N. Rena was on that page. Rena had been the housekeeper who had pity, then grief, for my father when no one had either. When Rena died, Letty didn't tell me she'd seen the obituary until after the funeral.

I had to be systematic, go from A to Z, possibly not that far. I had to skim. I would have to steal this book.

I went all the way to T before I found him. Tannenbaum.

I never had known that name, or I would have remembered it. A Jewish man named Christmas Tree. His four lines were barely legible. His address had changed countless times, and with it his phone number. *Nichtsnutz.* She had squeezed an asterisk next to an undeleted phone number, and when I looked down to the bottom of the page, the footnote read, "*Firtree Imports" with a 212 phone number.

I had two ways to reach him.

It was seven-thirty, too early to call, even to the East Coast. I thought about whether I wanted to phone from Letty's number or my own. The best, it seemed to me, would be to call him at his home and have the number at her house show up on Caller ID. I could wait until evening, come back. But I couldn't wait. I couldn't even sit around in that empty house for half an hour, waiting for business hours. Probably someone else answered his work phone; would he see Caller ID anyway?

I killed time stopping at Walgreens and buying Benadryl.

No matter what, I was going to sleep all afternoon. I walked the aisles, looking at a world of necessities for everyone, though foundation makeup and catnip and Frosted Flakes never were going to be necessary for me. I got home well after eight o'clock, lightly nauseated, rushed to the phone, dialed without plans.

A recording answered. I was thanked for calling Firtree. Just Firtree. If I knew my extension, I could dial it at any time. Otherwise I could hold for the operator. I had a lot of nerve, calling the owner. I held for the owner. Axel? Mr. Tannenbaum? "Firtree, may I help you?" The woman had a Queens accent in those six syllables. I told her I was calling for Axel Tannenbaum. Nice choice. Who's calling? Darby. She told me to hold a minute. *A* minute, not one minute. We were on the same plane.

"Well, well, well," came the voice seconds later. *Vell, vell, vell:* he sounded so much like my daddy. "And what can I do for you?"

"Is she there?" I started to tremble a little: this was the moment. He might say no. Or he might say, *who?*

"Good for you, my girl," he said. "I'm so glad you are calling. Your mama is here. Well, here in New York. Not right here in my office. But I am taking good care of her."

I couldn't have predicted what I would do. What I did was burst into tears.

\*\*\*

Axel didn't feel it was his place to give me information. "I understand there are two sides to every story," he said. I told him I had no clue what he was talking about. "You sound like a very nice young woman," he said.

I said I was hardly young, that I was old enough to be a

respectably old grandmother. It was the first time I'd seen myself that way.

"Oh, my goodness, you are right," he said.

He would do this much: he would act as an intermediary conveying messages. I gave him the phone number at my new old house. Letty didn't know anything about where to find me, though she did know I had escaped being washed into the Gulf of Mexico. The exchange was 896, TWinbrook 6 for anyone who'd lived in New Orleans long enough. We had had 891, 895, and 899 before the storm, and for some reason the phone company had had to add an exchange. That was strange, given that it seemed as if everyone was giving up landlines.

I told Axel that I had Caller ID and voice mail, so if I was out, she could leave a message, and if she didn't I'd know she'd called anyway. Letty had spent too much of the years right after my father died sitting by the phone waiting for Eddie Marino. I wanted her to know I was not giving away power. At least not to her.

Yet I did. I stayed in my house and tried to write, tried to write about a Letty I loved. The more time passed, the more I struggled with this fictional character, this young woman who wanted to be good enough for her own mother. She treasured only the right things, those that were full of memory and no particular monetary value. She loved her wrong husband, wrong-for-her-family husband.

I would type and look at the clock. After fifteen minutes, the first phase was over. Axel would have phoned Letty, and the logical result would have been for her to phone me immediately. But she didn't, which meant she deliberately chose not to. There was no other explanation. It was just a little past nine o'clock in New York, and Letty never went anywhere in New Orleans before eleven. In New York, where her only possible appointment could be at a beauty salon, she would still be lolling around wherever she had been lolling around since August.

I was now in the second phase, trying to concentrate on my work and wondering what Letty was thinking. I knew Axel was telling the truth. All stories about Axel pointed to a truth-teller. I imagined a phone call to Shoshana. I remembered reading *Herzog*, where he imagined writing letters. *How can I possibly write a sympathetic book?* I would say with a lot of accusation in my voice. Letty's silence was petulant, and the only Letty I knew was petulant. I was supposed to write about a young woman who didn't know she was going to lose her husband, and it was her fault. But not because she was petulant. Because she was earnest. Or the reader might learn she was stubborn, but only stubborn on her husband's behalf. *I can't reconcile that with what I see,* I would say to Shoshana, and she would say back to me that it was my job. To reconcile it? No, to ignore it and go back to my fiction-writing world.

I didn't need to do a physical description of the Lily-Letty character again, so for my purposes I created an image in my head of this person, as antithetical to my mother as possible. Could I make her plump? A little, as long as there were no meals, because a contemporary Letty character would emerge through self-deprivation. I wrote down "plump vs. anorexic." I made her five-eight because Letty was five-three. Wrote down "5'8". I gave her dark, stick-straight hair; young Letty had those unkempt reddish-blond curls. All right, I now had put a tall, plump, dark Lily into my mental population, not on the page, and I could keep writing my story with no prejudice.

Phase three took four days. I'd reached the point where I'd decided that knowing Letty was safe was enough, that in fact having her silent and safe was as good as I could imagine. When the phone rang it didn't even occur to me that it might be Letty. I looked at Caller ID, and I saw a 212 area code. Axel's home number was 917. This was not his office number. His office number ended in zero-zero, pretty good in Manhattan. Chances were good this was a sales pitch of some kind, though most promoters put their callers in much cheaper places.

"I understand you called."

Letty.

"Letty!"

"You found me," she said. "When did you bother to start looking?"

The only conversation more difficult than a regular one with Letty was a conversation which Letty had prepared for over the course of, say, four days. I was well schooled for this, but it didn't mean I would win. Or even hang up feeling well. Letty could give me psychosomatic symptoms, abdominal pain, headache. I never told her about them, having learned long ago that when my father had contact dermatitis she told him he needed a psychiatrist. Of course it had been true. If he had seen a psychiatrist, he would have learned that he needed to leave her. Rather, he needed to leave her and take me with him.

Today my symptom was going to be abdominal pain. I could tell. I let my belly relax. "I've been trying to find you since the flood water receded," I said.

"You're smarter than that," Letty said.

"You left your house—and your car—and took nothing but your luggage," I said. "I called William. You talk to William?"

"You'd know if you'd called him lately," she said. "No, I haven't talked to William. I don't need William."

My belly was clenching again. Relax, relax.

"Well, William told me you'd had zero activity on your financial accounts," I said. "So what am I supposed to think? You disappear and stay disappeared, and you don't use any money."

"You assume I've been kidnapped and call the authorities."

221

Letty clearly hadn't done as much thinking as I had.

"First of all, no kidnapper worth his shit tells his victim, 'You're coming with me, now get in the car, but first load up all of your Chanel luggage,'" I said. "And second of all, have you noticed that there was a small fucking disaster in New Orleans, and if you call the FBI and tell them, 'Oh, my mother disappeared, and nothing is missing from her completely intact uptown house except her and her Chanel luggage,' they will hang up the phone on you?"

"This is a fine reunion with your sick old mother," Letty said.

"Are you sick?"

"No, but I'm old," she said and hung up.

# Chapter Twenty Two

The list of people who might have wanted to know whether Letty was alive was longer than I thought. Evidently I had consulted quite a few, many of whom were strangers who I thought might be leads. I wrote a mass e-mail, with a huge apology for itself not being a phone call, and sent it to the likes of Shirley and William and Ted. As I hit send, I wondered what responses I would get. I didn't expect expressions of relief, paeans to Letty, and I didn't get them. Instead I got congratulations on my detective work. Except from William. He phoned.

"How is she living on no money?" he said.

I told him that his guess was as good as mine, that I'd had only one brief conversation with her, but that I'd sworn a while back I'd seen her slipping into Bergdorf's, so she wasn't starving.

In the e-mail I hadn't spelled out details of where she was or how I'd tracked her down. It was enough to announce that, after weeks of poking around in my memory, I'd figured out a connection, and I'd found her.

"Bergdorf's? Is that on Canal Street?" William said.

I told him it was on Fifth Avenue. I added New York City.

"I know where Fifth Avenue is," he said. "What were you doing in New York?"

I couldn't actually remember. I knew I'd seen Shoshana. I went to New York more than I went anywhere else. I would have liked to have said I was up there, hot on Letty's trail, but I knew that wasn't true. I told him I thought it was about a book. Then I remembered: a resurgence of interest in my last book because of the storm. "Yes, definitely, about a book."

"Your mother was missing, and you went to New York about a book?" William said. "Do you realize how easy it would have been to find a private investigator while you were up there? You can't get any help down here after the storm, but everything's normal up there."

"I fucking found her," I said. "And it didn't cost anything."

He was quiet. "Well, you could've found her faster."

I told him it would have done no good. I talked to her for three minutes, and she went back into whatever snit sent her up there.

According to William, I was the wrong person to have made the contact. I agreed. He was the right person. I didn't agree, but I didn't care.

*** 

William phoned two days later. I'd given him only Axel's work number so no one could fault me. With being the right person, it still had taken him two days.

"I'm not sure, but I think your mother is some kind of slut," he said. I thought I heard a little admiration in his voice.

I knew what that meant. I could believe it about Letty, but I couldn't believe it about Axel.

All he gave me were facts. Letty had phoned William and

given him facts, and William had drawn his conclusions. Axel lived in Queens because he always lived in Queens. But his business was an international conglomerate, it really was, and it had to be headquartered in Manhattan, so it was. And Axel maintained what he called a *pied à terre* in the city, on the Upper West Side, a fine two-bedroom apartment that was fully decorated and cleaned once a week. Axel used it only when his representatives came in from China or Brazil or somewhere and wanted a meeting at eight in the morning. Or wanted to have drinks late at night. Lately that was almost never. So Letty was living on West End, and Axel was giving her an allowance, because Letty was a refugee and shouldn't spend her own money.

"Why would a man sleep in Queens?" William said. "I've seen Queens on TV."

His reasoning was solid. Especially when he and I had unspoken shared background information. Letty was a college graduate who could have made her way in the world. She could have found work when my father was alive and saved him shame, though her reasoning was that her working would have shamed him, and it was the 'fifties, remember. When he died, her choice was not to go to work; her choice was to be the best consort she could be to the owner of a grocery store. Right away, starting at my father's funeral. Hardly a moment's consideration of starting over and working somewhere else with dignity, when so much more fast, easy dignity could be found spending a rich man's money. Except for the years she was married to my father, it seemed, Letty's best talent had been spending a rich man's money. She hadn't slept with her own father, but she had learned from him.

"Those people are past eighty," I said.

"Try telling that to Letty," William said. I forgot to whom I was speaking.

225

I asked him what he wanted to do, now that Letty was on a free ride over a thousand miles away. I knew I was having my own, different free ride, and yet I was waiting to be told how I could go back to a wrecked life.

"If your mother dies this angry at you, how are you going to feel?" he said.

I had to think about it. I told him that. He said he wasn't joking. I said I wasn't, either. Letty was going to die angry at me, no matter what. If she died on a beach with cool breezes and rainbows and puppies frolicking in the surf and dolphins frolicking at the horizon, her final words would be about me and my stinginess with the morphine.

I told William I'd been ready for this for a very long time.

"I think she's counting on me to do something," he said. "If I hadn't called, I wouldn't have crossed her mind."

"You didn't have to."

William's definition of family had a little to do with obligation and a lot to do with secret wishes of being remembered in a last will and testament. It helped, of course, that he gave free legal advice, and it was difficult to ignore him as an heir when he was sitting there at his desk, taking notes about beneficiaries and trusts and who had to die before whom.

"I feel a certain responsibility toward your mother," he said.

"You don't need to," I said. "She's a big girl. She can take care of herself."

***

I went into J.D. Salinger mode. That was my fantasy. Live in pure isolation, my only contact with people who knew I needed food or other staples and didn't want to talk about anything that wasn't right in front of me. I hoped Salinger was writing because he had the pure peace for his mind. I had it for mine. I didn't watch movies the way Salinger did, because they carried me too far into stories. I even found that reality shows on television pulled me into life histories that involved me too much in caring. I refused emotion. Game shows were all right. Talk shows were all right, as long as I didn't know about the guest. I didn't read. I still wasn't getting mail delivery. First class was slowly becoming available if I stood in line at the post office, but magazines didn't come at all. And books were out of the question. No emotional immersion. Nonfiction was a possibility, but much of it was full of energy, or why would people buy it? No, I lived in my book, sometimes eating, sometimes napping.

Axel's call came as a surprise. I didn't answer, just as I didn't answer any other calls, but I did check Caller ID and the message, just as I did with all other calls. He really needed to talk to me. He left his number. Then, as an afterthought, he said, "Oh, you might be thinking your mother is not well. She is very healthy. That is not why I am phoning. Please do not be alarmed."

I hoped this man was not in love with Letty.

When I said to the operator at Firtree, "This is Darby Cooper," she told me to hold one second before I even could say to whom I wanted to speak; before I knew it, Axel was on the phone. "Hey, I couldn't have gotten that treatment if I'd said I was President Bush," I said.

"*Especially* if you said you were President Bush," Axel said.

I wished he were in love with a mother I liked.

He was calling to tell me—*tell* was his word—that he and Letty were coming to New Orleans this coming weekend.

They sounded like a couple, traveling together. Did I need to make up the bed at her house? Did I need to pick them up at the airport? What would they like for breakfast? Did they know that New Orleans wasn't its usual self, that going out for dinner

227

and walking around the Quarter weren't exactly the same as before? Though the Quarter was pretty unscathed. Still, I could give them the disaster tour; they wouldn't believe the Lower Ninth Ward. But parts of the lakefront were horrific, just no one paid attention to that.

I didn't stop to breathe.

Axel told me to hold on, hold on, calm down, calm down. Everything was taken care of. He would call me when they were settled in, late Friday afternoon.

Were they going to synagogue? I asked because that was what I thought of when I heard late Friday, even though I knew no one who went to synagogue on Friday evening. No one in New Orleans, that was. I assumed a lot of people in New York did. And now Letty was some sort of New York person.

"Oh, for Chrissakes, no," Axel said.

***

It was a little after six. Caller ID said St. Louis Hotel. Axel and Letty were here on a honeymoon. Axel was supreme; his marrying Letty was dreadful. Though from what little I knew of the St. Louis Hotel, it was as low-cost as possible in the French Quarter. I thought I'd seen it on a list of hotels that were wall to wall FEMA evacuees. It would not be a tropic isle.

I said, "Welcome to New Orleans" to whoever was calling.

Axel was calling to arrange to meet for dinner at eight o'clock. Galatoire's. But would I meet him there for drinks before Letty came? He wanted to talk to me.

When I was younger, "I want to talk to you" stripped me of power. I would have to wait, and I would know that the talk was bad news. I would see Axel in two hours, and as powerless waits went, that was not much. But I hadn't had such a directive in a long time, and, really, Shoshana was the only person I could think of who was entitled to give me bad news that way.

I told Axel that I didn't like the sound of this, that he clearly was bringing me bad news, that I was too old to have to be polite. What was this about?

It was about Letty, he said, and I suddenly went from thinking she was married to thinking she was dying. And possibly not knowing she was dying. Either way, she was going to stay in New York, because Axel wasn't moving here to be married to anyone, and no dying person would come to New Orleans to die, unless she was on a gurney with her final morphine drip. New Orleans never had been a mecca for the medically complicated, and now New Orleans wasn't even a good place to break an arm. I knew Letty wasn't on a final morphine drip if she was going to eat at Galatoire's. I'd seen oxygen tanks in Galatoire's, but a morphine drip was pointless when the bar was already so good.

"Just about Letty?" I said.

"It's about me, too," Axel said.

That meant Letty wasn't dying, but it also meant I was back to their being married and my having to contend with it. I wondered why my mother had to go after men who were so close to my father. Eddie Marino had been his boss, the owner of the market where Daddy had wound up being a humiliated manager after my grandparents made sure he didn't thrive. Now she had gone all the way to New York to find Daddy's best friend in the world. Eddie and Axel were wealthy men, men who showed up my father. Daddy believed dead was dead, and he probably made no effort to swim up in the afterlife, so he never had to know Letty was showing him what she deserved. I was another story.

# Chapter Twenty-Three

Axel had the table in the front corner opposite the doorway. It was right up against the mirror and the window. He was on the mirror side, so I took the seat opposite him. Letty could sit next to him. I would be like a child with her parents. Galatoire's tradition. He told me to order a drink. I asked for vodka and tonic. Axel said, Grey Goose. I said I didn't care. The waiter laughed.

"I'm going to wait until you've had at least half of your drink," Axel said.

I told him I thought that was a good idea. I was a cheap drunk because I never drank, and tonight I needed to be slightly impenetrable. I wanted to hold onto common sense, but for me common sense often worked better when it was fuzzy. I took a gulp, forgot I hated the taste, looked around, emptied two packets of Splenda into the glass, stirred just a little, letting the sweet stuff go to the bottom, took a big draw from the little black straw. The sugary taste and pure alcohol hit me happily, and I said, "You can't possibly upset me."

"You need to take your mother back."

"No!" I went into a fit of giggles. I was so relieved for Axel that I could have strangled him until he laughed, too.

"Yes!" he said, and he broke into a wide grin.

I took another big mouthful of my drink, told him I'd be ordering at least one more and didn't care what kind of tab I ran on him. "No takebacks," I said.

"She is not a gift you gave me." He was still smiling.

He said he had expected a lot of outcomes, but not this one. "You're very much like Bernie," he said.

"Consider the alternative," I said. For a fraction of a blurry second, I got paranoid. What if Letty had turned Axel into her spy? *Go find out what Darby really thinks of me.* That was the fine part of being blurry. I couldn't think badly about a good person.

Axel looked at his watch. He had told Letty eight-thirty. We both knew that meant closer to nine. But we had to slug it out before she arrived, because if we weren't in agreement, she would divide us and conquer us both. I didn't see how we both could lose, since she could live in only one place. Aha! Axel said, that was where I was wrong. She would convince us both that she needed each of us to take care of her in a different way, and she would fill up both of our worlds.

Axel had thought it out carefully.

"Of course you have," I said. "I've been sitting here for days thinking you married her."

"What!" There was that W that sounded like a V.

"I don't know you that well," I said. "Letty can outsmart some smart people."

"Listen," he said, "I have lived in New York City since I was twenty years old. I have dated some very smart women. I mean, you're talking *smart*. Columbia Graduate School, the Sorbonne. And don't forget who was my friend as a boy. The smartest man there ever was. Except, of course, when it came to women. Be that as it may, I have lived my entire life without getting married. What would make you think I'd marry a woman without a thought in her head from the American South?"

"I should be insulted, but I'm not," I said.

Axel told me he was sorry to do this to me, but he had to return Letty to what he called her natural habitat. I could have let it go at that, because I had the basic fact, that since the day before the storm Axel had been taking care of my mother, and it was a thankless job. It was my place to thank him profusely and find a way to welcome her home and convince her that ravaged New Orleans at her own expense was a better deal than the glitter of Manhattan under the protection of the only man who ever came close to being Bernie. Well, Bernie's goofball twin.

I ordered a second Grey Goose and tonic. I finished off the first and lost all censors. I would take the second very slowly, watch my watch, be ready whenever Letty showed.

"How in hell did you wind up with Letty to begin with?" I said. Anyone looking at us from four tables away would have thought I was flirting with Axel.

He told me it was all over the news. By the time Katrina was taking aim for what might possibly be New Orleans, he phoned Letty.

"In God's name, why?"

"You don't remember after your daddy died?" he said. "You were a pretty big girl by then. In fact—"

I put my hand up, palm facing him. He knew about whose fault Daddy's death was. For the first time, I realized that I was the one who'd invited those girls to my house.

"I apologize, I apologize," he said. "So I came to your house. Well, I came to New Orleans, and I visited your house. I took care of Bernie's papers, do you remember that?" I nodded. "I told Letty I would set her up if she wanted to move to New

York. I thought she should honor Bernie, you know, live the life he wanted for her."

"She sure didn't."

"That's beside the point," he said. "What matters is that I felt a certain responsibility for you and your mother because Bernie was my partner. He was all I had in this country. We were like brothers with no other family. Really."

I remembered the fact of Axel if not the facts.

So my father had been dead over forty years, yet when a storm was raging in the Gulf of Mexico and threatening the woman my father had married after World War II, Axel had phoned her.

"She didn't know what to do with herself," he said. "So I told her, 'Look, you listen for your phone. I'll call the airlines. You go pack a bag. When I have a reservation, you just show up at the airport, take a taxi, I'll pay you back, I meet you at LaGuardia, you don't have a thing to worry about.' She says to me, does she need cash, the line at the bank is a block long, I tell her, 'You got cab fare to your airport, you're good to go.' That's how it went. She's worried for nothing since that phone call."

My father had a joke when I was a kid. If I did something that really pleased him he would bestow the highest honor on me. He explained that it was like being in the French military. I said to Axel, "If Daddy were alive, he would give you the Croix de Goose."

His eyes watered up just a little. "Some things you never get over," he said.

\*\*\*

When Letty walked in, the first thing she said was, "What are you doing here?"

"Aw, come on," I said and stood up and hugged her. I was full of drink and hugged tight, with actual sincerity. I thought she could feel it.

"The fare was twenty-three dollars, and I tipped him a five," Letty told Axel.

Axel leaned forward, pulled his billfold out of his back pocket. He gave me a look that said, *Not now.* He handed Letty a ten and a twenty. Letty looked at the two bills and said, "I think I'll go wild in the French Quarter." She smiled at Axel.

Axel knew Cooper women, or maybe women in general. He waited for Letty to get on her second drink, though she was much better schooled at holding her liquor than I was. Honor was a good drinker, too. It probably wasn't genetic; it probably had more to do with practice. Though my grandfather having been homicidally drunk without compunction possibly passed down genes we needed to watch for.

"Darby's here for a reason," Axel said.

"That's good," Letty said. Her voice was soft. Maybe she was expecting a marriage proposal. Maybe she decided he had been formal, asking me for her hand.

The waiter walked over and asked if we were ready to order.

"God, no," Letty said.

Axel looked past her at the waiter, giving him a look that said, *I know you get women like this every day all day.* "Maybe ten minutes," he said.

"So where was I?" he said.

"You were telling me why Darby was here," Letty said. Letty never was excited, but this was what Letty looked like when she was excited. It was more like impatient.

"Oh, yes," Axel said. He put his hand over Letty's. Good man. His other hand was on the table. No ring box. "Letty, I came here to help Darby bring you back to New Orleans."

"And?" Letty said.

Axel looked at me. That wasn't an answer on his expected list.

"And the city's back to being habitable, so you don't need to be in New York anymore," I said. "You can resume your regular life."

"I'm not asking you," she said. "What about you, Axel?"

"I'm going back to my normal life, too," he said.

Letty slammed her napkin down on the table. "I don't get it."

Axel's hand was left in mid-air, hovering over where the napkin-slamming hand had been. He quickly tucked it into his lap.

"It's time to come home," I said. "Honor's here. Oh, and she's married."

"Good for Honor," Letty said. "Wait, *what?*"

I told her Honor might have babies; wouldn't Letty want to be here for babies? What was I thinking?

"I'm not very good with babies," she said to me. "I'm very happy for Honor. I'm sure you know that." She turned to Axel. "Of course, I quit being able to get pregnant a long time ago."

Letty definitely expected a ring.

Axel had a lot of practice in these matters. He probably had brushed off scarier women than Letty over time. Women who could have lived many decades and brought parents or babies or challenges to his authority.

"I hope you didn't think we would become a couple," Axel said to her.

"We *were* a couple," Letty said. "You were just like my Eddie. With a lot of Bernie in you, too." Bernie was an after-thought; I dared her to deny that.

"Listen," Axel said, "when that hurricane was coming, I called you because I was committed to take care of you for as long as I live. It was a pledge I made to myself after I lost Bernie."

"That's like the Bible," Letty said. Letty knew as much about the Bible as I did, which was no longer anything. Axel looked at her funny. I didn't think Axel was a godly man, and he certainly wasn't one for Bible stories carrying any weight. "Anyway, you're the only person who cared about me," Letty said. "My own daughter told me that she didn't want anything to do with me. She was going to be alone for the storm, and she didn't want me ruining her space. You're the only person who loves me in the whole world."

I started to protest, but I closed my mouth because Axel had more to protest.

"I suppose that was some sort of love that made me phone you," he said.

"It sure was," Letty said. "You treated me better than any man I've ever known." She turned to me. "Darby, he put me up in a gorgeous apartment in the most amazing part of New York City, probably a lot better than where he lives, though I never went out there in the boonies. And he gave me a credit card and never asked me any questions. Can you imagine? Even Eddie, bless his heart, even Eddie would look at the statement and tell me I was spending too much, though I have to say he almost never did that." She turned to Axel. "Eddie loved me to death. That's how I know love when I see it."

Axel signaled the waiter. Axel was red in the face and needed to distract himself. In honor of Bernie, he said, he was ordering no seafood and no pork. I told him my daddy had learned to eat New Orleans food early on. "That's why I'm eating this way," Axel said. "I'm doing what he should have been able to do." Letty had planned on a lump crabmeat salad, she said, but she'd just have lettuce and tomato. I had the trout.

So did Axel. "To Bernie," I said, raising my glass with a few molecules of alcohol still left in it.

\*\*\*

Axel was silent, filling himself or time with fistfuls of warm French bread covered with dots of cold butter. I knew his problem was kindness. That was the trouble with Letty: she found kind men. There was no way Axel was going to tell her he didn't love her.

"Are you in love with Axel?" I said. I would have been, because he was so good and funny, and I could see in his bones that he had broken many hearts from across rooms. In the bits of Axel lore Daddy had shared, he had told how young girls in Stuttgart had fallen madly, deeply for blue-eyed Axel. Axel, who always had been in mischief before Jewish boys learned to know they couldn't do that anymore. I knew Letty wasn't in love with Axel. Letty was in love with Letty.

"That depends on your definition of love," Letty said.

Hadn't Prince Charles said that to avoid admitting he was marrying Princess Diana for selfishness?

"I could ask if you'd cry at his funeral," I said, "but you didn't cry at the last two."

"I was angry," Letty said.

Axel stuffed a huge chunk of bread into his mouth. I handed him his water glass. He surely wouldn't be the first to choke to death in Galatoire's over outrage. I was sure the waiters were trained in the Heimlich maneuver.

He chewed hard, swallowed hard. "I'm going home on a morning flight tomorrow," he said. "Alone."

"Well, I don't love you," Letty said.

She turned to me. "Where's that Whitney ATM?" I told her I wasn't sure, but it was one of the up-and-down streets like

238

Royal or Chartres. She fished in her wallet and handed Axel his American Express card. Not a black card. "You can have my dinner," she said to me, then she walked out of the restaurant. I noticed she picked up a pack of free matches by the door. Letty didn't smoke.

# Chapter Twenty-Four

Only after Letty was settled back into her house, working feverishly on integrating all her New York clothes into her now-dreary wardrobe, did it occur to me. I had sent out an e-mail to all of Letty's friends and family saying she was alive and well, but I had forgotten Honor.

It was an honest mistake. I had gone through the list of people I called on to help me in my detective work, and her name just hadn't come up. It wasn't a deliberate omission, and it certainly wasn't a matter of her not being important to me. I just hadn't connected her to Letty. That was an odd thing to say, given that I'd always feared that they were solipsistic confederates who easily could surround me, but right then Honor had been too present, and Letty had been too absent, and that made the disconnect.

Now it was a very good idea to call Honor. Letty certainly wasn't going to do so. It was Letty's mindset that word of her return would circulate in a city where no one else had had a disruption in recent months, of course, and everyone worth knowing at all would seek her out. As for Honor, no grandmother would call her grandchild when a *good* grandchild would call begging to visit.

Sciutto answered the phone. He was the gatekeeper. I tested. I asked for Honor. "Who's calling?" Darby. "What about?" Her grandmother. Whispers. "Your grandma." More whispers. "She alive?" Into the phone, "She alive?" I said to tell Honor that if she wants to know she better tell him to give her the damn phone.

A long wait in dirty air.

"Hey, Darby," Honor said. "I hope you'd've come over to tell me in person if Letty were dead."

"Actually, I hadn't thought about it," I said, "but, no, she's not dead."

I tried to imagine what kind of signals she was giving Sciutto to pass the news along to him. For all I knew he'd left the room.

"So, was she like one of those dogs you read about? You know, the family moves, like, two thousand miles, and they forget the dog or something, and the dog drags itself through God-knows-what and shows up on their doorstep maybe a year later?"

What?

I could hear Sciutto chortling in the background. He was built to chortle.

"You know what I mean. Like, she just shows up at her house one day, like it's completely normal."

I couldn't get angry. That was a possibility.

I told her my father's friend Axel had flown her to New York.

"What the fuck for?"

Surely Sciutto was impressed. Even I was a little impressed.

"He noticed there was a hurricane, so he rescued her," I said. "He took care of her and put her up and everything."

"Oh, gross."

I could hear Sciutto in the background, "What, what?" Honor told him, Nothing. Sciutto hollered, "If you think it's gross, it's gross." Honor said she'd tell him when she got off the phone. Next thing I knew, Sciutto was on the line. "She'll call you back in a little while," he said and hung up.

*** 

I almost didn't take the call the next time I heard from Honor. It was three days later. Caller ID said Ochsner Foundation Hospital, and I had absolutely nothing to do with Ochsner. But I knew that it was right at the parish line and never stopped operating because of the storm, so a lot of people were going there. Whoever was calling might be an in-the-marrow city person I wouldn't expect because she went to Baptist. No one called from a hospital with benign reasons.

"Hey, come see me, I'm fucked up in the head," Honor said. I could tell her hand was circling the mouthpiece.

I asked her what she was doing in the hospital. She said it was a long story, and she needed me to come see her so she could tell me her long story. I asked her what about Sciutto. Sciutto was all right. What about her? I was getting frantic. Was she all right? She was calling me, wasn't she?

Tchoupitoulas was the street closest to the river, and Ochsner sat between River Road and Jefferson Highway, so in a half-empty city I could follow the Mississippi and be there in ten minutes. As I rode along Leake Avenue, I did what I often did, looked at the buildings and the wild foliage and lamented the devastation. But as I passed the worst stretch, I looked closely and realized it had looked exactly the same before Katrina had hit. New Orleans was like a beater car smashed in an accident by a fancy insured vehicle: a lot of her old mess was passing off as new damage.

Ochsner had all its bricks and not all of its people; I could park on a lower level. I didn't know why, but I ran to Honor's room. It was a double, but she didn't have a roommate. Sciutto was sitting in a chair next to the bed. She had the window side, with a view of the levee.

Honor was in a hospital gown and covered by a sheet, so I couldn't see her torso, but I could see her arms and face. She was badly bruised on her arms, but her face was all right. I watched enough reality television to know that *Forensic Files* and *Dr. Phil* and everything in between had done this scene to the point of boredom. I didn't want my daughter to be a cliché or even a textbook case.

"Do you want me to ask you in front of him why he's not in jail, or do you want to wait until I throw him out of the room so we can talk?" I said.

"Honor knows if someone with my name gets arrested, it'll be all over the news," Sciutto said. "And she definitely doesn't want that. Besides, she's not exactly innocent. You of all people know that."

I told him I was counting to three, and then I was calling Security.

"I was hungry anyway," he said.

***

The first thing I did when he was gone was look at Honor's wristband. "Honor Cooper." Good choice.

"Who wants to be a Gotti when you don't have to?" she said.

"Well, I'm glad *you* don't." I took out a print I'd made of the photo of the computer screen at the library. I'd made four copies. I'd probably never use them, but I liked having a lot. I put the picture facedown on my lap. Honor didn't notice.

"Look, they're not giving me anything for pain, so I'm not in what you'd call a really good mood," she said. "Please don't get all hostile. I need somebody who can be objective. Really, I need somebody to take charge until I feel better."

Here was the girl I once had held so delicately because her newborn neck wasn't strong enough to support her newborn head. And now her baby skin was patched with dark colors because of huge, grotesque hands.

"He needs to be in jail," I said.

"I don't want it in all the news."

I felt the photo on my lap. But I wasn't ready.

"It's not going to be in all the news," I said. "I guarantee that. What happens in this city right now has to be catastrophic to get attention." I didn't mention that the first murder after the storm had made international headlines because New Orleans had gone so long without one, this, the murder capital of the nation.

"Well, it's trashy," she said. "You may think you're the only intellect who watches crap on TV, but you're not. I've seen those shows, and I guarantee there's never been a college graduate on your *Dr. Phil.*"

I asked her if she was saying that Sciutto should get away with beating her half senseless because she was a graduate student. I didn't point out that I had a feeling that if Sciutto had a high school diploma, it was only after several tries for the GED.

No.

I asked her why she was in the hospital. A person didn't go to the hospital for bruised arms.

"So Sciutto punched me in my stomach."

My mind went to anatomy. It found nothing. I only knew

where kidneys were, and only because they weren't in the belly. All I knew was that I imagined that was where a fist went to knock the wind out of a person. Fat was protective, but it would be a mean shock to the system. "You all right?"

She pointed to what I guessed was the lower part of her abdomen under the sheet. "So I'm pregnant," she said.

I knew that. But until she told me, I realized I didn't know that. Here she was, in the hospital, wanting to stay pregnant. "That's wonderful," I said before I could allow myself to imagine a tank of a child with bad habits. I got up and leaned over to kiss her. She didn't recoil. "How far along are you?"

She gave me that I-can-read-you expression that never was accurate.

What.

"You forget how well I know you," she said. I had no clue what she was reading into me. "You think I should have an abortion."

"Hey!"

She gave me the look of a protective mama. Honor's ferocity was going to serve her well, just as soon as she realized she was a vessel that needed to go a lot of odd places for the sake of what was right then a duck yolk.

"Listen," I said, "I'm no placard-carrying pro-lifer, but you know damn well I've gone out of my way to bring a baby into this world, so don't accuse me of pushing you into an abortion. I'm already adjusting to this kid looking like Sciutto with breasts.

"Really, I just was wondering if you were pregnant when you got married. But mostly I want to know what the doctors say. Is she all right?" I knew it was a girl.

"It's holding on," she said. "There. You've got a hint. I said 'it.' I know you watch enough crap on TV. I can't have an ultrasound until twelve weeks."

"I hope it's a girl," I said.

Honor's face almost was relaxing into pleasantness. "Another tough bitch. Letty, Darby, Honor, Gianna," she said. "You know what they say. Well behaved women rarely make history."

Gianna?

She and Sciutto were picking out names right up until he decided to risk the baby's life with a beating. I imagined this child born in Louisiana could wind up with Gianna Gotti on her birth certificate without Sciutto ever producing a driver's license that said Devin Morrow. Though he had plenty of time to bully the DMV into giving him one with Sciutto Gotti on it, too.

I asked Honor what I was there for. She had forgotten.

"This is a nightmare, honey," I said. "Why'd he hit you?"

She told me it was over money. It was always over money. He was waiting for his father to come through, and it made him angrier and angrier that she wouldn't just carry them until everything cooled off with his father. Everybody knew his father was richer than the feds knew, and Sciutto would never have to work a day in his life, though of course he'd work for his father. All he had to do was prove himself. Lately he'd been talking to his father on the phone, and from what Honor could hear, things were sounding friendly. "He said I owe it to him to have patience.

"I told him that if we were keeping some kind of ledger of who owed whom what, he was seriously in the minus column. So he pitched his voice all high, hollering, 'Who owed whom? Whom? And he started, like, hovering over me, saying, 'Say it, Honor, who owed *whom?*' And I didn't say it, and he kept at it, and I didn't say anything, and that's when he hit me."

This boy needed to be stripped of his power.

"What if this Gotti guy is not his dad?" I said.

247

"Aw, Darby, we've been over this a thousand times," Honor said. "Sciutto's mom is not his wife. That's why we don't read about her. And what more proof do we need than him talking to the guy all the time?"

I kept my mouth shut about a check for five hundred dollars with his name on it. If I ever got such a check I'd frame it, uncashed. Not a photocopy of the cashed check, either. I told her I had something to show her.

"Are you sure it's not something that'll get me fucking killed?"

"I think you're going to learn pretty soon that mothers kind of go out of their ways to make sure they die before their kids do," I said. *Well, all mothers except Letty.*

Either she had asked me to come to the hospital to use my judgment or she hadn't.

"Well, whatever you did, it's already too late," she said. Then she smiled. "I know, I know." I always quoted my father. His favorite expression was "too late."

I turned over the photo. It was self-explanatory. I handed it to her silently, and she studied it. A photo of a computer screen of one interchange required finding the names of the two correspondents as well as what they said and in what order. For me that would have been like translating Latin. For Honor it took five seconds. "Wow," she said. "How'd you do this?" No *why*.

I started to spell out the process, and she stopped me. "I know how a person would do this," she said. "I'm just surprised you figured it out. I didn't know you were so, you know, well, *young*."

I wasn't insulted. Being computer illiterate was a badge of maturity. "Adrenaline?" I said. "Like lifting a truck off a baby?"

She rolled her eyes, but they didn't go three-sixty; it was as if they stopped so the brain behind them could think. "He talks to his dad all the time," she said. "I guess he's faking."

I would have said everybody has a dad, but we'd have gotten sidetracked on that. "There's bullshit, and then there's bullshit," I said. I could see where the promise of great riches—say the heirship to a trucking company—would draw someone into a marriage, but I hoped the Gotti stamp on money took away its shininess.

"He's not just a big fat liar, he's a psycho," she said. "I mean, say you're descended from George Washington or Abraham Lincoln or even that you're third cousins with somebody alive like Brad Pitt who does good shit and maybe has the same color hair as you, but a mobster? That's fucked up."

I was about to say that no one needed the scariness of a mob name if he weighed three hundred pounds and could land a person in the hospital with a fist blow. But Sciutto walked back in.

She waved the photo in his direction.

"You won't believe what Darby got," Honor said.

He leaned into her in the bed and looked at the photo over her shoulder. "What the fuck is this?" he said.

"Carmine says he's never heard of you," I said.

"You mean some imposter saying he's Carmine told you that," Sciutto said.

"There's his name, right there," Honor said. "How do you explain that?"

"Oh, sweetie, how are we going to explain fame to your mother?" he said. He looked at me as if I were a teary-eyed fan and he were a rock star who long ago had lost sympathy. "Look, lady, no celebrity is going to respond to strangers, much less have his own page on Facebook. This is somebody using his name and pretending to be him."

"I guess you would know all about that," I said.

He leaned back from Honor so he could look her in the eye. "You see what I'm talking about? I told you what my father said. Your mother is a stone-cold bitch. You need to stay the hell away from her. Dad said she'll cause nothing but trouble." He turned to look at me. He was still right next to the bed. "You need to go away and stay away."

I looked at Honor to see what she would do.

She turned to me. "Call the police."

Sciutto sauntered out of the room as if he had no cares.

"I know your license number," Honor called after him. "So if you don't stay here, they'll be looking for you everywhere between here and my house."

# Chapter Twenty-Five

Right then Letty was a character in a book who eluded me. So I had been a daughter in actual life who had eluded her. But I needed her to know about Honor and all the cells that were going to be her great-grandchild, and about the father of those cells who right then was sitting in OPP without me to bond him out.

I didn't say why I needed to visit, but maybe the surprise made her ask no questions. She said to come over as if nothing had happened in as long as she could remember.

A plate of stale doughnuts was sitting on the kitchen counter when I walked in. The kettle was on, and Letty had two cups set out. "Evelyn came by day before yesterday," she said to explain the doughnuts. Evelyn had worked in the office at Marino's Market from as far back as when my father worked there, retiring long past her seventy-fifth birthday. Letty always swore Evelyn was secretly in love with Eddie, but Evelyn struck me as the type who was grateful to be able to go home at night to her little fluffy dog. She always had a little fluffy dog.

I asked her what was new with Evelyn, knowing the answer. Nothing was new with Evelyn. She had a new little dog. Evelyn was up in her eighties. Little dogs sometimes lived to be twenty, I said. "I told her I'd take him if anything happened to her," Letty said.

"You're no spring chicken, either," I said.

"So you'll take him."

"Hell, no."

I had nothing against little fluffy dogs. I had nothing against dogs. I just had decided when Honor got potty-trained that I never again was going to be involved in putting food into another being or dealing with what came out as a result. That mostly meant humans, but it worked its way down the chain all the way to goldfish. It seemed to me that Honor secretly had been relieved not to have pets after Ansel Adams and then FedEx had died. I wondered what she was thinking now, having a very high-end pet on the way.

Letty said to forget about it, women like Evelyn lived forever; they had nothing better to do. "So. Might as well get the big subject out of the way."

I looked at her blankly. A stunned kind of blankly.

She craned her neck at me, stared into my eyes as if I were simpleminded. "*Ax*-ul."

Oh.

"What about him?" I would give Letty her turn first.

"Well, I left the restaurant, but you had Trout Meuniere coming, and so did he, and I know neither of you walked out," she said. "So unless you tried to punish him on my behalf and sat there in silence, something must have happened."

I could have made mental notes during dinner, expecting a debriefing. But my loyalty that evening had been all to Axel, and everything I said was congratulatory. I wasn't lauding him for putting my mother in her place for the first time since my father died, though of course that was what he did. I was telling him that I liked his honesty. I didn't tangle myself up with men in

252

the unnatural way of marrying or living together because men weren't honest about what they wanted. But Axel wanted freedom. Or at least he wanted freedom from responsibility for another person. Or at least least, he wanted freedom from responsibility for another person who was ungrateful and acting entitled to everything she wanted.

"To tell you the truth," I said, remembering honesty, "I did most of the talking."

"I hope you tore him to shreds," Letty said.

I asked her if we could explore this with some kind of grasp of the truth. I wanted to ask if we could do it at another time, but I needed patience.

"I thought we were," she said.

"Look," I said. "Here is this man who doesn't know you except that you were married to his dear friend decades ago, right?" She nodded. "So he's like everybody all over the country, and he sees someone in New Orleans who needs rescuing, so out of the goodness of his heart, he gets you out of the city at the last second, right?" She nodded again.

"You realize his whole family was annihilated in Nazi Germany?" She shook her head, no. I didn't mention that Axel was estranged from his mother, though that would have pulled up worse guilt. She should have known all of this if she'd ever paid attention. "Well, saving someone was a natural act on his part. But what happens? You're not a refugee. You go on a tear in New York, spending a goddamn fortune."

"The man is a multimillionaire," Letty said.

"That's not the fucking point," I said. "If he gave you two-ply toilet paper, you should have been grateful and not asked for another thing. And you should have tried to stop taking help from him as soon as possible. You had your own credit cards with you, didn't you?" She nodded slowly. "What in God's name did you think you were doing?"

"I thought he was in love with me."

I wanted to let loose with a string of expletives. Instead I said, "What do you think now?"

"Obviously he wasn't."

"He never knew you. And if all he had to go on were sales slips from all up and down Fifth Avenue, he probably hated you."

Letty's eyes got a little teary, but only for me.

\*\*\*

I went through two terrible doughnuts before I got to the subject of Honor.

I brought her up. I didn't think Letty was such a bad grand-mother that she didn't care about her granddaughter who not only had married since the storm but also had survived. I thought Letty simply was in a dither. "So, you want to hear about Honor?"

"Oh, sure, sure."

I started right in on the subject of Sciutto. I wasn't going to remind Letty that Honor was married. Either she had forgotten, or she would be annoyed that I thought so. "He's dreadful," I said. "She needs to get an annulment."

Letty cut her eyes at me, as people in New Orleans said. Her expression said, *I know you are a eugenics shopper, and maybe your child knows better.*

"You need to believe me," I said. She didn't change her expression. "Look, I'm being honest with you. Honor is a pretty girl. And she's working on a doctoral degree. She can have her pick of men. So she goes after this guy who is way over six feet and weighs way over three hundred and looks like a goddamn Neanderthal who just crawled out of his cave and does nothing but grunt. And it turns out that's how he acts, too."

"Sounds like a guy who gets his way in the bedroom."

I did not want to know what got its way in Letty's bedroom. I'd already lived through her years with Eddie.

"The man is a nightmare," I said. "I mean, he might be good-looking for all I know, and he probably works out because he's solid muscle, but he's such a slob that all I see is a hairy mess. So you'd think he'd compensate by being a sweetheart, but instead he's a fucking brute."

Letty smiled. She was getting a good picture, it seemed to me.

"You could have sympathy," she said. "Though I don't know why."

I told her I wasn't judgmental except when it came to behavior, and he finally had gone too far. I wasn't ready to tell her he was in lockup. Yet.

"Oh! Did you notice Axel's table manners? The way he put butter all over the bread? I should have had a clue right then that we were a mismatch."

Finally enough was enough. "We're not talking butter here," I said. "The bastard beat the crap out of my kid."

"Oh, my God. Poor girl. Jewish people don't do that."

*What?* Since when was Letty Jewish? She and my father had had the most mixed marriage I'd ever known. She had been a fifth-generation assimilated Southern Jew, and he had been a first-generation immigrant, and it had been incendiary, but I was a hundred percent Jewish, and Honor, tracked by distaff line, was also Jewish, and somehow this story was now playing out in Jewish mores. As far as Letty and I knew, domestic violence did not seem to be a Jewish gambit, but Jews needed to be good at secrets.

The boy was not Jewish, not by a long shot, I told her. In

fact, he claimed to be Italian, as Italian as it is possible to be in this country without being deported to Sicily.

She was silent. "I'm trying to remember *The Sopranos*," she said. "I can't remember if they hit women."

I was getting exasperated to the point of being amused. "Look, this kid says his father is John Gotti, Junior, and when he beats up Honor, they don't call the police because he says all the news media will jump right on it and create a big disturbance, so Honor just sits there and takes it. Up until yesterday."

"He must have a lot of money," Letty said.

"*That's* your takeaway?" I said. There was no point in telling her anything else.

I picked up a third doughnut, went to the kitchen to get a paper towel to wrap it in, came back, and told her I had to leave. I promised I'd call her later.

***

Having this Letty make an appearance in my mind hadn't been too helpful for my writing. I had the world's best chance to kill her or fix her, and I wasn't sure what I wanted. My plan had been not to let Letty live in fiction any longer than my father. I would not kill her off, but I would make the reader tell her goodbye at the same point in time as my father went away. In *Werner Weiss*, Lily disappeared a few days after Werner, so what more was there to know?

Now I wasn't sure. Letty had become a different person for half a century—that half a century to which my father had alluded in his interview with the oral historian. "I do not want anyone reading my story for fifty years," he had said, protecting young me from what he thought was the worst of his life. Yes, the attempted annihilation of European Jews, and along with them his mother, was the worst of most lives, but he hadn't protected me from the bad that followed. I watched him annihilated by the evil of his new home. And then, when those fifty years began ticking away, I watched a new story, one he never would have imagined. I watched his quiet, self-denying Letty turn into the mother I knew now.

I was still at the part of the book where I had some chronology left in the sweet Letty years, and I needed to decide where my narrative was going. I wrote books with a simple trajectory: I had an opening and an end point, then I told the story that took me between points. The ending of any book had to be a milestone, sacrament, or sunset, but with this one, it would be ambiguous. I didn't need to tell what Letty's sign-off moment meant. In fact, it was best if I had no more idea than my reader would. But I had to choose it. From all I could see, I wasn't writing toward her death. Though this was fiction. I could kill her off at any point after my father died.

I thought about that. I let my mother walk my timeline; after all, this was from my point of view. Having Honor couldn't kill her; she needed indignation. My move to Mississippi? Hardly a blip. Something with Eddie? Eddie left her wealthy and unencumbered, so her dying might be fraught with irony. I would inherit everything. That was an unadulterated happy ending. I didn't write happy endings. Oh, wait, maybe I would grieve over my mother. No, not enough. I worked her up to present day, to Katrina, Katrina with a half dozen dramatic ways to kill Letty, most of which I'd considered when she was missing. That was possible. It also was possible that she could return safely, only to die trivially. Very cute. I didn't do cute, but any writer worth her nerve could turn cute into puzzling.

I had two choices in deciding my ending. I could phone Shoshana and tell her I needed an ending, or I could go walk a few circles around Letty and try to determine what was true about her. Having truth was a lot easier than turning Letty into a fictional character I loved and felt sympathy for. I wanted sympathy to jibe with actual feeling.

I had to call her back. It was still strange phoning her house number. It had been a long time since I'd done so with any regularity. I fully expected her answering machine to pick up. Letty was not one to stay at home, not when her credit cards had been resting for such a long time. She also was the type to let the machine answer, let the message start, then pick up if she felt like it. She answered on the second ring.

I asked her how she was doing.

"Why didn't you stay here after the storm?" she said. She'd had time to think since our visit. I wasn't sure whether I could detect accusation in her tone.

"I did stay there for a little while," I said. "But I got too rattled. First I thought you'd walk in any second and scare me to death. Then I thought *you* were dead, and that creeped me out."

"Sor-ry if my ghost scared you," she said.

"You weren't dead."

"Yeah, that's the problem, I'm not dead," she said. "Do you know how hard it is to be alive?"

I had no clue what she was talking about.

Evidently, when a person leaves a house unattended, some things go wrong. Letty had no indoor plants, so I hadn't failed her on that score. But it had been very dry after the storm, and all of her landscaping was dying or dead. I wondered if she'd noticed the parts of the city that had flooded. That might have explained why her gardener was too busy to replant her camellias. I should have watered them, though the city hadn't had water for weeks after the storm. Her St. Augustine was growing thick and wild; didn't that count for something? And what about the car? The car was dead, dead, dead when she got home. That's why she'd taken a taxi to Galatoire's. Did Axel or I care? No, neither of us had paid any attention. Did I know how long it took for Triple A to come jump her battery the next day? And her gas pipes! No self-respecting woman should have to drain water out of her gas pipes every other day, but what's she going to do, call the plumber every other day? She was lucky he came at all. If I'd stayed in her house, I could have gotten the pipes fixed before all these stupid people came back to town. Not from what I'd read, I told her. The water was in the street pipes; it was winter when everybody needed gas.

These are things a man should know, she told me. Not a woman.

"Where are you living anyway?" she said.

I told her I bought a little house. I was living in it until I decided what to do about Mississippi. She didn't ask what happened to the Mississippi house, and I didn't think it was because she knew the entire coast was washed away. She also didn't ask where my little house was.

"Why all this now?" I said.

"You come running over here with all this Honor mess, like it couldn't wait, never mind that I went through this storm, and my house went through it, and then you walk out, so why're you surprised?"

It was unnecessary to invite myself over for another visit. The truth of Letty could be found in a phone call. My imagination could pull up a full-blown account of what she would do if I went to her house again. Of what she would say, where we would sit, what she would offer me—in food, in hand-me-downs. I wanted a Letty I could carry to the end of a book. I already had what I wanted most, her perspective on men. That would be all she would talk about. If the subject of her granddaughter came up at all, it would only be to hear more about this husband of hers. *Really tall, huh? She met his father?*

I told her I would be in touch. I had a feeling she might bond Sciutto out, from simple curiosity. I hadn't gotten around to mentioning that he'd been caught in his little deception. With a second's thought she might have wondered why no one flew down from New Jersey with the cash. She could drift off so quickly into a fantasy of her granddaughter frolicking with rich, famous bad people: Honor would have one of those mansions in New Jersey with a lot of chandeliers, and her beloved grandmother would fly to Newark where a limo would be waiting, the driver holding up a sign bearing her name. I probably got my writing chops from Letty, who could spin gossamer cotton candy out of a sprinkling of pink sugar.

# Chapter Twenty-Six

I controlled myself for two days.

I phoned her as soon as I had washed down that lone stale donut with a cup of herbal tea. It wasn't Proust's madeleine, but it had its triggers.

I told her I had ended our conversation too fast, and I apologized. I offered to come over, knowing she would say no. The other three doughnuts probably already were in the garbage. "Just tell me what I need to know," she said.

"And you'll believe me?"

"Maybe," she said. This was her friendly voice. I could recognize it in two syllables.

Damn. Here I was again, not having prepared my speech. Sciutto was not an easy story to tell. I might have been someone who knew how to build a narrative, but I always had the luxury of time, of unconscious time, of sleeping and organizing so I woke up ready.

"I'll give it to you in bullets, okay?" Oh, wait, Letty didn't speak writing jargon. To her, bullets were what mobsters used. "I mean, I'm giving you a list," I said. "You want to write all this down?"

"I'm not senile," she said.

So I took notes on what I said, making sure I didn't miss anything. He beat Honor so badly she wound up in the hospital. Would I tell why? Yes. Honor was pregnant. Letty said, *Oh, my.* What more could anyone say? He always was asking for money. Why? He said it was because he was trying to get back in his father's good graces. Yes, he said his father was Junior Gotti. Yes, Honor overheard him talking to his father.

And then I went into the long, complicated explanation of how I had contacted Carmine, who had said he had never heard of Sciutto, whose name when he went to jail the first time was Devin Morrow. *What?* I forgot about that. I bonded him out of Central Lockup. "Jews do not go to Central Lockup," Letty said. I knew that was not true. Tulane had an attorney on retainer to bond out students who got too drunk in public places, and Tulane was loaded with loaded Jews. Besides, I told Letty, this boy wasn't claiming to be a Jew. "But he married one. And her baby will be Jewish."

Now he was in Orleans Parish Prison. Jews surely went to OPP.

"Why am I telling you all this?" I asked.

"Think," she said, as if she had been one of those mothers who successfully had reared her child using the Socratic method.

Given two seconds to think, all I could come up with was that Letty had a right to know. Honor was her grandchild, and this so-called Gianna would be her great-grandchild. It seemed to me that if you didn't write books, this was a good shot at immortality.

"I forgot to tell you," I said. "They plan to name it Gianna if it's a girl."

"Pretty much anything goes with Cooper."

"Pretty much anything goes with Morrow," I said. "I'm just

wondering if he's going to try to put Gianna Gotti on the birth certificate."

"You never answered why you're telling me all this."

I shrugged, even though we were on the phone. "I'm kind of liking talking to you," I said.

"I'm not the ogre you think I am."

"Not today," I said.

"People change."

People do not change. I once had tried psychotherapy. I had been tentative about it. I'd felt the way Barbra Streisand had felt when people suggested she have her nose fixed. She'd said she was afraid that if she changed anything about her face it would ruin her voice. Then I'd told myself that Michael Jackson had done himself no harm, and he'd in effect begun to remove his nose. I hadn't wanted to lose the unhappiness that drove my writing. With Michael Jackson's disappearing nose in mind, I went to the therapist to whine and brag in alternate weeks. When I complained about Letty, she had been well into her fifties. The doctor had pronounced that no one after a certain age was capable of change. I had seen patients with gray hair in his waiting room. I'd asked him what kind of scam he was running on them. They could adjust, he said, but they couldn't change. *Nice save*, I'd told him, and I'd terminated soon afterward. But I'd begun to look at Letty as set in stone after that time. She might have become a different person when she was widowed at a young age, but that different person was her life character unto death.

"That's not it," I said.

"Well, good, because there was nothing wrong with me to begin with."

My stars realigned. I was pushing sixty and never had had a mother friend, at least not in this particular person. I wouldn't know what to do with her. I had Charlotte, and in a way I had

Chelsea in Mississippi, even though she was the same age as I was. We had reared our girls in circles that intersected as often as they could until she got tired of being black in the South and moved to Tacoma ten years ago. With no husband, I tried not to rely too much on women friends nearby. It was a matter of pride. I hadn't told Charlotte or Chelsea about Sciutto. Oh, they would laugh. I wouldn't be ashamed. But I wasn't on the phone with Charlotte or Chelsea.

"Listen, this has nothing to do with you and me," Letty said.

This had to be good.

"You may not like this, but Honor doesn't have very many relatives, and really, I'm almost all she's got."

I did a quick family tree in my head. No father. Was that it? Possibly. But our side was pretty free of branches, too. William was about it. Sad.

"Before you get all sorry for her, don't forget she thinks I'm all right. In fact, she respects me. A lot."

So Letty had picked up on my having produced an over-educated, motivated descendant who carried some of her DNA in recognizable ways.

"Bring her over here, and I'll get her all taken care of."

"If you think throwing money at her will do something, I can do that as easily as you," I said. "It takes more complex thinking than knowing how to write a check."

"I know better than to ask you to give me a little credit," she said. "Or to ask you to trust me. But just get her over here. It can't get any worse. And I still have three doughnuts."

\*\*\*

The first thing Honor had done when she got out of the hospital was give up her belief that she didn't need ADT. She thought wrought iron at the windows and double-bolt locks kept her safe, but now, she told me, she wanted a siren that screamed if anyone other than herself opened any entry point. ADT didn't change locks, so she had a locksmith out, too. Honor had a way of talking to whoever answered a phone that got a work crew at her house immediately. Even if a woman answered.

Honor wasn't neurotic. She was a girl who dealt in her own very real assessment of the truth. She expected Sciutto's key to try the lock as soon as he was released to await trial.

"He hasn't got a nickel, and he's far too healthy looking to panhandle," she said to me when I phoned her.

"And OPP's too far from the standard panhandling intersections for him to walk," I said.

She made me comfortable, but only in a temporary way.

I was calling to tell her to meet me at Letty's. That was what Letty wanted. Honor wasn't flapped about the request. This equilibrium was biochemical. She could think there was a chance her grandmother was dying or dead, and she would consider that important, but she wouldn't worry or beg for information. "You need to meet me at Letty's" was all I told her, and her only response was about the time. I told her tomorrow, and she said that was good, which would have meant she now figured Letty wasn't dead or dying. Or that Letty was long dead, and this was no emergency.

I arrived at three, the set time. Honor wasn't there. Honor never had gone through that Piaget literal stage, which had included being precise about time. She never had wanted a watch. Now that no one wore a watch, she never looked at her cell phone. She thought she had a good enough relationship with the sun.

"What are you doing here?" Letty said when I came through the door.

I said I told Honor to meet me there. I thought if I said to meet me at her grandmother's she might think that something was dreadfully wrong and wouldn't say no.

"You don't know your kid very well, do you?"

I shrugged, but I didn't turn around to leave. I wanted to watch Letty perform magic. I was fairly certain that my description of Sciutto alone would have Letty warming up the car for a trip to the abortion clinic. Letty scoffed at my eugenic pickiness that she always said would have killed my father, but Letty didn't want ugly around her, either. When Honor had come out beautiful, Letty eventually had found her a delightful fashion accessory. How could she brag about a great-grandchild who looked like Big Bird?

"Are you going to keep your mouth shut?" she said. I nodded.

She had set out a platter of fresh fruit and a plate of Pepperidge Farm cookies. "No coffee for her," she said. "No tea, either. I've got pineapple juice. And apple juice, in case pineapple juice gives her heartburn. Any little thing can give you heartburn, but maybe not this early, you know?"

Letty had served me nothing but silence or contempt at this stage of my pregnancy. At every stage of my pregnancy, but I wasn't going to revisit something that had happened more than Honor's lifetime ago. For all she knew I'd been drinking battery acid with no side effects.

When the doorbell rang, I got up to answer it, but Letty told me to remember I'd promised to keep quiet. I took a nice little branch of green grapes, rubbed a finger over a stem to be sure Letty had washed them, felt wetness, leaned back and started eating. I could hear Letty in the doorway. "Your mother's here, but she's going to be furniture."

Honor shrugged. "She's all right," she said. All in all, it was a good endorsement.

Letty had done all the nurturing in her power in advance. Going to Marino's and setting out two plates was a big deal to her. When she offered Honor some juice, Honor knew to give her order to me, and I served quickly, not wanting to miss a word. Letty was talking about New York when I came back. Not the circumstances, definitely not Axel, but the availability of every designer Honor might ever have seen in any magazine she could imagine.

I sat down, moved on to the cut strawberries on the plate. "Napkin," Letty said.

"They're linen," I said.

"Go get a paper towel."

I popped the strawberry slice into my mouth, sucked the juice off my index finger and thumb, sat back.

"What are we going to do with your mother?" she said to Honor. I heard affection, no conspiracy. Honor shifted a little on the other end of the sofa from me. I couldn't see why. She looked perfectly comfortable.

"Okay, look," Letty said to her. "This is going to be easy. Unless you make it tough. Believe it or not, you're outnumbered, two to one."

"You're kidding," Honor said.

"You're kidding," I said.

"Hush," Letty said to me. "You hush, too," she said to Honor. "I've thought this all out for you, and someone is coming to help us any minute now."

Letty looked at her watch. Instinctively I looked at my watch, too. Honor had no watch. I was the only one who had anything to do, but even I had no schedule. The doorbell rang. "Right on the minute practically," Letty said, almost crowing with pride.

Both of us stood to see who was coming to help, and there stood Sciutto in the doorway.

"Get him the fuck out of here," Honor said.

"Are you out of your mind?" I said to no one in particular, but I was calling toward the door.

"You're not who I was expecting," Letty said.

I had to give Letty credit. She used whatever sharpness she had saved up her entire life to figure out who this was. And then she filtered it through what she had thought passed for clever her entire life.

"You must be Sciutto, and I'm pleased to meet you, but this is ladies only," she said. She was using the nice old Southern woman gambit. She didn't know that Sciutto didn't respect old or Southern or women. "You're going to have to excuse us if we ask you not to participate. Honor's mother will drop her off at her house when we're finished. It shouldn't take long."

Honor leapt off the sofa, placed herself in front of Letty, who jockeyed back in front of her. Letty always was the one with protective hands on her shoulders.

"Get the hell away from here before I have you arrested," Honor said to Sciutto.

"Baby, I'm not doing anything wrong," he said. "I've just been trying to see you. You won't let me see you at home."

"Home?" Honor said. "Home is somewhere in Florida, buddy." She tried moving Letty aside so she could close the door around Sciutto, but Honor wasn't exactly a girl with muscles or dexterity. All Sciutto had to do was take one small step, and Honor had to retreat into words.

"You know, we're still married, and if your grandma is doing any kind of business with you, you better remember this is a community property state," Sciutto said. "I probably should be here."

I wanted a closed umbrella in my hands at that moment. I'd have had no compunction about going right over my daughter and mother, risking injury to both of them, and taking a good, unpulled swing at Sciutto. My raisin left brain refused to take in legal facts, but I knew this much, that the moment Honor and Sciutto no longer were a community, they no longer had property together.

William came up behind Sciutto right then. This was Letty's surprise.

"I've been listening," he said. He was half a head shorter than Sciutto. Sciutto didn't startle; he just turned around as if a Girl Scout had come up with cookies.

I expected William to recoil in uselessness. But I'd seen William only as an attorney sitting at desks and tables. William with his white hair had that same puff-up trait Sciutto had, of scaring his prey in the wild, even when the wild was litigation.

"As the family attorney at law, I have an appointment here," William said to Sciutto as he worked his way smoothly past Sciutto and into the house. "You on the other hand are working your way into criminal trespassing."

Sciutto hesitated for just long enough, then took a step back. He looked at William to see if he'd obeyed the law yet.

"Property, son, I thought you knew all about property," William said. "You're on the property." He turned to Honor. "You have this guy's contact number?"

Honor nodded. She had his cell number, she said.

"I promise I'll be in touch," William said. "I've got your number. It's time for you to get moving. Right?"

Sciutto lumbered down the steps. When he got to the sidewalk, he hollered to Honor. "Don't forget how much I love you."

Honor said nothing.

"Hey," he hollered, "I don't have anywhere to recharge it when I run out of gas."

"Go to Catholic Charities," Honor said. "Just tell them about the good Italian family you're from."

***

William stayed just long enough to show me he knew what he was doing. To my surprise, that took probably less than forty-five minutes. This was William, who I thought was the most wrongheaded, lazy attorney in the city, and wrongheaded, lazy attorneys were New Orleans's primary crop. "I think loathing fuels William," I whispered to Letty.

"More like contempt," Letty whispered back.

"I hope not," I said, thinking first of my father, and then of how little William had to look down on, given that he was supposed to be cerebral.

William planned to give Honor a solid gold divorce "as a wedding gift," he said. This boy was looking at garnished wages and an electrified fence at the parish line if he, William, had anything to do with it, and since he knew a Jewish judge in family court, he could come damn close. Honor had made sure to tell William that Sciutto thought *Jew* was an epithet. She also had made sure William knew what an epithet was.

Honor gave him a goodbye kiss without flinching and said she had a couple of things to sort out; could she get back to him?

"She won't have anything to sort out when I get finished with her," Letty said.

***

Letty had more plans than just bringing William over with his pro bono gift.

"Now no interruptions," Letty said. "Just yes or no. You got me?" Honor nodded. "Good. Okay, for starters, I know what's going on with you. You got married and got pregnant, possibly in that order, right?" A nod, yes. "And now I've had the privilege not only of seeing this husband but of hearing a little of what he's like." I heard a little kick when she said the word *husband*. "Now tell me, are you finished with this man?"

"You mean, do I want a divorce?" Honor said. "Well, *obviously*."

"And you think that's all there is to it," Letty said, and Honor looked at me with eyes wide in a way she hadn't looked since before she started school and routinely saw new things. I put my index finger to my lips, *shhh*.

"Your mother went to a shrink a long time ago and came running back to me telling me that I was never going to change and she was stuck with me the way I was, and she didn't know what she was going to do," Letty said. "She told me the only thing people can do when they're past fifty or something is *adjust*. Well, I may not have changed, but I sure have *adjusted*. And I'm here to tell you that I know about men now. If you're smart, you'll listen to me."

"Can I talk?" Honor said.

Letty said, "No!" at the same time as I said, "Yes!"

"You both need to hush," Letty said.

I told her Honor knew everything wasn't cut and dried. Oh, yes it was, Letty said. Just wait.

"Before I tell you what I know about men," Letty said, "I'll tell you about you. I'm sorry, but I will never understand how you're carrying that man's child."

"Hey, a kid's a kid," Honor said.

"Try telling that to your mother," Letty said.

I hoped she wasn't thinking that she, Letty, had given birth to just any man's child. I was grateful every time I was competent and goodhearted that I had had my particular father. My only possible endowment from my mother came from flights of fancy, and I parlayed those into making money instead of spending it.

"I'm not talking about your child," Letty said.

"Is this going somewhere?" I said.

Letty nodded, reached out for Honor's hand. Letty probably hadn't reached out for anyone's hand since she and Eddie went shopping in Paris.

"Listen carefully," she said. "I learned from Axel that I didn't need a man. And the person who already knew you don't need a man is your mother. Now her reasoning was that she didn't want to lose someone the way she lost her daddy, but it meant being alone. She had you by herself, and she did a wonderful job. You need to get sole custody and raise this child by yourself. No visitation. Severed rights.

"You can do as well as your mother did. This time you'll have a mother and grandmother to help you out. I don't know how good the grandmother is with children, but the mother is the best."

I almost didn't hear what Honor said. I was so swell-headed with Letty's approval. It was true approval. Letty was many things, but she was no liar.

"God, you'd think my mother would have known how important a father is," Honor said. "It'd be worth the risk of losing him."

I looked at Letty, who wasn't going to take the body blow. So I looked back at Honor.

"Not having a father was the absolutely worst thing in the world," Honor said. "I mean, like deliberately not having a father. And I'll give you this much: it wasn't all Darby's fault. What fucked me up was what *he* did. That bastard never tried to find me. He never wanted to know me. And love me. That amounts to pure rejection. Even if he never saw me, he had some idea of what I looked like. Maybe even what I thought like—if he had even a little understanding of genes, and I'm sure Darby didn't pick an idiot.

"Sciutto is a piece of crap to me, but you don't think he'd take care of his little girl? Maybe I'd feel like shit if he dies. It's all I'm thinking about, a fatherless girl."

"What happened to your mother was tragic," Letty said to Honor. "What happened to you was not. Your mother made mostly good choices. Remember that."

# Chapter Twenty-Seven

I was well past fifty, well past the age when I could change.
All I could do was adjust. Oh, could I adjust. I woke up
adjusting, and I went to bed adjusting. Letty approved of my
life, understood my life. I would lie in bed and superimpose that
fact on the time when she told everyone I was a blight, and I
revised my past, at least in shadows. I was a woman ahead of
my time. I found that out when a generation passed, and cele-
brities were doing what I had done. I knew that, but I didn't
believe it until Letty said she knew it, too. I pictured myself in
that hospital bed, alone on a ward because I was a pariah,
though no one said so. Now I was on that ward because I was a
harbinger of the future. I had nothing against men. They had
their place, but their place was passion, not tranquility.

The person who needed to hear me adjusting was Alyce. I
wouldn't tell her anything around me was different. I wasn't
changed because I was too old to change; I was *adjusting*, and
she would have to hear the echoes around me. She was my test-
peer.

I told her I wanted to start switching a chunk of my
portfolio from mutual funds to stocks.

"I'll be damned," she said.

"Very professional," I said, and she laughed.

"I guess if I said it's about time, that wouldn't sound professional, either, huh."

Alyce was a big advocate of mutual funds. She hadn't gotten where she was by being a big risk-taker, and the market was too volatile for much game-playing. She had had one client, she had told me, who had nothing better to do than puts and calls all day long. He might as well have been in a casino, she said. And he would have gone home at the end of each day stone-cold broke if she hadn't refused to put in his orders after he reached a certain amount of extreme ignorance.

"I had no idea you'd changed your philosophy," I said.

"Just about you," she said. "I think it's pretty cool that you're not scared to death. You've probably made more money than anyone else we went to school with, but you act like you're going to be homeless if the Dow Jones drops five points."

"Are you serious?" I said. All I heard was a fact. A speculative fact, but a measurable, quantitative fact. Anyone who had gone to school with us had a piece of brain that relied on measures, how much money, what kind of grades. Out in the world past age eighteen, I had tried to gauge myself more abstractly, but it was impossible not to keep that piece of brain. Alyce was using that piece of brain, too, saying I'd made the most money. And she had the tools for knowing this was true, possibly by being the manager of everyone's finances. Except, of course, those who also called themselves financial managers. Though Alyce surely knew how they were doing. She had her ways.

"Serious about what?" she said.

I told her never mind.

"Oh, you mean how successful you are compared to everybody else." *Everybody else* should have meant a very wide universe, but it didn't.

"Not an issue with me," I said. Adjusting, adjusting.

\*\*\*

By the time I hung up, Alyce had logged two instructions. She had determined that she would reinvest half a million in stocks as long as they weren't the earth-destroying companies my drunk grandfather had enjoyed so much. It had cost me a fortune in capital gains to unload them to begin with.

And I had told her in no uncertain terms that I was going to have nothing more to do with reuniting with school classmates. Linda in Houston was all I needed—first, last, and forever. I did not need ever again to think about any of the other people Alyce had paraded in front of me in recent months. I was a fluke, Linda was a fluke, and, I told her, it was possible Alyce was a fluke, but I was beginning to have my doubts. Oh, Zachary was good, but Zachary was a biological mutation.

Alyce had laughed, and I'd said, "All right, you're on your way to flukehood."

\*\*\*

Alyce would be in town in two weeks for the reunion. I wrote fiercely during those days. I had to rein in the latest Letty image. She had gone from her longtime self to the one Shoshana had made me manufacture to Honor's excellent grandmother, and a writer needed a consistent character, or readers would write on Amazon that something was really wrong. Or the editor would throw the book away. Julie probably would catch my bipolar Letty and send me back for one more chance. I didn't want Julie to know I was sloppy. I took a slip of paper and wrote down a few bullets for the widow Letty. Every time she made a choice, I would look at the list. It was working, but she wasn't appealing. I found another slip of paper. I made a new list. I took it all from when Letty still had Bernie—her clinginess and insecurity and unworldliness. There! That would ward off touches of the brand-new Letty, who knew the world and stood right up in it. She would evolve. Though evolution was about the biggest form of change I'd ever heard of. Just kind of slow and imperceptible.

\*\*\*

On my calendar I wrote down the times of the phone calls I received that night. I'd penciled "reunion" in that square and erased it. I saved all of my calendars.

Alyce called at eight-thirty. She already had left the reunion party.

"Well, you were there even if you weren't there," she said.

Reuniting my spirit with those people was wrong.

"Hold on," Alyce said. "I did nothing. People came at me."

Alyce was friendly with everyone, but she also had shown up in public with me. It made sense. "You know I don't want to hear this."

"Maybe you do."

I'd been surprised when I went to Houston. Now I was home in my nightclothes. No one could see me. Though I did have memory. I let her speak.

"It seems that when you've gone to school with somebody famous, you want to be able to go home after a reunion and say you saw her," Alyce said. "People wanted to know why the hell you weren't there."

I asked if she told them. I would have liked to know why myself.

Of course she told them. It was a lot better than their all thinking I was a snooty bitch who thought I was too good to mingle with people I knew in the past.

"Well, crap, so you said I was scared shitless that they'd be mean to me?"

"You ought to be glad I'm not there to hit you," Alyce said. Okay.

"I told them to ask Louise," she said. "And after maybe the tenth person, Louise came after me and asked me what the fuck I was telling people about her and you. I said I bet she didn't talk like that at her daughter's coming out party."

Oh, Jesus, oh, Jesus, oh, Jesus. "Oh, Jesus," I said.

Alyce became gentle. Alyce never had been so slow with her words in all the years I had known her. "It was amazing, Darby," she said.

"Okay, okay," I said.

"I swear, probably a half dozen people were watching. You know, all these people I'd told to go ask Louise. So I said, 'Look, Louise, Darby finally might have decided she was tired of hoping you'd figure out you owe her an apology, you know?'"

"Let me guess," I said.

"Mmm, hmm."

"Something to the effect of 'what the fuck for?'"

"Pretty much verbatim."

This was why I did not go to the reunion. This was why I had decided to have no further use for schoolmates. Memory was not necessarily a place to visit. Loss of memory might very well have been a great gift of the process of aging. It just wasn't coming fast enough, and I was going to have to make it a conscious choice.

"All those people—and they were guests in her house, remember—basically told Louise she was out of her goddamn mind. No matter who they were, they all remembered she was the ringleader of the girls responsible for your father's suicide.

"And the weird thing was, Louise was the only one whose father wasn't dead. So they all started yelling at her about their dead fathers and how they couldn't imagine what it would have been like if they'd lost their fathers in tenth grade and it almost felt like they hated Louise because her father was still alive so she couldn't understand what in hell she did to you."

"Were they serious?" I said. It sounded a little like bullshit, but then I'd never lost a parent in adulthood.

Alyce was silent. "Better late than never?"

"You have to wonder if that's really ever true," I said.

I was feeling as if I'd been elected to something after I'd withdrawn from the race. I wouldn't have to serve.

"Don't you want to know what happened to Louise?"

I said no. I was sure Louise had run off crying in indignation for the rest of the party. If there had been any other outcome, I'd have had a phone call.

We were quiet for a while. My good fluke Alyce and me.

"You know, if I could have had a reunion, I would have wanted to ask everybody just one question," I told her. "I just wanted to know if they remembered the tour of the National Cathedral in ninth grade."

Alyce had no idea what I was talking about.

"The guide said it would take until after the year 2000 to finish the construction," I said. "I thought that was the way to have perspective."

"I would have liked that," Alyce said.

\*\*\*

Honor phoned an hour later, nine-thirty.

Was something wrong?

"I could have asked you the same thing. Why didn't you answer your phone?" I told her Alyce was telling me about my class reunion because I hadn't gone. She asked why not, and I told her she wouldn't understand, thank goodness.

"I've been wanting to tell you, I have some news," she said.

Her tone was a holding-back kind of neutral, so I couldn't tell her to save it until tomorrow. If it was good news, I needed it.

"You're not calling to tell me anything about Sciutto, are you?"

"No."

Then it had to be good news.

"Well, it's kind of *different* news," she said. "I had the ultrasound."

Oh, God. Wait, it wasn't bad news. It must have been gender news.

"They told you what it is? You let them tell you what it is?" I was sure it was a girl. I had a vivid imagination, but it didn't go beyond baby girls.

Honor was silent. A teasing kind of silent. "You ready for this?" I didn't answer. "All right, get ready. It's a boy."

"Holy shit."

For once Honor could read my mind. For once Honor let herself go to eugenics the same way I did. "Calm down, that guy is not bad looking when you get past the way he looks. And probably not stupid when you get past his dumbness."

"I know," I said, "but a boy?"

"And I've already named him."

I could take anything right then. I'd had weeks of adjusting to her having accepted the name Gianna for a girl. I liked Gianna cookies, imagined buying her little Gianna frog cookies, telling her they were baked specially for her.

"I don't know if his last name will be Morrow or Cooper," Honor said, "but I'm naming him Werner."

"Werner."

"I think Bernie doesn't work in this day and age, but Werner's a straight-up tribute everyone would know."

Werner Cooper. No more girls. It was about time. He would be a good daddy.

THE END

## WE GUARANTEE OUR BOOKS...
## AND WE LISTEN TO OUR READERS

We'll give you your money back if you find as many as five errors. (That's five verified errors—punctuation or spelling that leaves no room for judgment calls or alternatives.) If you find more than five, we'll give you a dollar for every one you catch up to twenty. More than that and we reproof and remake the book. Email julie@booksbnimble.com and it shall be done!

**Want to go back to the beginning?
Here's the FIRST in
The *Too Jewish* Trilogy!**

http://amzn.to/1vV8FQH

**What they said about TOO JEWISH:**

"A powerful and emotional story of a Jewish family here in America."

*—Life in Review*

"Flows like cold water down a parched throat...Her readers are thirsty for this one, and they won't be disappointed."

—*Critique*

"Friedmann writes with a sensitivity that can touch the heart without falling prey to the sentimental."

—*Kirkus Reviews*

## Or...

**Buckle up for a bumpy ride with PATTY FRIEDMANN's compelling fictional heroine, Eleanor Rushing in *Through the Windshield***

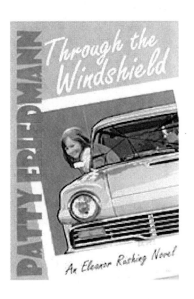

http://amzn.to/13oTiJS

## Also by Patty Friedmann:

## A Respectful Request

We hope you enjoyed *Do Not Open for Fifty Years: Too Jewish Trilogy Part III* and wonder if you'd consider reviewing it on Goodreads, Amazon (http://amzn.to/1BvuHQF), or wherever you purchased it. The author would be most grateful.

## How About A Free Book?

Keep up to date on terrific new books, and get a freebie at the same time! First go to **www.booksbnimble.com/contact/** to join our mailing list. Next, choose any book you want from the booksBnimble website – **http://www.booksbnimble.com** – and drop a note to mittie.bbn@gmail.com letting us know which one to send you. We'll get it to you immediately. **The password is: Mailing list.**

Or request a review copy of any book on the booksBnimble website. Just write mittie.bbn@gmail.com and we'll send it right away. The only thing we ask in return is an honest review. **Be sure to say the password:** *review copy.*

**Important: Don't forget to tell us whether it's a free sign-up book or a review copy.**

# About the Author

PATTY FRIEDMANN is the author of the literary perennially bestselling e-novel titled *Too Jewish* [booksBnimble ]. Its sequel is *Too Jewish: the Next Generation*, formerly *The Exact Image of Mother* [Viking Penguin 1991]. The third book in the *Too Jewish* trilogy released in both print and electronic format is *Do Not Open for Fifty Years* [booksBnimble].

She also is the author of several other darkly comic literary novels set in New Orleans: *Eleanor Rushing* [1998], e-book *Through the Windshield*; *Odds* [2000]; *Secondhand Smoke* [2002]; *Side Effects* [2006], e-book *Pick-Up Line*; and *A Little Bit Ruined* [2007] [all hardback and paperback from Counterpoint except paper edition of *Secondhand* Smoke from Berkley Penguin], released in digital form through BBN; as well as the humor book *Too Smart to Be Rich* [New Chapter Press 1988]. Her novels have been chosen as Barnes&Noble Discover Great New Writers, Borders Original Voices, and Book Sense 76 selections, and her humor book was syndicated by the *New York Times*. Friedmann's manuscript titled *An Organized Panic* took first runner-up in the Faulkner-Wisdom competition (out of 406 entries in the novel category) in late 2012. Her other books since Katrina are two YA novels,*Taken Away* and *No Takebacks* [TSP]. *Taken Away* was a finalist for ForeWord Small Press Book of the Year in 2011.

She has published reviews, essays, and short stories in *Publishers Weekly, Newsweek, Oxford American, Speakeasy, Horn Gallery, Short Story, LA LIT, Brightleaf, New Orleans Review,* and *The Times-Picayune* and in anthologies *The Great New American Writers Cookbook, Above Ground, Christmas Stories from Louisiana, My New Orleans, New Orleans Noir, Life in the Wake, My Funny Valentine,* and *Something in the Water*. Her stage pieces have been part of *Native Tongues.* Friedmann wrote the foreword to Wendy Rodrigue's *The Other Side of the Painting* in 2013.

In a special 2009 edition, *Oxford American* listed *Secondhand Smoke* with 29 titles that included *Gone with the Wind, Deliverance,* and *A Lesson Before Dying* as the greatest Underrated Southern Books. With slight interruptions for education and natural disasters, she always has lived in New Orleans.

CPSIA information can be obtained at www.ICGtesting.com
Printed in the USA
LVOW11s1319200515

439217LV00001B/40/P